I0664605

PAYING for IT

By JR Wylder

Paying for It

Two men. Two women. Two couples. Too many secrets.

Axel

I can have any woman I want, except for the one who has broken my heart more than once.

Jameson

When I fall, I fall hard. The woman I yearn for can't be mine, and if even she could be, she would never accept my secret.

Shondra

Big girls don't find love easy and it takes a special man to handle what I dish out. Too bad my soulmate hates the sight of me.

Vegas

Love has alluded me for so long, until one night, I meet the perfect stranger who turns everything around. Trouble is, he's taken.

A story filled with humor, heartbreak, and angst, follow these characters on a journey to discover if love can really be everlasting.

** This story jumps from past to present. This story has mature themes and triggers not meant for younger audiences. There is a HFN ending with no cliffhanger. This book contains only fade to black scenes.**

Paying for It

TABLE OF CONTENTS

4

Paying for It

Paying for It

Paying for It

Paying for It

ACT ONE

~Do you ever wish
you had a second chance
to meet someone again
for the first time?

CHAPTER ONE

Two years ago

"Are you Timothy James?"

I set my martini down. Placing my palms against the hotel bar, I pushed off, swiveling on the stool to face the speaker of those husky notes. The woman was stunning. My mouth fell open at her beauty and the olive I had just been about to shift to my molars, fell from my tongue, bumped off my jeans, and landed on the bamboo floor.

Hope I don't slip in that shit.

She moved closer and her perfume hit me—a bouquet full of sweet notes, like a botanical garden in the spring. I stopped contemplating the olive and started sizing up the woman before me. Smooth sepia skin, filled with rich red undertones. Dark natural hair hung in tight curls down her back. Upturned hazel eyes gave her a feline effect...

My scrutiny must have unnerved her. She frowned, backing away. "I'm sorry. I must have the wrong person."

"Wait! Yes." I halted her with a hand to her shoulder. "I'm, um, Timothy James."

Her smile at the news was unbelievable—rainbows and sunshine. A far cry from my wife's—*ex-wife's*—pinched grimace. Her beam captivated me with its winsomeness, and for the first time in over a year, I seriously considered having sex.

"Nice to meet you, Timothy. I'm Vegas. Vegas Shipley."

Vegas? The name suited her. A sizzling lucky seven with long legs, small waist, and tits I'd love to get my mouth on. *She is ...*

"Sin and Sugar."

Heat crept from my neck up. *Way to go ... Timothy.*

Her laughter, a sweet tinkling sound, stirred me south of the border. I crossed my legs at the ankle, shifting in my chair.

"You're not the first one to equate the two, but you are the first one to say it so ..." Vegas lowered her eyes, scanning me from bottom to top, "*so deliciously.*" Her tongue hovered between her teeth and a slight smile, seductive ... *sensual*, played around her lips.

There was no mistaking her vibe. She was *into* me.

Now, if I can just dust off my lines, maybe I'll get lucky tonight.

She spoke first, saving me from an embarrassing attempt to get her upstairs. "I have a room if you are ready?"

"Ready?"

"Well... um, yes, um, if you are ready to... you know." She shuttered her eyes in a slow blink and traveling her tongue over her top lip and halfway over her bottom before it disappeared like a rabbit in its hole.

Paying for It

I'd have to have an IQ the same as my shoe size to misinterpret her look. *She is ready to ...*

"Have sex?"

What's with my mouth today?

Vegas let out a girlish giggle, fluttering her hands. Embarrassment cast her eyes down and her lips curled in amusement.

I couldn't believe my luck at the surreal moment.

A beautiful woman is propositioning ... me?

Propositioning?

Was she a prostitute?

"Do you do this a lot?" I asked, lifting a brow.

Her eyelashes, naturally long and thick, blinked double time in surprise. She shook her head in staccato jerks, clutching her thin bag under her arm so hard something cracked, and she fiddled with the strap on her shoulder, her hand slightly trembling. "No, no. This is the first time, ever."

Running over everything she said, I was quick to figure out the situation.

This woman thinks I'm a ... gigolo.

Why not if it gets you laid?

This had to be a joke. Axel had played them on me before. Albeit nothing like *this*.

"Are you sure you want to go through with it?" There was a price to pay if she said 'yes' and I would gladly accept the cost, but in doing so, I wouldn't allow harm to come to her.

Vegas threw back her shoulders and lifting her head high, her body language told me, and the world, she was a grown woman... with a *grown woman's* desires.

"Yes, I do." A pause and then a sheepish grin. "My friend paid the agency directly. She knows I would try to weasel out otherwise."

Her accompanying giggle thawed my insides, giving me the courage to move ahead. "She must be a wonderful friend."

Her eyes clouded over, and her words dripped with thanks. "She is the best."

I downed the rest of the martini in one gulp—moral fortitude in a glass. "Well, let's not waste her money." I slid off the stool and Vegas took in my height, looking up at me in awe. "Time is ticking."

CHAPTER TWO

JAMESON

Present day

Vegas?

That's not her, right?

Here, of all places.

Vegas Shipley. That sexy siren who had ended my yearlong drought. The woman who had turned me out, leaving me sated like a fat man with a belly full of smokehouse ribs.

Vegas.

She was the best sex I ever had.

Not a day went by when I didn't think of her. How her beautiful face transformed into something ethereal as she shuddered around me. The way her jazz-infused voice called my name each time she came undone. Walls so warm and tight, she had wrung completely dry. With each position we explored, she took in all of me, begging for more. Unlike—

"Shelia!" A petite woman with the body of a ten-year-old boy flung herself into the toned, tanned arms of my ex-wife.

"Gertrude!" My ex said, peeling herself out of the woman-boy's embrace. "It's been *too long*, really."

Paying for It

Even as I watched Vegas and the hulk of a man she was with, I had to laugh at Shelia's tone. In *Shelia speak, too long*, wasn't long enough.

I listened to their catch up chatter with half an ear while surreptitiously watching Vegas from across the room. The guy by her side *had* to come from football stock. He either played professionally or it was in his past. He had a thick neck, bald head, and his hands were the size of Christmas hams.

His tanned skin was a perfect foil for the expensive charcoal grey suit he wore. *Armani, by the looks of it*. His size twelve's, encased in black Italian leather and shinier than a newly minted penny, seemed to shudder the ground on which he walked. He was *somebody,* this guy. Already his impressive figure had several pairs of female eyes following his every move.

Vegas lifted a canapé to his mouth, feeding him from her hand. The bitter jealousy that coursed through me like a tsunami had me nearly biting through the glass of my Champagne flute. He smiled down at her, and holding her hand up, he licked her fingers. I turned away with a curse on my lips and my chest tightening with a sharp zig-zag like pain.

My refusal to ogle Vegas didn't last long. Her bell tinkle giggle had me staring like a stalker once again.

So beautiful.

The jeweled-toned pink, slightly above the knee cocktail dress she wore, flared out, accentuating her small waist. The dress's halter top, studded with crystals, left her smooth back bare.

Paying for It

I *knew* it was smooth. I had kissed and suckled every inch of her body—at *least* twice.

"Jameson?" Shelia's call to attention had me nearly clicking my heels and bowing. "This is Gertrude Eisenberg. You remember her? Her family donated a wing to St. Vincent's."

Shelia was an ER doctor at St. Vincent's. That meant long days and even *longer* nights. Her work had contributed to our marriage's demise.

No, not her work.

It was her many, *many* extra-marital affairs, including the one I had witnessed with a resident doctor on her staff.

I nodded my greeting at the diminutive woman. "Yes, Mrs. Eisenberg. So nice to see you again."

Mrs. Eisenberg latched onto my arm, exerting enough pressure to raise my diastolic reading by twenty points. "I hope you know your wife is a gift from heaven. She saved my little grandson, Abel." Gertrude's watery blue eyes grew even mistier and her gravelly voice faltered, "Our family will *always* be in her debt."

CHAPTER THREE

VEGAS

Present day

After he handed the car keys to the waiting valet, he turned to look at me. As usual, his eyes lit up, filling me with wonderment.

"You look great tonight, Vegas."

"Thank you, Terence."

Circling his arm around my waist, he guided me into the hotel. We nodded at the doorman. He wished us a pleasant evening.

Before we entered the hotel ballroom, Terence kissed my temple. The soul-patch under his lip scratched my face. I smiled up at him, wiping with my finger tip the bit of foundation that clung to his facial hair.

"Am I wearing too much makeup?" I had applied more war paint than I usually did–concealer, blush ... *everything*. It was important for him, *for us* and our future, that I make a good impression at his fundraiser.

Terence stepped back, giving me a leisurely once over, starting at my silver sandals and ending up at the top of my curls. When his gaze flickered back to my breasts, I slapped his arm to get him to focus.

Paying for It

"Well?"

"Baby, you always look good." When he smiled, his teeth flashed under the lighting of the hotel lobby like those old-fashioned camera bulbs.

I love his smile. I love him.

***

Being the fiancée of an up-and-coming politician had its drawbacks. Parties like these were one of them.

Expensive cologne and perfume mingled with a maze of faces and a plethora of names. The grasping, the clutching, *the clawing,* had me at my wits' end. With each new introduction, my smile grew less and less in wattage until it became more or less a perfunctory grin. I didn't know how much longer I could keep up the pretense...

"Terence Kovack! There you are."

An elfin woman, dressed elegantly in a silver sheathed dress that showed off her perfectly toned legs, made her way toward us. The woman, both compacted in height and width, seamlessly parted people that stood in her way.

I squared my shoulders, determined to get through yet *another* introduction.

"Mrs. Eisenberg," Terence beamed, "this is my fiancée, Vegas." Terence nudged me forward and into the spotlight of the woman's gaze. Up close, I noted that time had stood still on the woman's face, even though her hands were rivers of veins and boulders of age spots.

Paying for It

Mrs. Eisenberg's gaze traveled my entire frame and bore into my soul in less than a second. From her dismissive glance away from me and back to Terence, I gathered her critical eye had picked up on my flaws and weaknesses.

There were so many...

"So nice to meet you, dear." Mrs. Eisenberg circled her thin arm into Terence's beefy one. "Come Terence, I want you to meet some people." Almost as an afterthought, she turned to me. "Vegas dear, do mingle. I'll bring him back as soon as I can." Terence threw an apologetic glance over his shoulder at me before Mrs. Eisenberg led him away.

Now what?

My eyes darted around the room. I didn't recognize not one person I could latch on to. For me, small talk *wasn't* an inherent gift. I always found it difficult to start a conversation with a complete stranger. I seized up like a deer in the headlights, my mouth working in confusion while my brain searched for an intelligent answer, often coming up empty.

Just be yourself, Terence had always told me. Easier said than done. I did not know who Vegas Shipley *was*.

In college, I worked on finding myself when Terence *found* me. He was a hurricane force, catching me up in me such a whirlwind of emotions, I let him consume me. Two days after my graduation, we broke up. I'd hurt before, but at that moment, I went through serious pain. Six months ago, Terence called me out of

19

the blue, and we took up where we left off. It was as if we were never apart.

But this time, we were in it for the long haul. The ring on my finger proved it. Nothing and no one could stop us, not even ... *Timothy James.*

The glow of a newly formed sun warmed me and my heart *double-dutched* in my chest.

That is him.

I would recognize him out of an identical twin line up. There was no mistaking the thick, dark hair I'd clutched while my body languidly twisted in euphoria. Those swimmer shoulders and still flat waist. He even had on the same silver wire-rimmed glasses. That night I had admired the way they suited his chiseled, angular face. When I'd told him so, he laughed. The deep boom released a thousand butterflies in my stomach.

When he'd taken them off and placed them on the nightstand, the temple pieces clicked like the polished boot heels of a soldier. Without them, his dark eyes were enormous and liquid, yet they burned every inch of my naked form...

Without so much as a start of recognition, he moved toward me. Confidence in every stride.

I grabbed a passing flute of sparkling wine from a server's silver tray, sucking it up like a vacuum on the highest setting. What courage I hoped to gather from the quick intake of alcohol didn't work.

The closer he got, the more apprehensive I became. My legs grew weak and rubbery. An Arizona summer, hot and dusty, swirled in my mouth. My tongue felt like a slug on a warm piece of concrete.

But I was happy. No, *ecstatic.* And worried, and afraid, and—

He enveloped me in a hug, his embrace so familiar, it hurt to let go. A maelstrom of emotion swirled within me, making my eyes fill with tears. I dabbed at the wetness before he noticed.

"Vegas," he said in that deep voice of his. The one I heard in my dreams. "It's so nice to see you."

CHAPTER FOUR

VEGAS

Present day

"Vegas, it's so nice to see you."

His words barely registered. I was too busy inhaling his scent of mint, sandalwood, and musk. Drinking it in while I had the chance. The moment I pressed closer, he dropped his arms from around me. I bit back a sigh of frustration. Jae still had those clean notes and hard lines. At least he hadn't noticed my tears.

"It's nice to see you too, Jae." I dredged up the nickname I had given him. I'd come up with it after he confessed he wasn't the man Shrondra had paid for. More embarrassed than angry at his duplicity, I uncharacteristically let him feel my wrath.

***

VEGAS-Reliving the past

The light in the hotel room reflected on the lenses in his glasses, hiding his dark eyes from me. "I'm sorry, Vegas," he said, hanging his head like a dog that ate the cat food. "I wanted you so I thought ..."

"You thought what?" I asked, buttoning my blouse up to my chin. "What were your intentions exactly? To get some and go home?"

Paying for It

Timothy James was a transaction between consenting adults, nothing more. But with this man, this stranger ... It was different. It was seedy and—

"Oh!"

He gathered me up in a hug, crushing me to his chest. I was so startled by the movement; I didn't protest. He felt good, like a warm blanket on a cold winter's night. It had been ages since a man had wrapped me in his arms. I let a sigh of contentment escape my lips, and I freely let my body revel in the experience.

"It wasn't like that, Vegas," he breathed. "I came to the hotel intending to get drunk at the bar, then sleeping it off." He pulled out a card key with the image of downtown pictured on the front. It was just like the one the clerk had given me when I checked in. "I was celebrating my divorce."

He paused, waiting for my reaction. I didn't know what to say, but I knew what I didn't want. And that was to break our contact. So, I simply nodded for him to continue.

"It wasn't really a celebration so much as a mourning. My ex-wife and I haven't lived together for over a year. It hurt like hell when I signed the last bit of paperwork. I came here..." he let out a weighted sigh that stuttered through his chest. "I just want to forget."

I moved to look up at him. Jae's dark eyes were sad, every slight crease weighted with anguish. My heart swelled for this unknown man. He was feeling the utter destruction I had felt when Terence called it quits. That numbing of the heart, that all-consuming feeling of hopelessness that struck like a wrecking ball. Our pain bound us together. And despite his subterfuge, my comforting gene took over. I was willing...no; I wanted to see it through.

***

The noise of the fundraiser came back before my senses did. When Jae reached out to touch my elbow, I didn't resist. "Talk to me, Vegas. Tell me what you're thinking." Our gazes met. His eyes held concern. To him, mine probably looked bewildered.

He pulled me closer...

Snap out of it V! You're engaged!

I stepped back. Out of harm's way. "Um, I was just thinking I needed some air."

Jae nodded so vigorously, he dislodged a piece of hair from its coif. The dark strands hung over his brow and curled over one liquid brown eye.

Damn, I love his eyes.

"Let me go with you." Without waiting for my reply... or giving me a chance to escape, Jae propelled me through the crowd and out the doors. Once we were away from the sea of faces, he grabbed my hand.

My left hand...

The ring!

His thumb moved in a slow arc across my knuckles. When the enormous diamond halted his progress, tension crept over his back like a cat stalking a bird, and he dropped my hand as if it had scalded him.

Paying for It

In the hallway, a few people milled around talking and laughing in quiet tones. Jae whipped his head first left, then right, searching for what I assumed to be an out of the way place.

"There," he said, pointing his head to an alcove behind a few leafy potted plants. He stalked off without another word.

After a beat, I followed him a few paces behind.

CHAPTER FIVE

JAMESON

Present day

She tipped toed into the alcove, her feline eyes wary. "Um, Jae, can you give me a moment? I really need to use the restroom." Before I could reply, she left in a flash of a pink skirt and silver sandals.

The tension I felt at finding out she was engaged (Dear God, I hoped not married) must have radiated outward and caused her to bolt. I cursed myself for letting it show. Given what I knew about Vegas, I should have waited for her to make the first move.

***

JAMESON-Reliving the past

"Can we talk ... for a bit?"

I smiled down at her curls. They set me on fire with their tickles on my chin.

"That would be fantastic, Vegas."

The hotel room had a small dining table. On opposite sides stood two uncomfortable looking hard-backed chairs. I moved in that direction, but she pulled my hand in the other direction... the direction of the bed.

Paying for It

Vegas kicked off her shoes and climbed up, her knee digging into the mattress. She leaned back into the pillows, her dark hair spilling out behind her—a sharp contrast to the white bedding.

That woman was a true vision. She was a new dawn after a hard night.

Vegas tilted her head and poked her pink tongue from between her lips. Her seductive entreaty caused a warm rush of desire throughout my body, effectively heating me up after a two-year cold spell.

"Do you mind?" I asked, pointing to the cashmere blue sweater Shelia had gotten me last Christmas.

"No. Not at all."

The soft material ruffled my hair, pulling it back from my forehead. A sudden coolness floated around my midriff. The removal of my sweater had loosened the cotton tee from my jeans. It clung in a bunch, just under my pecs.

Vegas's eyes scanned my torso. I didn't have a bulky gym body like my best friend Axel, but I had definition. My hip bones jutted from above the top of my jeans while the black band of my tanks hugged my flat abs.

I tossed the soft blue ball into a chair and joined her on the bed, grabbing the remote from the nightstand. Twirling it in my hand gave me something to focus on while I waited for her to speak.

"So what is your actual name?"

I flipped the remote from one hand to the other, the red colored off switch catching my eye.

Paying for It

"It's Jameson."

"And you last name, Jameson?"

"Thijssen. It's Dutch."

"How do you spell it?"

I told her. The remote warmed in my hands as I continued to avoid her gaze.

"And how do you pronounce it again?"

"The 'thij' is like 'thigh' and then 'sen' like 'sin'."

She giggled. The remote skipped the rhythm and landed in my crotch area. Right on top of my growing member.

"I bet many people get that wrong." She snatched up the channel changer, her fingers lingering a little too long on my puffed out front.

"Vegas—"

She sprang from the bed. The memory foam pillow slowly lifting from her indented form. Her sudden movement cooled my passion, but not my want of her.

I followed to her place before the ceiling to floor window. She gazed out at the darkness, seeing nothing. Still as a statue, her silhouette was a relief in beauty. I marveled at the way the night carved the supple strength of her arms, the turn of her slim calf, and the thin length of her fingers.

"Are you hungry?" She asked, staring into the frosty night. "I could go for something to eat. I was too nervous..." Her hands fluttered in an intricate dance. She stilled them by wrapping them around her waist. "I haven't eaten all day."

28

Paying for It

"Sure," I said, sitting up. "Let me get the room service menu."

I placed the order for buffalo wings and a Caesar salad to share. At Vegas's nod, I ordered a bottle of Riesling to go with the spicy meal.

"Please charge it to my room, number 643." I turned my back on her pursed lips and scowling eyes. I wanted to pay. God knows I had money enough. At least my wife...ex-wife didn't get her claws too deep into that.

The in-room dining operator drew in a breath. "Um, Mr. Jameson ... oh boy, um, Thigesin?"

"Thigh - sin," I said with the practiced voice of a person who had long suffered the mangling of their name.

The operator let out a shrill giggle. "Oh, I never would have guessed that." She must have realized I wasn't laughing along and she cleared her throat, becoming professional once more. "Will that be all, sir?"

"Yes, thank you." I ended the call and put the receiver back in its cradle.

"You didn't have to pay for it, Jae," Vegas said from her spot on the bed. In her reclining pose, she was once more the picture of ease. "But thank you."

I shrugged, refusing to acknowledge the flutter in my stomach because of the nickname she had given me. No one called me "Jae". It was Jameson (the ex-wife and close friends) or Mr. Thijssen (practically everyone else).

It wouldn't due to lie so close to her. Neither of us were ready for that. Instead, I took refuge in a chair and yes; it was indeed as uncomfortable as it looked. And I suffered for nothing. Just looking at Vegas had me growing hard again.

Vegas's full lips poked out prettily above her scrunched chin. "Why don't you lie here?" she said, her hand smoothing out the rumpled surface of the bed.

I imagined her palm running along my thigh and up my stomach, and it took only a matter of seconds before I was stiffer than a pair of cheap jeans.

"I'm fine here, Vegas." I pulled down my tee, covering up my obvious excitement. "I thought you wanted to talk?"

She rolled forward and crossed her arms underneath her breasts, pushing them up. My mouth watered, and it wasn't because of the forthcoming chicken wings. I wanted this woman. I needed her. At the moment, I didn't know if finding a release in her was my way of escaping the pain of my divorce or if it was more.

Only time would tell.

"I want to talk, Jae. But over dinner and a bottle of wine." Her amber eyes pierced me and her voice became honeyed. "In the meantime, why don't you pack up your stuff so you can stay here with me?"

Her wish was my command. In under ten seconds, I was out the door with a mumbled, "Be back in a few." I didn't even bother to put my shoes on.

While I was in my room, haphazardly stuffing my overnight bag with my spare shirt and toiletries, a bitter chill went down my spine.

Would she still be waiting for me, or would she run?

CHAPTER SIX

VEGAS

Present day

"Um, Jae, can you give me a moment? I really need to use the restroom." I dashed off before he could reply, my stomach heaving and rolling like a ship tossed on stormy waves.

Just as I sank to the floor, the pasta primavera Terence, and I had shared for lunch, spewed from my mouth in an Exorcist arch, splashing the pristine toilet bowl in chunks of red and partially digested white.

When the dry heaves were over, I stood on shaky legs and wiped everything down with the antibacterial cloths from my purse. After dumping them into the silver bin on the wall, I plunked down on the toilet lid and pulled out even more of the wet clothes to use on my mouth and trembling hands.

The toilet seat shifted with a slippery creak as I bent over and held my head in my hands, moaning softly. The toilet seat shifted with a slippery creak the more I moved around by alternately raising a foot on my tiptoes, I had hoped the movement would relieve the fist-sized knots in my stomach. It didn't work. Nothing did. I had to face the music.

Jae.

Paying for It

After two years of working as an Emergency Room resident — through sweat, tears, and blood — I dulled the memories of my past, Jae included.

At one glance of his broad shoulders, trim waist, messy hair, and lazy smile, everything came rushing back. Instead of fuzzy black and white, the images of that night were once more in vivid living color.

***

VEGAS-Reliving the past

Jae licked the spicy sauce off of his longer fingers, leaving his thick thumb for last. He finished with a resounding smack, wiping the last bits of sauce on his stained napkin. He then set his empty wineglass and plate on the nightstand.

"So you start your residency next week? At the same hospital they brought JFK to in Dallas?"

I nodded and took a sip of wine.

He fixed his eyes on my moistened lips, and I resisted the urge to lick them again. "Have you ever been to Dallas before?"

"I was born there, or so my birth certificate says."

"What does that mean?" he asked, picking up a carrot stick.

I elaborated, giving him the dry toast version. I wasn't quite drunk enough to give him the meat and potatoes. "My mom died of a heart attack when I was two. Her sister, my aunt Mae, raised me until I was eight."

Paying for It

A drop of condensation, like a tear, slid down the outside of my goblet. I collected it with my finger and wiped it on my jeans. "The company she worked for needed her in Japan. She wanted to take me, but she thought life in America would be better." I took a healthy gulp of Riesling, pausing in the middle of a tale I was in no hurry to finish.

When I fiddled with the delicate stem of my wineglass, Jae prompted me by nudging his sock covered foot against my bare one. "And?"

I took a deep breath. Only my best friend knew of all the shit I went through. Why should I tell this man?

All I knew is that I wanted to. He was hurting like I had hurt. Besides, I'd never see him again, anyway.

You want to. You already know you want to.

Perhaps.

The guy just got divorced. You would be nothing more than a rebound. Just like you were with your football player senior year.

Jae nudged me again. "I'm here, Vegas. Talk to me. I want to know everything there is to know about you."

"Why do you want to do that, Jae?" I took another sip of courage. "We're strangers attracted to each other at best and at worst... we're two people who want to escape our pain."

Jae leaned forward, drawing up his long legs and circling them in his arms. His eyes fixed on his knees. "I came here tonight to do just that, escape my pain. You're right. In the end, I did much more. I feel a connection to you Vegas, something I can't explain. All I know is I want to see you again after tonight, I want..." Jae leaned his forehead on his knees. His t-shirt pulled up, showing a bit of his erector spinae.

So damn hot.

I licked my lips in my want of him.

Yeah, he was handsome, and he made my heart stutter. More than any man I'd come across. Even more than the man who took my virginity.

Jae was also a good listener. He seemed like he cared, and he wanted to get to know me. I believed he was sincere in that. My upbringing, shitty as it was, gave me a sixth sense in judging people.

Jae was one of the good ones.

The silence that stretched between us had gone on long enough. It was my turn to prompt him into a confession. I did so by running a finger along the valley his t-shirt had exposed. "What do you want, Jae?"

CHAPTER SEVEN

VEGAS-Reliving the past

He looked up. A red spot had formed on his olive skin where his forehead had rested on his knees. I want to smooth it away and the worry in his furrowed brow.

"I don't want to scare you off, Vegas. Why don't you ask me that question another time?"

I made an exaggerated pout with my lips. Jae fixed his gaze on them as he spoke. "I hope you'll allow me to show you how much I like you. I hope that in time, I'll be able to say what I want. Deal?" He met my eyes. The worry (of rejection?) still lingered in them.

I wasn't quite ready to make that deal, but I trusted Jae enough to continue with my story... after taking another sip of wine.

"My aunt handed me over to my Chicagoan father and his adoring wife." I let out a mirthless laugh, then drained my glass dry. The sweet wine mixed with my bitterness, making the retelling of my story almost palatable. "You should have seen their faces when I showed up. They never even knew I existed." The chilled wine bottle almost slipped from my grasp when I grabbed it from the nightstand. In my rush to drown out the terrible memory, I nearly overfilled my goblet with the contents, stopping just short of the rim.

Paying for It

Even at eight years old, I recognized what my arrival meant, and it was nothing good. My dad's face had been a mask of shock. The blood had pooled in his forehead and his cheeks, turning his caramel skin the color of weathered bronze. As my aunt provided proof — letters and my birth certificate. Tina, my dad's wife, had narrowed her eyes into slits and her mouth thinned into nothingness. Over the years, I would become very familiar with that look.

Jae curled his fingers briefly over mine before he removed the empty wine bottle from my clenched hands. He set it on the floor. "I take it your home life wasn't great," he said, his voice full of compassion.

"Nope. Not by a long shot," I whispered, rapidly blinking back the excess moisture that had formed in my eyes. Jae lifted the wineglass from my hands, took a sip, then set it down next to his on the nightstand. He stretched out his long legs, draped his arm around my shoulders, and curled a hand around my arm. I leaned into him, placing my palm on his chest. He was so warm and comfortable...

"Was it your stepmom that gave you trouble or your dad?"

"That woman was never a mother to me." The facts behind the words weighed me down like an anchor, sinking me into the ocean of my past. "My dad, when he was around, was great. He was a pilot for an airline and he flew a lot. Every time he came back, he would bring me a souvenir, usually a magnet or a t-shirt from the cities he overnighted in. Everything was fine when he was there."

Paying for It

"What happened when he wasn't, Vegas?"

I moved from him and yawned, feigning disinterest. "Typical wicked stepmother, the same story heard a thousand times over. Enough about me," I said, closing the subject by changing it. "What about you? What do you do?"

"My parents are alive and well. Like you, I have no siblings. As far as work goes, I do nothing. I don't have to."

I turned my head to see him fully. "Okaaaay, so what does that mean?"

The force of his sigh caused his chest to heave under his t-shirt, and I ached to hear his heart. One day, I wanted it to beat just for me.

Crazy, Vegas. That's just crazy.

"A few companies bought my patents, and now, I don't have to work."

My mouth gaped in surprise. "So you're pretty smart, huh?"

Jae rolled his eyes to the heavens before returning his gaze to mine. His lips lifted into a wry grin. "Says the girl who graduated medical school at twenty-one."

I shrugged. "Yeah, well. Things just worked out for me."

We lapsed into silence. Time passed. Eventually, we laid down, shoulder to shoulder. My head migrated to his chest. The quietness between us, comfortable as it was, had brought more memories of the past to the forefront.

Paying for It

They coated me in melancholy like a shriveled newborn's caul.

This will end just like your last relationship. You know that, right?

Those were my thoughts as Jae brushed my curls with his hand. That, coupled with the wine, lowered my eyes to half-mast. Dipping my head down further, I listened to the steady beat of his heart.

Mesmerizing. He had an excellent heart rate for a twenty-six-year-old. Fifty-nine beats per minute.

And it will never beat for you.

I was about to rise, to call this whole thing off when Jae tilted my head up with his finger. Our lips met. Soft and urgent and needy.

And until the morning, I forgot all about the bad because he was just that damn good.

CHAPTER EIGHT

JAMESON

Present day

"What are you doing hiding behind that plant, Jameson?" Shelia's blue eyes grew playful in an attempt at bedroom charm. I knew what she wanted. Crowds and admiration always turned her on.

Too bad.

She would have to look elsewhere. We hadn't slept together since before Vegas, and now that I'd found her again, Shelia was nothing more than an annoyance I had to get rid of... and fast.

"I just wanted some air, Shelia. You know I'm not good with crowds."

Shelia's eyes turned downward like they did when she knew I was lying. She could always tell. Hell, anyone could. I wore my emotions on my face and my heart on my sleeve.

I crossed my arms, waiting for her to call me on it, but all she asked was, "Are you ready to go home?"

"Sure," I said, "let's go." It was obvious Vegas wasn't coming back. For over thirty minutes, I'd kept my eyes trained on the hallway, waiting for her return while the past we shared kept me company.

Paying for It

Shelia linked her arm through mine, her nails resting lightly on my forearm. The facets of the diamond I gave her winked in the light. Once a cherished heirloom, I now hated that ring. It was a stark reminder of our sham marriage. We kept up pretenses in public, but behind closed doors, we led separate lives.

Outside, Shelia left my side to speak to an elderly couple, both with snow white hair and botched face lifts. Their expressions were so fixed, only the suit he wore identified the man from the woman next to him. Given time, my ex would be the same. When the ravages of age kicked in, Shelia would gladly lay under the surgeon's knife.

A lanky teen with a constellation of acne came up to collect my valet ticket, breaking me out of my thoughts. "I'll have your car right out for you, sir."

I nodded and patted my pant pocket. His eyes drew down and widened. He dashed off, smiling.

Damn shame how few people tip the valet these days.

It wasn't so long ago I had the same job. Miles I'd run, night after night, in the snow, the wind, and the heat. Oh... that heat... and the humidity was hell. I hated how the sweat formed on my forehead and under my arms, trickling down my back like a scared toddler on a slide. That was bad, but what was worse were how the fat, rich men acted like assholes just because they could.

"Keep it close," they would often say, their barbed tongues lashing out over their veneers. "And no scratches, boy." The young bimbo on their arm would giggle, entertained by the sugar daddy's wit.

40

Paying for It

Thank goodness those days are over.

My medical patents kept the coin rolling in, and my secret passion kept even more money coming my way. Too bad Shelia used it like a weapon, threatening me with exposure if I stepped out of line. Before Vegas, I didn't think of doing so—there wasn't a reason. Now that she was back, well... I was going balls out to get her back.

And Shelia could do her worst.

The valet drove up. I slipped the teen a twenty for his effort.

"Thank you, sir," he said, scrambling out. He went around and opened Shelia's door. She got in without thanking him. Not even a fucking nod. Secretly, I hoped he would close the door on her thousand-dollar jacket.

"I need to stop by the convenience store on the way home and get a few cigarettes," Shelia said, tugging on her coat. A hiss of hot air escaped through my ex's teeth. Shelia clawed at the handle, opening and closing the door before the air conditioner escaped. Her head whipped around for the valet, gnashing her teeth.

Since he'd disappeared, I received the full brunt of her tirade. "Would you look at what that idiot did?" I glanced down and bit my laughter back at the long black mark that slashed a line across the bottom of the white silk.

My secret wish had come true.

"It was an accident," I said, inching the car forward. "Let it go." She wouldn't. She never did.

Paying for It

Shelia huffed, no doubt thinking of a creative way to get her revenge. It wouldn't be the first time she'd ruined a life... or stunted one like she had mine.

Yeah, my ex was truly a dirty piece of work.

I pulled into the nearest gas station. Shelia begged me to go in. I turned up the radio, drowning out her pleas. She cursed me under her breath, slamming the car door a moment later.

I briefly thought about leaving, but I didn't. Instead, I watched her through the windshield as she stood in line, tapping her expensive heel on the dirty tiled floor. The closer to the counter she came, the more I let my mind roam free on exactly what I wanted to do to Shelia. My jailer. My executioner. My ball breaker.

Snorts escaped me at the image of me peeling out of the parking lot, leaving her ass in the less than stellar neighborhood. I laughed until tears fell at how her blond head would whip right and left as she looked for me, the man who was nothing more than arm candy and the driver of her silver Audi. A car I'd bought and paid for.

And how I was still paying. Day after day. Night after night. I was alone and without the love of a wonderful woman, the only thing I've ever wanted in life.

In the beginning, Shelia blinded me. I thought I had achieved my happily ever after with her.

Not so.

After I caught her cheating on me with a resident doctor, I lawyer-ed up the next day. Within a week, I'd her served with divorce papers. I expected a fuss. A damn fight, at least. That didn't happen. In fact, Shelia had readily agreed. Her only stipulation was that she tend to my needs until the divorce was final.

Naïve me thought I was getting the best of both worlds. I'd get a no fuss divorce, and I wouldn't have to look far for quick gratification.

Little did I know it was Shelia's way of keeping me under her thumb. When I'd finally figured it out, I ended all physical contact, but not before she had what she needed to ruin me.

Why had I let her suck me in again?

It was my fault. I knew what a manipulative bitch she was. Three years of marriage had taught me that. I should have never let her spend the night with me when someone ransacked her apartment. My first instinct was to drop her off at a hotel and wash my hands of the whole situation. We were getting a divorce; I had no stake in her. It was stupid of me to come to Shelia's rescue, but her pleading wore me down.

The next morning, I awoke to the shuffling of papers and the clacking of a keyboard.

Her name soured on my tongue even as my mind spoke it in terror. When I entered my study, the one I stupidly forgot to lock, there she was, behind my computer, rifling through my files.

I stood helpless in the doorway while impotent rage and shame alternating for dominance of my soul. Shelia's triumphant smile told me she'd found what she was looking for. The very something that would once again bind me to her, despite us on the road to Splitsville.

Paying for It

Shelia had turned the laptop in my direction and when I saw what was on the screen, I died a thousand deaths.

All I could think about was Vegas and how she would react. Once I found her, that is.

Vegas.

I'd never stopped believing in her...in us. We became fated with her tap on my shoulder. That one simple touch struck an ember in me and ignited a fire I thought had long since died out.

Vegas.

She disappeared that morning after, and I had no way to contact her. A few days later, I'd hired an investigation firm run by an old friend of mine and they found... nothing.

Not so this time.

Her ditching me at the fund raiser only prolonged the inevitable of us being together. Her boyfriend ... no, her fucking fiancé would lead me to her all right. The prick was easy to find. He was running for mayor, after all.

CHAPTER NINE

VEGAS

Present day

"Would you like to come in?"

Now why did I ask that?

The excuse was always the same.

"No." Terence shook his head, averting his baby blues by fiddling with the radio. "I need to get up early." He leaned over and gave me a dry kiss on the cheek. It was the last act before he left me- like he usually did. "I'll call you tomorrow."

My hasty exit didn't compare to Terence's. I stepped from the car, closed the door, and turned for a final wave goodbye. I barely caught the gleam of his taillights right before his car disappeared around the corner.

What's the hurry?

Since I moved back to Chicago, Terence and I have shared a total of three passionate kisses and half a dozen cuddles. He said he wanted to wait for the night of our marriage to do more. I agreed with no reservations. My reasoning was: if he loved me enough to want our second-first-time to be special, who was I to argue?

Paying for It

Only recently had I questioned his choice and try to wear down his determination. Against all my feminine wiles, he'd held steadfast. A solid rock of iron that couldn't break. This night, my feelings had changed. As I watched his car zoom away into the darkness, I breathed out a sigh of relief. I wasn't angry that he didn't say "yes".

***

Shondra greeted me when I entered the double iron and glass doors. Her manicured hand was finger deep inside a tub of buttered popcorn. She wore a purple nightgown, the one with the small white polka dots that reminded me of tears. On her face, the makeup she applied for the party she'd attended was absent — and still she was beautiful.

"So how was it?" she asked, eyeing me from head to toe. What she was looking for, I could only imagine.

I started in without preamble. "Jae was there."

The handful of popcorn that was on the way to her mouth fell back into the bucket. Her eyes grew round under her eyelashes and her wide mouth broke out into a grin. "What happened? What did you say? When are you going to meet again?"

I sighed and kicked off my heels. "Nothing happened. I said little, and we aren't."

Shondra crossed the marble foyer and grabbed my arm, leaving a greasy print on my skin. "What dafuq you mean by that?"

Paying for It

She won't let it go until she knows everything.

I broke from her grip and rolled my neck and my shoulders, preparing for a grilling of epic proportions.

"If I'm going to give you a blow by blow account, I want to make a cup of tea first."

It will give me time to figure out what to say.

Shondra eyed me suspiciously. "You won't disappear in your room, will you?"

"No, I want to talk. I need your advice."

She rolled her eyes in disgust. "You ran away, didn't you?"

"Tea first." I turned and headed to the kitchen without waiting for her reply.

***

The copper pot whistled its ready tune. Shondra, with a humph in my direction, sat down on a kitchen chair, which creaked under her bulk.

Shondra was a big girl. She was the size of a high school linebacker, and she weighed just as much. Her even-toned skin was the color of a seventy percent cacao bar, and her eyes were a natural Kelly green. My girl had a shape like an hourglass, with a triple helping of T and A.

The men that laughed at Shondra when she first approached them, soon wished they hadn't. From her first words, she held them captive, and by the time she turned them loose, they were on their knees.

Paying for It

Shondra could get any man anywhere, and they always wanted seconds. When they called her up the next day, begging to go out again, it was her turn to laugh. She rarely went out with the same man twice.

"Okay, Vee, spill."

"Maybe I should check—"

Shondra lifted an eyebrow—a perfect arch. "Now, Vee."

As I sipped my tea, and she munched her popcorn, I told her everything. I withheld not a single detail. Out of pity, Shondra kept her eye rolls and tsks to a minimum. When I came to the part about Jae's wife, Shondra started asking questions.

"So you were in the bathroom when his wife entered."

"Yes." I blew on the contents of my cup before taking a small sip. "That's why I didn't leave. I wanted to hear what she had to say."

Shondra shifted. The chair whined. "How do you know she was his wife?"

"Because the woman asked if Shelia, that's the wife, and Jameson would go to the Bakers' party on Saturday night." I gave her a pointed look. "How many people do you know have the name Jameson?"

Shondra tapped her lacquered purple nails on the wood of the kitchen island, staring off into space. It was her way of thinking everything through.

48

Paying for It

While I waited for her thought process to finish, I held my cup in both hands, trying to warm them. Seeing Jae again had left me cold. There was more at stake than just me. All the entanglements that surrounded me would eventually come out. The trajectory had begun from the moment I saw him.

"Well, you have a point," Shondra said, conceding. "Then what happened?"

I quickly swallowed the tea in my mouth. "They discussed her ... Shelia's, new job at the hospital." Shondra didn't make the connection, so I added another clue. "Her Emergency Room duties."

The light bulb over my best friend's head grew to full wattage in less than a second. She leaned forward and slapped my knee. "Nuh uh. No way. You mean to tell me his wife is gonna work with you?"

I shook my head. Shondra leaned back, relaxed.

"She won't work with me," I said, setting the cup down. "I'm working for her. Shelia Caldwell is Shelia Caldwell-Thijssen. My new boss at the hospital."

Shondra jumped straight up. Her chair fell backwards, clattering to the floor. "Dafuq you say?"

CHAPTER TEN

VEGAS

Present day

"Well, you know what we have to do, right?" Shondra said, bending down and picking up her chair. "We need to go to that party." She sat down delicately, like a princess on her throne.

Shondra was indeed that—more than. "A Queen among mere mortals," one of her "dates" told her a few months back. We'd laughed about his cornball sentiment, but it was true. Shondra, who'd come up from nothing, had an empire. She was royalty.

"I think I can wrangle an invitation," she said, nodding to herself.

"Wrangle? You must have been looking at an old western or something." I took a handful of popcorn. It was cold. I winced as if it burned me and dumped it back in the bowl.

Yuck!

"Cold popcorn is so gross." I dusted my hands over the table, trying to get rid of the nasty, shivery feeling.

"Gurl don't be correcting my words and don't be f-wuckin' with my popcorn." Shondra's fine brow scrunched like torn up concrete and her mouth rested in a scowl. "Did you even wash your damn hands?"

"Uh, f-wuckin' is too close to the real thing and you know I don't like you saying 'b' and 'd'." I shook my head in mock disgust. "I suggest you moderate your language, Triple T."

Shondra shook her finger at me, leaning forward in her chair to speak her piece. "She won't get what I'm saying, no how. And don't 'Triple T' me in my home, dagnabit."

I pushed the popcorn bowl closer to her. "Hey, just because you own a company with thousands of employees, don't think you can lord over me." I smiled at the end to let her know I was kidding. Shondra had saved me a thousand times over. I owed her more than I could ever repay.

I rose to make another cup of tea. Shondra rolled her eyes before drumming her fingers once again on the table. Sho, lost in deep thought, worried about the turn of events.

Hell, I was too.

Lifting the copper kettle, I poured steaming water into my china cup. The Earl Grey I removed from the metal tin had come from Harrods of London.

Shondra might have grown up at the low end of the middle class spectrum, but she was doing more than fine now. Her kitchen alone was the size of my college apartment.

Paying for It

The maîtresse de la maison snorted behind me and I moved so she could throw her popcorn into the stainless steel recycle bin under the sink.

"Let's get back on track." Shondra placed the bowl inside the dishwasher and shut it with her hip. The door closed with only a whisper of a sound. I loved her appliances—actually, the entire room. The kitchen was a chef's paradise with all the latest top-notch equipment. Though she could cook, Shondra barely used it. That was what the cook, Ms. Richfield, was for.

"What is there to discuss?" I said, blowing on the brown liquid. "I'm up for going to the party." My stomach fluttered at the thought of seeing Jae again.

Just seeing him was enough. I can make do—

"Won't your man say otherwise?"

The weight of an anchor replaced my good feeling.

Terence.

I had completely forgotten about him.

Don't you love him?

I do. But Jae ...

Hands, lips, tongue... soul.

Shondra snapped her fingers, bringing my thoughts back to the matter at hand.

"Terence knows about Jae," I said, pouring the rest of the tea down the drain. "Uh, um, we talked about him.

We had to, after all. He wanted to know... well, let's just say we discussed Jae in great detail."

Too much detail. I'd told Terence everything before I moved up here. I wanted there to be no secrets between us. When I was through, Terence not only offered to help me find Jae, he suggested something so preposterous, I still couldn't wrap my head around it. I had declined his offer, but told him I would think about his suggestion.

Oh yeah. I will think about it. A lot.

Shondra leaned back on the island, one hand on her hip. "I know that look, Vee. What did he say?"

"Terence said ... "At Shrondra's impatient look, I rushed through the rest. "He wants to give me closure if that's what it takes."

Shondra's mouth gaped open and her neck swiveled back in surprise. It relieved me not to have to explain. Shit was too deep.

When my roommate gathered her composure she asked, "And what did you tell him?"

Of all the questions she could have posed to me, that was the easiest one.

"I told him I wasn't sure."

Yet.

After seeing Jae in the flesh...

Still lean. Still handsome. Still a part of my life... for years to come.

Shrondra flapped a hand. "Damn ... oops! I mean darn. I'd have to take him up on that." She winked. "At least twice." Shondra started fanning herself under her arms, eyes rolling in her head. She was acting a fool to get me to laugh and relieve the tension.

I let out a chuckle or two before reality hit, as swift and as sudden as nightfall, and my face collapsed into seriousness once again. One night with Jae wouldn't be enough. The fire he'd lit three years ago still burned within me. Just seeing him had rekindled the embers of my feelings.

Shondra stopped her antics and her president-in-the-boardroom attitude came out to question me.

"What are you going to do, Vegas Shipley? Are you going to accept your free pass and end whatever it is between you and Jae, or will you run again like last time?"

I jutted my chin out. "I didn't run."

Shondra patted her hand over her scarf, twisting her lips and looking up at the recessed lighting. "Mmm hm."

"Look, I-I don't know, all right? I'm still not sure." The equation for the best outcome had so many variables, it would take a supercomputer to work everything out. "Before I can decide on Terence's suggestion, I need to talk to Jae."

Shondra perked up.

"In private, Sho."

Paying for It

My best friend, my sister, deflated. Shondra had played a part in every big decision I've made, but in this one, I had to do alone.

Shondra smiled, lighting the way in the darkness. "Then it's settled. We'll hit that party. You and me."

CHAPTER ELEVEN

VEGAS

Present day

After we made a few vague plans on how to *'wrangle'* an invitation, I left Shondra foraging in the fridge.

Crossing the marbled foyer, I headed upstairs, running my hand up the intricately carved wooden banister. When Shondra had this house built, she worked with a top architect and designer to bring the home life. She wanted light and air, and a showcase for her wealth.

And they delivered. Ten fold.

Original art from several African and African-American artists hung on the walls. Modern furniture (costly and comfy) graced every room. Each window, most floor to ceiling, let in as much light as possible. Before I moved in, the house and grounds featured in several magazines and talk shows. Shondra had declined further offers, even one she'd received from People Magazine, out of respect for my privacy.

Not for the first time had she put my needs before hers. And as much as I didn't want her to, she would continue to do so. Shondra rarely budged, and she usually got her way. Like when I told her of my plans. The words of "I'm thinking about moving back to Chicago" were no sooner out of my mouth when Shondra took over. She helped me get my last two years of residency switched to a hospital she donated to and insisted I live with her— rent, utility, and food cost, free.

My best friend. My sister.

On the last riser, my gratitude for Shondra, something I felt every day, welled inside me. I stood in awe at how perfect my life was in these moments. With a heart filled with love, I rounded the corner and opened the door.

And inside ... a miracle.

Kae was fast asleep on her back in her wooden crib. A chubby hand pressed against her head. The nanny had dressed her in one of her many, many sets of pink pajamas.

Shrondra had insisted on a pink. "I'm going to give my goddaughter everything I wanted, but my mama couldn't afford," she'd told me.

I tried to argue with her, but she shot me down so much, my behind leaked lead.

In the end, Shondra had her way and pink held sway.

Kae had a room fit for a princess. Baby-doll pink paint graduated from the floor to the ceiling, ending in a whitish-blush. A quilted patterned rug, pink of course, spanned almost the entire width of the dark bamboo floor. All her stuffed animals were pink, her strollers—pink, and most of her clothes were pink. Pink *was* my baby's color. It went well with her olive tinted complexion and dark curls.

Paying for It

My arms ached to hold her soft, warm weight. I settled instead for brushing my fingers through her mop of thick hair. Her pink bow lips pursed and my heart nearly burst through my chest when she laughed in her sleep. Her timbre was as light as air and sweeter than Dutch apple pie.

Jae is half Dutch.

That made my baby a quarter. When I first found out I was pregnant, three weeks to the day after Jae and I were together, Shondra hired a top investigation firm to find him. By then I was ready to search all of Chicago, I missed him so much. We had more than sex that night, we connected, like two old souls separated by time and space. Even during, I knew it was more than just physical. I must've cursed myself a thousand times for running out on him because I was too damn scared to give him a chance. Even if I was ninety-nine percent sure we'd end up like my first and only relationship, Jae deserved a chance to prove me wrong.

Trouble was, the firm dug up a lot on Mr. Jameson Thijssen.

It *was true* his net worth was more than I, as a doctor, would probably ever see in my lifetime. It *was true* he'd started divorce proceedings, but *he hadn't gotten divorced.*

Learning that minor detail had caused such a pain to blossom over my heart, I feel to my knees, right there in the detective's office. The detective, a balding man with wisps of white hair and jowls like a hound dog, had gazed at me with sympathy while Shondra patted my back.

Paying for It

Amidst their sounds of compassion, a steely resolve overtook me. I mentally put on my big girl panties and pulled back my shoulders like the woman I was. *"No matter his marital state," I said, switching my gaze between the blinking detective and commiserating Shondra, "Jae deserves to know about his child."*

The detective offered to set up a meeting. Shondra did as well. I declined. My problem wasn't theirs.

I came up with a plan and put it into place. I put off my residency by a year and carved out a bit of time here and there to stalk Jay. With my binoculars around my neck, I parked in the first row of the upscale strip mall outside of Jae's apartment. It took almost six months before he exited the front doors at the same time I was there.

My heart jumped when he came into view, only to crash when I saw who was on his arm. An unpleasant taste, like cold popcorn, filled my mouth. My baby moved within me, kicking in protest at the sight.

Jae's *wife* chatted like a magpie while he smiled down at her. Another couple walked with them and from the expression on their faces, they admired the lovebirds. That was bad enough, but what really broke me was his wife's diamond ring. I caught the flash through my binoculars. With the magnification of the lens, the rock looked as big as a robin's egg.

Morning sickness, something I didn't suffer from until then, started that day. *That moment.* My Starbucks latte and chocolate chip cookie had splashed my lap and the floorboard while something inside me broke.

That *something* was my belief in happily ever after and love at first sight. After two strikes, first Terence and then

Paying for It

Jae, I promised never again to put so much faith in a man. Once Kae was born two-and-a-half months later, I left Chicago and *ran* to Dallas.

I was content to stay there and would have if Terence hadn't called me, begging for another chance. I was ashamed to tell Shondra it took only a week for him to convince me when she had been trying every day for the past two years. Truth was, it was neither of them. I missed Chicago and the people I'd left there. Chicago was my home.

The people in charge of the residence program didn't give me static. I told them my father, who'd finally divorced the bitch of his wife, needed help to get into a nursing home. The doctors had diagnosed him with the beginning stages of Alzheimer's. His wife had stayed true to form by honoring her marriage vows and sticking by him through thick and thin—note the sarcasm. When I found Daddy, Tina had taken his money, his baseball memorabilia, and his dignity by moving him into a junkie-infested building in the worst part of Chicago.

I settled him into one of the best facilities in Chicago and with a trusted nanny to watch my child, a fiancé, and a residency program arranged by Shondra, I lacked for nothing.

Except for Jae. He was in town. Somewhere. Maybe the same place? All I had to do was stalk him like I did before. No one had to know. No one had to discover the longing I still harbored in my heart...

But I pushed those thoughts down. Way down. So far, they didn't resurface... until I saw him again.

Paying for It

Terence was to be the answer to my prayers. I wanted a stable life with someone who had a stellar background, and Terence was it. There were no skeletons in his closet. I had Shondra make sure.

Yes, Terence was perfect. And no matter how often I needed to say it to *convince* myself, Terence was the man I loved.

But when did convincing ever guarantee believing?

CHAPTER TWELVE

JAMESON

Present day

The Bakers' party was in full swing. As Shelia made a show of air kissing a group of men by the entrance, I slipped away on the pretense of getting her a drink. I doubted she would notice I had left. Shelia liked to be the center of attention wherever she went, and those men would fill that need. If they didn't, she would find some group or *someone* who would. When she got bored (or ran out of victims) she'd come and find me. That was how it usually worked.

Never one to worry about entertaining myself, I easily found friends who I liked to hang out with. And after leaving Shelia, I went on the hunt for them, starting outside. The day was perfect for a garden party. The sun was bright, and at four in the afternoon, the September had turned pleasantly cool. I waved to a few people I knew and chitchatted with a couple more. Tate Harvey, one of members I sat with on the board of directors for a tech company, crossed the lawn and called out my name. "Thijssen, you are just the man I was hoping to see."

We shook hands warmly. "Mr. Thijssen, I'd like you to meet my son, Trevor." He pushed a nondescript boy with pale skin and black hair forward. The father a rotund man had hair redder than a firetruck and a florid complexion and I vaguely wondered if he had adopted the boy.

Trevor held out a limp hand. "Hello..." he mumbled something, probably a mispronunciation of my last name. I was used to it and let it slide.

"Pleased to meet you, Trevor." I let go of his slightly clammy hand, smiling inwardly.

I had been the same way at his age, which I guessed to be about thirteen. A shy introvert, I still found it hard to fit in during social gatherings.

"Trevor will go off to college soon, right after he graduates on his eighteenth birthday, a full five months early in December."

Damn, was I wrong about his age.

"Uh, that is an impressive achievement, Trevor."

Trevor hung his head and shuffled his feet on the grass.

"Trevor," his father boomed, "Mr. Thijssen is a solid engineering man. You could learn a lot from him."

Trevor peeked up at me through his stubby lashes and resumed a slouchy stance.

"Trevor is going to study engineering down in Texas. He got a full-ride scholarship to A&M."

"That is a wonderful school. I'm sure you will do well."

Trevor mumbled something which his father understood, but I didn't. "That's right, Trevor. This is the man that is on three boards of directors and has won the Draper Award twice in a row. No one is as admirable as he in your field."

Paying for It

And that was the crux. Neither Trevor nor Mr. Harvey would look at me the same way again if my secret were to come out. The one Shelia was only too happy to spill if I crossed her.

And I would do that... when Vegas came back into my life. She was worth my ruined reputation.

That and a lot more.

***

Eventually, the Harvey's, and I parted ways. Soon after, I found Axel in the solarium, just off the garden. We shot the breeze for just a second before the venom in my best friend's voice had me spinning around to see who he was angry with.

"I hate that fat bitch."

A beautiful, curvy woman at the end of the hallway turned her head this way and that, looking for someone. Her skin was a shade darker than Vegas's and she wore her long hair straight. The dark strands framed her oval face and the curls at the end clutched her ample breasts like a lover's hands. The woman Axel shot daggers at wore a dark pink dress, which hugged every curve. She was big. She was beautiful. And she was *hot*.

If I weren't so into Vegas ...

"Are you talking about her?" I tipped my head in the woman's direction.

"Yeah. That's the bitch." Axel's lip curled as if he smelled something rotten. "I can't stand her fat-ass."

Paying for It

His words flabbergasted me. Who could hate such a lovely creature?

"Why?" I asked, perplexed.

"You remember the contract I had so much trouble with last year?"

Axel was one of the top contract lawyers in the country. Blessed with riches and good looks, he hadn't experienced trouble in his career except for once. Around Christmas last year, Axel had to iron out a contract between a defunct testing lab and a cosmetic company. Axel represented the lab pro bono as a favor to a senior partner.

The negotiations should have only taken a couple of weeks, but the owner of the cosmetic company, "Ms. Fat-ass Bitch" as Axel had called her, kept changing the terms.

My partner in crime had to cancel his Christmas trip to Antigua with a swimwear model to iron out the details. The model was so mad; she took off with an Indie 500 driver to a chateau in the French Alps. Axel had bitched and moaned like a lost ghost for months afterward.

"Don't tell me she's the cosmetic company owner?" I asked, watching as the woman's slim fingered hand plucked an appetizer from the tray of a passing server.

Axel's ice-blue eyes narrowed in disgust and his long arms flexed under his jacket.

"Yep. That bitch forced me to cancel my vacation to Tahiti with ah ..." Axel scratched the blond stubble on his angular jaw, his eyes still hard, "you know ..." he clicked his fingers and tilted his head. "Ah ... what was her name?"

I smothered a snicker. Axel never remembered the details, and it never occurred to me to question why. Once I saw who he was up against, I understood.

She's gorgeous.

"The trip was to Antigua, not Tahiti, and her name was Jasmine," I said, muffling another laugh behind my teeth.

Axel crossed his arms over his broad chest, his lips curled up in a sneer. "Who gives a fuck?" he growled. "I was going to bang *Jasmine* six ways to *Saturday*. That week in Antigua was going to be a stay-in-bed-fest with a gorgeous swimwear model who promised to do many things to my buffed body." He turned from the woman's direction, dropped his arms, and raked an angry hand through his unruly blond hair. "But what did I have to do? I had to spend Christmas in cold-ass Chicago with Ms. Fat-ass Bitch who couldn't decide what she wanted."

"Stop calling her that, Axel." Whatever she did, she didn't deserve that name.

I glanced over at the woman in question. She was bearing down on us and closing fast. "And keep your voice down, she's headed our way."

Axel's face tightened in anger, and his eyes had turned into shards of ice. "I don't give a fu—"

CHAPTER THIRTEEN

JAMESON

Present day

"Axel Sexton, so good to see you again." Up close, she was even more beautiful. Her green eyes sparkled and her mouth curved into a genuine smile. Whatever beef Axel had against her, she held none for him.

My friend morphed his face into a nondescript mask. The tick in his jaw, however, gave away his dislike. "Hey, Shondra. How's it going?"

Shondra's beautiful smile widened, exposing her even white teeth. "Good, good." She rocked back on her pumps and shot me a questioning glance, clearly waiting for an introduction.

Axel, it seemed, wasn't in the mood.

"Jameson, I'll catch you later." My best friend, *my brother*, left us without another word. His abrupt departure caused an awkward silence in the space he'd vacated.

After a few seconds, I took the plunge and introduced myself. "Hi, I'm Jameson Thijssen."

Paying for It

Shondra's green eyes popped. She shifted her hand in mine and stepped back, looking me up and down.

"Jameson, Jameson. You look different with your glasses." She squeezed my hand. "I've only seen pictures, but the real thing ... my, my, no wonder."

Did she know me?

Her words made me wary, as if I were waiting for the sound of thunder after the bright flash of light. My hand grew clammier than Trevor's under her regard, and I disengaged from her clasp.

"Have we met?" I asked, lifting a questioning eyebrow.

Shondra tossed her long hair over her shoulder and planted her hands on her wide hips. "Oh, don't mind me." She fluttered her lashes. I lost my train of thought. "How do you know Axel, Jameson?

Except for Vegas, I wasn't normally loquacious with strangers. Shondra's seductive aura, like that of a siren's song, prompted me to speak. "Axel and I went to college together."

She gave me a sage look and stepped forward, closer into my space. "Oh," she said, her voice lilting, "that Ivy league thing."

"Yep," I said, shifting my stance from one foot to the other. Only Vegas had made me more nervous, and this woman was a close second.

What was it about her?

Shondra gave me an impish smile. "Is Axel always such an ass?"

Paying for It

A disquiet tingle rose within me. I felt the need to defend Axel like I had defended her against him. "Normally, he's a good guy, but it seems *you* are the exception. Why is that?"

Shondra looked off into space and her eyes turned down as if she were witnessing a tragedy. "Your friend Axel is a little boy accustomed to getting his way, especially with women." Her eyes changed into the scorching color of GOT's wildfire and she shifted them on me. "When he finally grows up, he'll be one hell of a man."

I silently agreed, sensing something bad had happened between her and him. I doubted whether I would find out the "what". Axel *never* 'kiss and tells,' and I respected that. As close as we were, I never told him about Vegas. Some things were better kept private.

But there would be no more of that. I needed Axel's help in dislodging Shelia from my life. Thinking of our long-standing friendship and what it meant to me, my words to Shondra flew from my mouth, coming out a lot harsher than I intended.

"I guess you must not know him too well because he already is a hell of a man." I bite back the rest I wanted to say. I didn't know this woman, and without getting into his personal details, I doubted she would understand why Axel was the way he was.

Shondra let out a huff, her round globes rising. "I'm sure he is—when he is not chasing skirts all over Chicago."

Is she one of his conquests?

Paying for It

Shondra didn't look like Axel's normal type. He went for models, actresses and...that was it. All one-nighters from my understanding, but then again, I didn't know for sure. Since our sophomore year at Harvard, and that incident with Tabitha Moore, Axel had been tight-lipped with his sexual prowess.

"Look, Shondra, Axel is an adult. If he wants to play the field who are we to judge?"

"Do you play the field, Jae?"

WTF?

The conversation had just hit the outer limits.

"Call me Jameson, please." I said, fixing her with a curious stare. "And I'm married."

For all intents and purposes.

I hadn't had sex since Vegas, mainly because I hadn't felt such a connection to anyone, and before her, Shelia had been my first and only for the three years of our marriage.

And although Vegas didn't know it, *she* would be my last.

Shondra gave me another coy smile, and my slight anger dissipated under her engaging charm.

"Being married doesn't stop attraction, does it?"

Heading into dangerous territory, but I want to see where it goes.

"No," I answered shortly, my mind firmly on Vegas. "It doesn't"

Paying for It

Shondra moved lightning fast. Before I could blink, she was a fingertip away. Honeyed breath fanned my face. Her perfume, flowers and musk danced in my airways. Shondra's large breasts grazed my chest and the outline of her pebbled nipples revealed themselves under the silk of her dress.

Damn.

If I didn't have Vegas on my mind, I would drag this woman into the nearest darkened space and give her what she so badly wanted.

Shondra looked up at me from beneath her lashes, a small smile on her lips. "You're attracted to me, aren't you?"

"Yes, I am." Some inner voice told me not to lie to this woman, so I bared it all. "You are beautiful, confident, and sexy as hell. But like I said, I'm married."

She cupped her chin and tapped a manicured nail on her cheek. "Hmm. You keep saying you're married, but you say nothing about love. Interesting."

Shondra stepped away, giving me breathing space. I nearly sagged in relief that the temptation she presented had faded. Only with Vegas had the pull towards a woman been so irresistible. Though with Shondra, it was as if she were excreting some sort of pheromone that had me under a spell.

Go. Now. Before you do something stupid...

"Uh, it was nice meeting you Shondra, excuse me." Heady with the victory over the little brain in my dick, I took a step back in preparation to run for the hills.

Paying for It

Shondra's soft voice stopped me just as I reached the door. "You passed *my* test, Jameson. You are welcome to see Vegas *in my home*, anytime you wish."

ACT TWO

~The deepest hurt
is when the story
is not finished.

CHAPTER FOURTEEN

AXEL

Twelve years ago

"Hey, Mom?"

"Yes, Axel?"

"Can I unpack later? I want to go to the park and see if I can get in on a game." Football was where it was at, but basketball would do in a pinch.

My mom sighed and sat heavily on the bed, one of my dad's undershirts clutched in her thick hand. "I don't want you going alone."

"Let the boy go, Marjorie," Dad said, packing tobacco in his pipe. He didn't smoke often, but the drive down from Vermont had worn him out. Mom wanted to stop every few hours to stretch her legs. I know the trip was hard on her. Being as big as she was and cramped in a car seat for hours couldn't have been easy. "Axel is sixteen and can take care of himself." He winked at me from over Mom's head. "Can't you, son?"

I raised my long arms, flexing my biceps. The muscles strained under my skin. Daily workouts in the gym had me ripped. Even Coach said so. Anyone tried to put the jump on me, I would hand them their ass on a silver platter. "No one is going to mess with these guns." I kissed my right bulge and waggled my brows.

Dad laughed outright while Mom repressed a smirk.

"Axel," she began, "you'll have all Thanksgiving-week to play in the park."

It was a weak excuse, and we all knew it. I backed up a step, inching towards freedom.

"Go on, son." Dad tipped his pipe towards the door. "Just be back by six or your Aunt Liza will have you doing dishes."

"Yes, sir."

I thundered down the stairs, not giving Mom a chance to change her mind.

She called after me, "And don't slam the screen door."

BANG

"Axel..."

Her admonishment faded into the crisp wind. I hated to worry her; she had a heart condition, after all. Yet I needed a rest from the stuffiness of the house and the log car ride. Fresh air and exercise beckoned. I couldn't resist their pull any more than I could resist breathing... or looking out for the hotties.

I picked up the pace, jogging the two blocks to the park. Green ash and maple leaves crunched under my feet.

Chicago differed from the small Vermont town I grew up in—much more diverse. If I could sample a few of the local delicacies while I was here, I would go back home a fortunate man.

Paying for It

I'd been playing streetball for an hour when a girl sat down on a bench near the swings. Even dark skin, thick as fuck, with plenty of jiggle in all the right places. She kept twirling her long hair around a finger. I'd looked up just in time to catch her giggling at a funny part in her book and damn if her smile didn't beat back the sun.

I had competition, though. Several guys had gone up to her, but she politely shooed them away. I didn't think I had a chance until I turned on a pivot and saw her checking me out, too.

"Don't even bother white boy. That fat-ass don't give it up for no one."

I narrowed my eyes at the lanky African-American dude giving me lip. He'd been one of the first she'd turned down. "The name is Axel, and don't call her that, *prick*."

He held his hands up in surrender. "My bad, *Axel*. Why don't you go over there and see what you can do?"

"I think I will." The ball I tossed at his midsection made a satisfying *smack* as he caught it a second too late. He cursed me under his breath. That was fine. As long as the fucker said nothing to my face.

The girl's exquisite almond-shaped eyes, the irises as green as the field behind our mansion in Vermont, lifted from her Kindle Paperwhite and widened at my approach.

My swagger slowed. The view of her was just too beautiful to rush. Her cheekbones were higher than the Alps, and her lips were juicier than an overripe mango.

Paying for It

I could feast on those for days and still have some to take away in a Styrofoam container.

She giggled.

Did I say that out loud?

She straightened her shoulders and frowned at me, but the shining laughter in her eyes was unmistakable. "To what part of my anatomy are you referring?"

Way to go, Axel.

"Um ... I mean your lips are ... um ... very nice."

She regarded me for a moment, searching my soul for its sincerity.

My knees trembled. I sent up a silent prayer, hoping she'd let me get to know her. I'm rarely entranced by a girl... hell, I never have been, but something drew me to this one and I wanted to find out why.

She turned off her Kindle with a click. "If you had said boobs, I was so outta here." Relief coursed through me when she patted the space next to her.

I parked my ass, leaning back like I was at ease while a wheel of nervous fire churned my insides.

"Well," I said, keeping my eyes on her face. "I will not lie, girl. Those are nice."

She giggled again, hiding her mouth behind her hand. At her openness, my nervousness quelled enough to allow me to take in the melodious sound her braces did little to muffle.

"Very nice, indeed."

She play-frowned at me.

Damn. Girl even frowned prettily.

"Don't get any ideas ... "Her lifted eyebrow asked my name.

"Axel, Axel Sexton," I said, taking her warm hand in mine. Even before I lifted her hand from her lap, I knew it would fit perfectly in my palm—and it did. "Uh, what might be your name, angel?"

"Shondra," she said, dazzling me with her smile. "Shondra Williams."

CHAPTER FIFTEEN

AXEL

Twelve years ago

"Shondra. Shondra Williams," she said, turning our hands over.

Shondra the big.

Shondra the bold.

Shondra the beautiful.

She wore a light pink T-shirt, a gray leather jacket zipped to her mountains, and ripped blue jeans. Small silver hoops dangled from her earlobes and small glinting diamonds, three on each side, rose into her cartilage. Her makeup was over the top, like that of an Instagram model, but the bone structure underneath supported her fineness.

"You're beautiful, you know that?"

She smiled, her braces glinting in the sun. I hadn't seen the metal kind on anyone except in old sitcoms. All the people I knew could afford the invisible ones. I found the uniqueness made her even more attractive.

"Thank you, Axel."

I like the way she took my compliment and put it in her pocket.

Paying for It

Shondra trailed a finger down the back of my hand, raising gooseflesh on my arms. "You have nice skin."

Her matter-of-fact tone did nothing for me. Her touch, however, caused a hitch in my throat. I had to clear it before I thanked her.

A hint of a smile graced her face before it disappeared under her concentrated brow. "Your hands are very smooth, but your palms are rough."

That summed up my personality too. Smooth with the ladies and rough on the field ... and between the sheets.

Take it easy, Axel.

My playa-instincts told me to slow down with this girl. Hell, woman. She was rockin' her style and makeup so well; she had to be over eighteen.

"Is that why you are holding my hand? To give me an analysis?" I squeezed her fingers. An acceptable substitute for the other parts of her anatomy I desperately wanted to explore. "She cocked her head, elongating that beautiful neck I wanted to make my mark on.

She giggled. "Nooo. That's not why."

"Then why?"

Her gaze was on our hands as she spoke. "I just want to is all."

The contrast between our skin tones was striking. Mine had the tint of a northern tan while hers was like a rich, reddish brown.

Damn, how I want to taste it...

Paying for It

A child's shriek from the swings broke me from my lustful thoughts and I said the first thing that popped into my mind.

"So what's going on around here." My "here" came out as "he-ya".

She giggled again, laughing at my accent, which was more pronounced when I was nervous. I couldn't help it. True beauty always wound me up.

Still, I couldn't look weak in front of her. Shondra had displayed no hesitation in rejecting the guys who delivered crap lines and sported big egos. I wasn't about to be among the losers.

Palman qui meruit.

I straightened my spine and gave her the look I reserved for my opposition on the football field. "Are you laughing at me?" I growled.

Her eyes grew wary, like two Victorian plates behind the window of an antique shop. She tugged her hand from mine. The cold rushed into my palm like an Arctic blast.

"No." She looked over the field, past the players on the courts and into the distance. "I wasn't. I was just thinking."

Say something dumb-ass.

"Hey. I was just kidding, Shondra." Forcing a laugh, I and twisted on the bench so she could see my candor. "I can be fake mad too, can't I?" Girls back home loved it. They said my bad boy look made them throb.

81

Paying for It

Shondra kicked her feet out from under the bench, crossing her legs at the ankles. The shoelaces of her tattered gray Converse trailed the ground. "I don't know you like that," she pouted, biting the corner of her plump lower lip.

Hot damn, that's sexy!

Usually when a girl played hard to get, I was out. Axel Sexton was above the chase. Not so with Shondra, I wanted to know the woman behind the stellar beauty.

"Will you give me a chance so you can?"

She skipped my question and asked one of her own. "So where do you live? I've never seen you at the park before." Her gaze flickered to mine, and I became lost for a moment, busy imagining them full of sleep after I'd taken her all night.

"Um. I-I'm here with my parents, visiting my aunt and uncle. They have a house a couple of streets over."

She nodded. Gathering her hair together from the base of her neck, she threw it over her shoulder.

No tracks or nothing. Shit is real.

I didn't mind wigs, weaves, extensions or braids. It was just helpful to know the lay of the land so I wouldn't tug them loose during sex.

"So... Axel, are you just here for Thanksgiving?"

"Yeah."

I sighed, already wishing we were staying longer. It was kinda funny that normally for the break; we went skiing. Well, Dad and I did. Mom sat by the fireplace and read books all day. Anyway, when Mom first proposed this trip to visit her great Aunt, I threw a fit. I had been looking forward to the new crop of snow bunnies I'd plow all week. Last ski trip, I was in so many girls' rooms, I barely spent time on my own. To solve the stand-off, Dad promised to take us to Aspen for Christmas. I reluctantly relented. Now, the thought of leaving filled me with a drudgery sort of sadness, like sludge at the bottom of a drain.

I know already that I'll miss her.

Shondra sensed my moroseness and leaned in closer, bumping my shoulder. "So where are you from?"

"Vermont."

Her face lit up like a department store Christmas tree and her voice held awe. "You are so lucky! I've always wanted to see the abscission of the leaves there."

I swatted at a fly that buzzed in my ear, and my annoyance at the insect laced my words. "The what?"

She leaned away from me, probably thinking I'd directed my pique at her. "Abscission is the shedding of a tree's leaves." Her mouth curled into a defensive frown and she tossed her hair back. The parts the sun dappled on glowed like auburn fire. "I'm a girl who likes science and math. I won't apologize for it."

Shondra reminded me of the queen Nana Yaa Asantewain I'd read about in my World Culture class—proud and fierce. In that moment, I ached for her like no other.

CHAPTER SIXTEEN

AXEL

Twelve years ago

"Hey, I'm not asking you to," I said, hastening to reassure her. "You're right. The *abcession* of the leaves in Vermont is pretty cool."

Again with the smile that stole my breath. "Abscission."

"Yeah, um, that." I quickly changed the subject to hide my lack of knowledge. "So... uh, what are you reading?"

"The Alchemy of Air by Thomas Hager."

"I had to read that for an AP class last year. It's an influential book."

She barely hid her scoff. "What did you like about it?"

"Why? You think I haven't read it?"

Her lips quirked up. "Sum it up in a few words, then."

"If I do, will you let me take you out?" Mom would throw a fit about me going out at night, but Dad would talk her around.

"When?"

"Tonight." I said, hoping I didn't sound too eager.

"As long as it's after eight, that's fine."

Paying for It

"Deal," I said, turning so her warm, sweet breath fanned my face. "Do you want to kiss on it?"

She pursed her juicy lips, making me stir down below. "Shaking hands will do." We shook. Longer than necessary, but not long enough for me.

"Well..." She cocked a brow, reminding me of my challenge. "Give it to me. Twenty words or fewer."

Easy. I don't have a 4.3 GPA for nothing.

I cleared my throat, then launched into the task. "Haber and Bosch, came up with an alternative way to make fertilizer, saving future generations from starvation."

With her nod of deference, I felt like I'd won a billion-dollar lottery. Elation coursed through me. I was already planning on having a night to remember, hopefully with plenty of kisses and cuddles, but I didn't plan on rushing things. With Shondra, I wanted to take things slow... to savor every moment and take those memories back to Vermont. Shondra was different. She wasn't trying to impress me. She just did.

And for once, I wanted to do the same.

"What film production would you like to attend? Personally, I wouldn't mind a documentary or indie film." I mentally patted myself on the back, thinking I was all that.

"Oh, really?" Her look told me she was not fooled by my frou-frou answer. "There is a marathon of art films based on the female and male reproductive system. How does that sound?"

Paying for It

Fuck no. I knew everything there was to know. I had started at thirteen and would probably would finish at a hundred, dying in the middle of sex with an enormous smile frozen on my face. My love of the act didn't mean I wasn't overly careful. Given my background, I had to be. The thrill of riding bareback wouldn't have me paying eighteen years plus for a one-night mistake.

Not this boy.

"Um, not so interested in that. Let's stick to a mainstream genre. What about a comedy or action?"

She wrinkled her nose. "Hmmm, I don't mind a romcom, but please no action."

Anything you want.

I pulled out my phone, and under her direction, we searched the movie listings for the closest theater. Good thing she lived close by, just on the other side of the park. Mom wouldn't like it if I had to travel farther than a few miles in a strange city. I wouldn't either, to be honest, but for Shrondra I would.

"Oh, that one looks good," she said, pointing a manicured nail at my screen, leaning into me.

Thigh to thigh, shoulder to shoulder, and I took the opportunity to stalker-ly breathe in her scent. A mixture of jasmine, vanilla, and some other aroma I couldn't name.

She popped up, catching me. "Are you sniffing me, Axel?"

Damn.

Paying for It

Her expression wasn't angry (thank heaven) just curious.

"Um, no."

Her eyes narrowed.

"Yes. Okay? Yes. It's just that you smell so good. What kind of perfume is that?"

Her gaze was steady, and there was a hard line to her mouth. "It's my own. I made it and never lie to me, Axel."

Shame burned my cheeks. She didn't hit me, but the sting from her words felt like a bitch slap.

"Sorry, Shondra."

She bumped her shoulder into mine, forgiving me without words, and her accompanying made everything right with the world.

Damn, do I want to taste those lips...

Shondra was of the same mind. Her chin tilted up in slow motion and she lowered her lashes.

This is it!

The anticipation of laying my lips on hers sent a tremor down my spine.

I moved in.

So soft.

And she tasted like cotton candy. I tugged and teased on her juicy goodness, coaxing her for more. A moan escaped me when she opened her mouth wider. I plunged inside.

87

Paying for It

Our tongues twisted and turned like a canoe going down a whitewater rapid. We rocked and groaned, clutching on to each other in our need to survive. Eventually, we came down into calmer waters; the thrill lingering even as we broke apart.

"Axel," she said, catching her breath, her long lashes fluttering. "That was—"

"Shondra!"

Three guys headed towards us, kicking up dirt and leaves with their shoes. Evil intent splashed all over their faces.

"What is it?" I asked, tensing my thighs to spring.

In the fifteen seconds it took for the trio to reach our bench, Shondra gave me low down while removing her hoops from her ears. "The blond has been after me for months. Damn bastard won't take no for an answer. I'm going to end it today."

She placed her earrings and Kindle in her bag, setting it on the bench. A car radio blasted Eminem's *Till I Collapse*. I smiled, cracking my knuckles. The song was the perfect mood music for stomping some ass.

"So... you too good for the guys around the way, huh Shondra?" said the leader, a bleached-blond with a donut of flesh around his middle. Dude also had the biggest nipples I'd ever seen on a man, a woman, or a cow. Shit resembled like close pins.

The clowns who flanked him (the ass-hat who'd given me lip earlier and a somewhat buff Latino guy) carried off the expressions of crazed-hungry hyenas. Their leader, looking between Shondra and me, was the lion getting ready to enjoy his meal.

Not today.

I had been fighting since the first grade and I hadn't lost yet. These three pussies would be no exception.

Better make it quick 'cause Mom will hate it if I come back bruised.

Shondra and I stood as one. I moved in front of her, rolling my neck.

"What do you want, Duke?" Shondra said, moving to my side. Again, I angled my body in front, not realizing what she was doing.

"Name is Daquan," Lard Belly said, spitting on the ground and wiping his mouth with a dirt smudged hand. "You know that, bitch."

It's on now. No one messes with my angel.

"Daquak," I said, stepping all up in his space. "Why don't you and your buddies get dafuq outta here.

CHAPTER SEVENTEEN

SHONDRA

Twelve years ago (one hour before)

I shuffled my feet, crunching the leaves under them. The fir trees, dead leaves, and wet earth, combined to make the perfect scent to herald the death of summer and the coming of winter or what I called the fragrance of fall. I stood still and tilted my head to face the sun. Drawing in a deep breath, I savored the smell of Heaven.

Summer, with its oppressive heat, made people act up in the summer. There were more shootings, more robberies, and during a summer barbecue my uncle—

"Hey Shondra!" Ms. Jenkins called from her stoop, putting an end to thoughts I always tried to suppress.

Round, doughy, and on disability, Ms. Jenkins was a permanent fixture outside. No matter the weather— blistering heat or frigid wind—she sat in her weathered rocking chair like a bird on a wire. Her keen eyes taking in *everything*.

Ms. Jenkins was by far the biggest gossip of the neighborhood. She had no qualms about spreading juicy tidbits she'd gleamed about her adult neighbors, but she let nothing slip about their children.

Like what happened to me when I was eight.

Paying for It

And for that, I was eternally grateful. To show my appreciation, I did what I could to take care of her.

Placing a foot on the first step leading up to her stoop, I raised my head much as I'd done toward the sun. After all, she was my hero.

"Yes, Ms. Jenkins?"

"Do you have a new batch of that perfume you make? My boyfriend is comin' round tomorrow night and I need some in the worse way."

"Yes, Ms. Jenkins. I'll bring it around after I get back from the park."

My neighbor nodded, satisfied. "You've got a talent there. The way you make all them different scents... you're a miracle worker, baby girl." She rubbed the mole on her chin and beckoned me closer so she wouldn't have to shout over Mr. Sutherland's leaf blower. "Now, my crotch can sometimes be funkier than fresh chitterlings, but one drop of your perfume has me smellin' like a springtime daisy." Ms. Jenkins reared back and cackled, slapping a plump, be-ringed hand on her expansive thigh.

I shook my head, but spared a laugh for the foul mental picture. "Ms. Jenkins, you are something else." I adjusted my bag over my shoulder, waved goodbye, and headed up the street. Crazy and crass as she was, Ms. Jenkins was right. Mixing *was* my talent.

The bug for mixing bit me when Mr. Jacobs, my AP Chemistry teacher, bought a perfume starter kit. He wanted to make a unique scent for his wife, for Valentine's. The day after, he brought the leftover ingredients to school and let the students in his AP

91

chemistry class use them for an extra credit project. I was the only one who went for it. Through trial and error, I made a sweet smelling scent...at least that's what everyone in class said and even Mr. Jacobs nodded his head, impressed by my efforts. He took me aside after class and encouraged me to sell it. I thought about it for a few days, and since I had nothing to lose (well...not too much), I went for it. Later that day, I took the two hundred dollars I had in my bank account and started my empire.

With the glass atomizers I had bought of Amazon, I mixed three scents. I took the stash to school, marketing them from my locker. In two days, I sold out. I ordered a new kit and made two fresh scents, for five in total. Those went fast as well. This went on for a month before security got wind of my dealings. They caught me selling my "drugs" and took me and my remaining vials to the Principal's office.

Principal Moore, fairer than most, let me off with a "talk" and a warning. I also had to swear not to "distribute" on campus since doing so "sent the wrong message." With a wink, a finger to his lips, and a twenty-dollar bill, he bought the four remaining vials for his daughters.

My brush with security didn't stop me or slow me down. I bought a bigger kit, filled with tons of scents. I gave a sample to Ms. Jenkins, and within a week, I was back in business with orders a mile long. In the eight months that followed, I opened a business bank account, registered my company, and converted (with the help of Mr. Jacobs and permission from my mom) a spare room into a home lab. With the week off from Thanksgiving, I planned to make the biggest batch yet, hopefully selling out before Christmas.

My mom deserved a gift. At twenty-nine, my mom looked as worn and faded as a forgotten newspaper left out in the sun. She often worked two, sometimes three jobs at a time. Except for her company now and then, I never wanted for anything. And as much as she was able, she was there for me, encouraging me in my dream.

If I could earn enough, I'd take her to a day spa, get a few treatments, then go to dinner afterwards at some place a lot better than McDonald's.

"Have fun," Ms. Jenkins called after me, "and watch out for that Duke. He left up the street, headed that way 'bout a half hour ago."

Damn.

Duke, a neighbor boy and classmate who lived a few houses away, had been sniffing around me since the first grade. I ignored his advances, friend zoning him time and time again. I wasn't interested in guys. Not in Duke's kind, anyway. They reminded me too much of my uncle.

The pawing. The grabbing. The *arrogance.*

Until I found a guy who treated me like a person instead of a piece of meat, someone who was as intelligent as he was sincere, I'd stay single. Besides, I was too busy with my business. I was going to make it in this world. Come hell or high water.

I walked the length of the park, looking for a seat. In this fine weather, and with many people free from work, they took all the benches... except one, and I hurried over to claim it. From my seat, I watched the little kids in the distant playground, jumping and sliding, squealing and laughing. With no sign of Duke, I slowly lost the tension from my shoulders.

After a shake of my head at my paranoia, I pulled the Kindle from my bag and dug into the last few chapters of the mystery book I was reading. From time to time, catcalls from different guys interrupted my reading with shady lines. Sitting this close to the courts, I couldn't expect much less. If I didn't hear a wolf-whistle or a "give me yo' number", it was a slow day indeed. Damn shame girls had to put up with such shit, but that was the way of the world that men ran. Still, I didn't let it bother me too much. I needed a break. If I could have a few hours in the sunshine with my book, I'd be happy.

I stared off into the distance, thinking how a simple word brought up the ugliness I could never escape. What happened to me as a little girl no older than most playing on the swings had made me lose some of my joy. How could I keep it knowing what evil walked the world?

He's in jail. He can't hurt you.

Yes, he can.

He was in every candy bar, piece of cake, and pizza slice I ate as I tried to make myself unseen.

Let it go, Sho. Enjoy the day.

Bit by bit, I let the sunshine heal me. The laughter of the kids—

Wait...

Paying for It

Is he looking at me?

CHAPTER EIGHTEEN

SHONDRA

Twelve years ago

I'd snuck more than a few glances at him. More than I had at any man. I liked the way he moved... gracefully, as if the ball were part of his hand.

Tall, with wavy blond hair and light eyes, he knew he was handsome. I could tell by the way he had taken off his Harvard hoodie, carelessly tossing it on the ground. It was there in the slow *look-at-me-way* he'd run a hand over his abs before flexing his sculpted arms, stretching them towards the heavens.

Yep, this Mr. Harvard *knew* he was something.

Duke was like that as well—even to the point he was working on his body to back it up. When he'd cornered me in the janitorial closet last week, Duke had made a point of planting his muscled arms close to my head as he tried to steal a kiss.

Tried being the operative word. I kneed that fool so hard, he'd dropped like an anchor, straight to the floor. I left him there in the dark, coughing and moaning like a little bitch. Served him right. No man would take from me what I didn't want to give—not any more.

Paying for It

When I have my first **real** kiss, it will be with someone **I** want to be with.

Unlike the only kiss I'd received, my first *real* kiss wouldn't taste like beer and cigarettes.

My sight turned inward, thinking of that day. When the past grabbed a hold of me, I spaced out for a few minutes, sometimes longer. Eventually I'd snap myself from my trance and go about my business. This time, when I came back to the world, Mr. Harvard's eyes were on me, searching, probing, taking me in from head to toe.

Guys had tried to devour me before, sure, and I brushed it off like I would an insect crawling on my arm. This boy, *this man*, had my heart lurching and my stomach pounding. Puzzled by my instant attraction, I bent my head and pretended to read. Seconds later, I hazard a peek to see if Mr. Harvard was still looking. He wasn't. He had the ball under one long arm while he used his mouth (and what a beautiful mouth it was) to argue with Michael.

Michael's thin brown lips moved in ugly strokes and his beady eyes shot daggers in my direction. That damn fool was probably calling me all sorts of names because I'd turned him down. Clown was mad because he couldn't get some. Lousy *pig*. All Michael and his type wanted was to break me in, not build me up.

I'm not about to settle for that.

Mr. Harvard seemed of the same mind. He threw the ball at Michael, hitting him square in the gut.
The *smack* the projectile made when it connected with his flesh made me smile. Michael was part of Duke's clique and I hated him almost as much as his fearless leader.

Paying for It

They ran through girls like berries through a goose, their droppings, or victims, left on the pavement.

Mr. Harvard turned his back, missing Michael's scowl. He picked up his hoodie, dragged it over his head and down his long torso, watching me, watching him. His smile grew wider. He left the court, headed my way.

All right, Mr. Harvard. Let me see your worth. Are you strong steel or weak-ass chaff that I'll cut and let the wind blow away?

The confidence Mr. Harvard exuded as he swaggered towards me like a sailor back on shore didn't win him any points. In fact, I barely kept from rolling my eyes.

Chaff then.

However, I gave him a little leeway when he didn't sit down without asking, plant a dirty shoe near my bag, or lean in to grab my attention with a tired-ass line.

As we talked, the man...Axel won me over with his sincerity, his intelligence, and his abundant charm. He didn't make me feel less of a person because of my affinity for math and science, and he didn't try to undress me with his eyes. He *seemed* legit. When he asked if I wanted to go see a film, I readily agreed.

"Oh, that one looks good," I said, pointing out a romcom my mom had said she wanted to see. Axel moved in closer, bending his head and—

What is he doing?

Is he sniffing me?

I never had a guy *sniff* me before.

Cute!

"Are you sniffing me, Axel?"

"Um, no."

He lied.

Damn! I wanted to trust him too.

CHAPTER NINETEEN

SHONDRA

Twelve years ago

He gave me a contrite look with a rushed apology. "Yes. Okay? Yes. It's just that you smell so good. What kind of perfume is that?"

I narrowed my eyes. I *hated* liars. Axel needed to know this above all else or we would end before we had gotten started. "It's my own. I made it, and never lie to me, Axel."

"Sorry, Shondra." When he hung his head, something inside me crumbled. The warm blush coloring his sandy cheeks, reminded me of a little boy that got caught stealing sweets from his mama's purse.

Kiss-ably adorable.

A kiss?

Maybe ...

First, I had to make him smile so he would look at me again. I bumped his arm. *Solid.* Axel had those thick arms I wanted to wrap myself in so they could protect me from all hurt, harm, and danger. He was strong, respectful, and I liked the look of him.

Should I let go of my past and let him in?

Yes ... just a kiss.

Never had I wanted something so much as his lips on mine. Wishes for the success of my business, hopes of taking care of my mother, even the hurt I wanted to inflict on my uncle, paled in comparison. Without further hesitation, I tilted my chin up and lowered my lashes, leaning forward to meet him halfway.

His lips were as soft as butterfly wings and warmer than the rays of the sun.

More.

Damn, he was good. Nothing like *before*. No stale breath or groping hands.

This is how it should be.

"Axel ... "I stopped to catch my breath, trying to gather the words to describe all the magic that I felt. "That was—"

"Shondra!"

Dookie and his dickheads, their faces set in scowls, walked towards us.

Axel watched the guys approach, his body tense.

Poor guy. He's probably never been in a fight.

Those guys didn't scare me. Growing up in Chicago, I knew how to stomp heads into the ground.

I took off my earrings, and planned my strategy of attack, explaining the situation to Axel as I did so. "The blond has been after me for months. Damn bastard won't take no for an answer. I'm going to end it today."

Axel's face was blank. With fear? I wasn't sure. If he were to run, it didn't matter. I planned on taking all three.

Music blasted from a radio, drowning out Duke's mutterings. He raised his voice to make himself heard. "So you too good for the guys around the way, huh, Shondra?" Duke scowled, his blue eyes hard like stones.

He got the same look from me for his attire. In forty-five-degree weather, Mr. Dumb-fuck had only a thin shirt covering his chest. Seemed like he was just asking for some battle scars.

I tensed, ready and able. Axel joined me, stepping into my line of fire. I stepped around him, willing to take the first blow to save that beautiful face. "What do you want, Duke?"

"Name is Daquan," Duke said, spitting a glob of yellow phlegm in the dirt. "You know that, bitch."

Before I could open my mouth, Axel got right up into Duke's space.

"*Daquak*," Axel said, eyes colder than frost. "Why don't you and your buddies get *Dafuq* outta here."

I would have laughed if I wasn't so afraid Axel would get hurt.

Damn weird that.

This morning, I only cared about Mom, Ms. Jenkins, and myself. The rest of the population consisted of objects who co-existed with me. Axel had snuck in and had broken down my defenses to become a part of my world. I'd protect him, even at detriment to myself.

Duke blustered. I cut him off, stepping around Axel once more. "Duke, I'm not interested in you, don't you get that?"

"No, Shondra, I don't. And I also don't understand why you gotta hang around this pretty boy, like you too good or sumpthin' for the men 'round here."

While he spoke, Duke waggled a dirt smudged finger in my direction. At least I *hoped* it was dirt. Duke had gotten the nickname "Dookie" because in the third grade, he'd dug in his pants and smeared a line of crap down his desk, mad at the teacher for telling him to pay attention. The name Dookie had stuck to him like body odor. At least until last summer, when he grew seven inches and told everyone to call him Daquan. After a few after a few fights after school (and a couple during), Daquan stuck.

Not with me, though. He'd forever be Duke or *Dookie*.

"Listen, *Da-prick*, I suggest you get your shit-smelling finger outta her face," Axel said, his eyes spitting blue fire.

Duke advanced, bumping his chest into Axel's. "Or what."

"Keep your udders away from me, dude, or there is going to be a problem."

Duke poked Axel in the chest, smudging the white shirt under his hoodie with a dirty dark spot. "Are you *gunna* make me, asshole?"

Axel's smile was as chilly as the wind blowing through the trees. "You bet I am, mofo."

It was on.

Duke took a step back to get in some room, He then swung a hard haymaker at Axel's head.

Axel ducked and then charged forward, ramming his shoulder into Duke's belly. Duke flipped on his back like a turtle. Before he could think about getting up, Axel straddled him, pinning Duke's arms to his sides with his thighs.

Axel delivered punch after meaty punch to his opponent's head. Blood spurted from Duke's nose and lip, coating Axel's Harvard hoodie in a fine mist.

Michael dove in, his arm around Axel's neck, choking him.

My eyes stung with rage. Adrenaline made my heart pound, and I didn't think or hesitate. I grabbed Michael by the hair, yanking him backwards, tearing out tuft after tuft of his dry-ass fro.

The Latino that made up their motley group of three sniggered from behind his hand. "Damn. She kickin' yo ass, man."

Oh, I haven't even started.

I pushed Michael face down in the dirt. He coughed and sputtered, trying to squirm. I gave him an elbow-fist combination to his back, putting all my weight behind it.

A rib *crunched*. The sound was sharp and flat, like a can of exploding biscuit dough. Michael screamed like a little girl. I didn't stop there. Oh, no. I delivered lick after lick until powerful hands pulled me back and I heard a voice that made my blood run cold.

"Stop it, Shondra. And don't make me tell you twice."

CHAPTER TWENTY

JAMESON

Twelve years ago

"Jameson," my mom said as she came into the kitchen. "A sixteen-year-old shouldn't be working so hard... one job during the week and two on the weekends. You'll burn out before you turn eighteen." She moved closer. Her robe, a blue silk kimono style, went well with her elfin features and dark hair. At thirty-six, Mom was eight years younger than my dad, yet her eyes had small crinkles around the corners. I chalked them up to worry over me, her antisocial son.

My deep sigh betrayed my annoyance. We'd had this conversation before. Though we lived well (with my dad being a doctor and my mom an interior designer) they expected me to work for what I wanted.

And I'd wanted nothing more than the money for the 1967 Mustang wasting away in his garage. The body and interior were in an excellent state, the engine... not so much. After haggling back and forth for a week, we'd come to an agreement on the price.

With my parents' permission, I closed my bank account of the money I'd saved up from birthdays, paper routes, and cleaning dad's medical office every day after school.

Paying for It

It was just enough to cover the $6000 down payment. The remaining $6000 was due in three months, and one way or another I'd have that and some left over to get a few engine parts.

"I'll stop working so many hours at the grocery store and the country club when I get the money for the car, mom. You know this." I wasn't trying to be an ass. I was just tired. Work had been brutal. Private parties with an open bar made some people think *everything* was free. And though I'd maintained a smile, a pleasant attitude, and was quick to get the cars, it was a futile effort. The tips I'd received were dismal.

Mom regarded me silently as I took a gallon of milk from the refrigerator. My face heated under her disappointed gaze. I could count the number of times I'd talked back to my parents on one hand. Exhaustion had made me snap, and shame made me open my mouth to apologize.

Before I could, mom said, "Jameson... your father and I think you're spend too much time working and not enough hanging out with friends... doing things normal teenagers do."

A ghost of a smile touched my lips. "Do you think I'm *abnormal*, Mom?"

Spots of red appeared on her high cheekbones. "No. That's not what I'm saying... but if you wanted to tell us *something*, we'd be open...we'd be accepting. We'd listen."

Paying for It

Something in her look—resignation yet embarrassment—clued me in on the direction her thoughts had taken.

"Do you think I'm gay, Mom?" I asked, slightly amused. Mom calling my sexuality in question didn't anger me. I was more surprised she and Dad hadn't asked me sooner. I had few friends, and I worked all the time, whether at a job that paid, or on my patents that didn't.

Yet.

"No, Mom." I shook my head slightly for emphasis. "I like girls."

It was an understated lie.

From the time I entered kindergarten, I'd been in love with the female form. All shapes, all sizes, and all colors. All of them were beautiful. Some more than others, true, but if a girl carried herself with confidence and poise, I was halfway in love.

That was why I wanted a car. A *chick-magnet car,* my middle-aged neighbor had said, giving me a lewd wink. I'd get female attention driving a car like that. A guaranteed icebreaker to the shyness that engulfed me. In my Mustang, I would cruise the city.

And maybe, just maybe, find someone who would love me.

By her composed expression, my answer hadn't phased Mom. I counted my blessings for such an understanding parent. *Two* understanding parents. Dad, a *Nederlander,* was more liberal than most.

"Jameson, how you choose to live your life doesn't matter to us." She shook a thin finger at me. "As long as you are abiding by the law, that is."

I laughed.

She reached up and patted my arm. "We are here for you, and we support you in anything you want to do. If you ever want to talk, you come find us. Okay, sweetie?"

I nodded. "Sorry, I snapped at you."

Mom smiled, and everything was right with the world. She stood on her tiptoes and I bent my head so she could give me a kiss. With one last pat, she left me with my milk on the counter and trouble in my heart.

What I did in my room, on my computer, wasn't *illegal*. But to some, it was *immoral*. And as open as my parents were, given their standing in the community, I wasn't sure how they'd feel about it.

CHAPTER TWENTY-ONE

VEGAS

Almost twelve years ago

"Don't go, Daddy."

"Vegas, I'll be back in less than a week. Home in plenty of time for your ninth birthday." Dad circled his long russet arms around my thin frame. I squeezed him tighter. I didn't want him to leave. Bad things happened when he left.

"Now, come on. Be a good girl and let me go."

I resisted... until my step-mother, Tina, pinched me, making a *tsk*-sound behind her teeth. I jumped back, rubbing my upper arm. Following the direction of Tina's narrowed light-brown eyes, I saw the sketch of wrinkles around my Daddy's belt line. Wrinkles I had caused.

Tina was in charge of my father's appearance, from packing his clothes for every trip to the cleaning of his uniforms when he was back home.

And I'd ruined her hard work.

That's what she'd told me when she sent me to bed without dinner and the right side of my face momentarily numb from where she'd backhanded me. There wouldn't be a mark. Seemed she had a knack to never slap me hard enough to leave one.

Paying for It

I flipped my light out and crawled into bed, sleeping on my left side. It was a month before Thanksgiving, and the weather had turned cold. I buried deeper into my thin blanket. Tina had removed my quilt and turned off the heat in my room as soon as my dad left.

When she was in charge, I was too cold, too hot, and always hungry. I didn't know what I'd do when Thanksgiving break came around. Tina was a housewife, so if Daddy had to work, which was a strong possibility, it'd be Tina and me.

Not for the first time, I wished my aunt had taken me to Japan. She'd gotten a promotion and her company sent her there. My aunt Clara told me at the time that she would share an apartment with a colleague and she couldn't bring me. There was no room.

That was a lie.

I overheard Tina and Daddy talking a week after I'd arrived. They were in the kitchen. Tina was making bread. I thought it tasted like sawdust most of the time, but I didn't complain. Not after the first time when she'd pinched me so hard she'd broken the skin.

***

VEGAS-Reliving the past

Tina flipped the dough over and over. It made a smacking sound on the countertop that reminded me of the slaps she'd give me when my dad wasn't home, or if he wasn't looking... and sometimes when he was.

"Couldn't one of your relatives take her?" she asked.

110

Paying for It

"Who can I send her to? My parents live in a house half the size of ours. Besides, they're in their eighties. They can't raise a little girl —"

"Shut up," Tina snapped. "You're useless like always."

The way my dad had hung his head and shrunk in on himself, made my stomach pound. I was both embarrassed for him and fearful of Tina. If she could make a strong, tall man like my daddy small. What could she do to me?

Tina looked up from her deflated dough at me peeking around the corner from the living room. I scurried away, afraid she'd come after me.

She didn't, but her words did. Carried on an evil wind. Her hatred found me halting my tracks.

"I don't know why you didn't have the balls to say no to that woman. Just because she didn't want her, didn't mean we had to take her. I never wanted kids for a reason. You knew that when you married me five years ago. We agreed on it. Now, someone off the street throws papers in your face and you believe you have a brat. Well, not me. You may be simple, but I'm not. You and the little waste of space are getting a DNA test pronto."

A month later, the DNA letter arrived. I was his.

And Tina never let me forget just how upset she was with the results.

CHAPTER TWENTY-TWO

AXEL

Six years ago

"Axel, you'd better get up or they'll leave without you." Jameson yawned, his long arms stretching over the covers.

It's too damn early. Why the hell did I schedule us to leave for the conference at early as-fuck dawn?

"You have no right to sound tired, Jameson Thijssen," I rasped in his general direction.

"I'm not tired," he said, yawning again. "I had plenty of sleep."

Our Harvard house party had just gotten interesting when Jameson pussied out and headed up to our room. When I came in at the break of dawn, he was sound asleep. His phone, with no notifications on the screen, lay by his ear. He probably wanted a quiet place to talk to that she-devil, Shelia.

I mirrored his yawn and stretched, cracking my neck and arms. "And why did you leave the party, anyway? Was it to call your girlfriend?"

Jameson had it bad for Dr. Shelia Caldwell. She was a hot little number with a petite athletic body, bobbed blond hair, and a pedigree almost as impressive as mine. *Except,* her family had very little money in the bank.

Shelia was as sweet as a spring strawberry to my best friend's face, but she didn't fool me. Shelia and I came from the same ilk. We cloaked ourselves in subterfuge and bathed in deception. We were the type to go after what we wanted, smiling like a wolf the entire time—even wider when we ran over whom ever got in our way.

What separated us was how long we continued our path of destruction. Once I achieved my goal, I was done.

Shelia Caldwell kept going until there was nothing left.

She was an opportunistic, ball-busting bitch, and she had Jameson by the short hairs. He'd met her our freshman year when she was in her last year at medical school. Shelia had stood with a few other med students, handing out flyers for a community blood drive. Jameson and I sat under a tree on the commons a few yards away. We had different majors but shared a few core classes.

Getting good grades came easy for me, but for Jameson...it was like he wrote the damn textbook. He read something once, and it hunkered down into his brain, *forever*. Like a combat solider in a bunker, the information came out fighting when needed.

On the day we met Shelia was beautiful-not the experience, but the weather. It was near spring and the first good day after a dreary-ass winter. The sun was out. The clouds fluffy white. Girls on campus had given up their raincoats and boots for shorts and skirts.

A pleasant sight.

Paying for It

Never one to miss an opportunity, I dragged Jameson outside on the pretense of studying.

Like we *needed* to. My plan was to get my roommate laid.

Jameson was far from ugly and although his physique was nowhere near as developed as mine, he could hold his own. He also came from money and had a kick-ass muscle car. True, my looks and wealth didn't impress everyone. Girls turned me from time to time. Mostly, though, going home with a random (a one-nighter) was a done deal.

For Jameson, it wasn't about sex; he went straight in for love the day his eyes latched onto Shelia. He'd taken sneak peeks at her while he pretended to study, watching her chat up those that looked like they could do something for her, and turning away those that couldn't.

Unaware of the witch Shelia was, I encouraged Jameson to make a move.

"Go one, dude. She won't be handing out those fliers forever."

"Yeah, yeah. I know."

He didn't move. I nudged him in the ribs. Hard. "Move, chickenshit."

Jameson placed his textbook on the ground and rose fluidly to his feet. He walked over to Shelia like he was approaching his doom. She shielded her eyes against the sun and watched him approach. When he started talking, she gave him a smile I'd seen only twice. The kind that said, "I'm going to be nice, but I'm not interested."

Paying for It

Sure enough, Jameson came back with his head lowered to his shoulders, kicking up grass. "Yeah," he said, folding his tall-ass body to the ground, "she thanked me for my invite for coffee, but she's too busy with medical school to go out with anyone."

Especially my boy, it seemed. Jameson didn't see Shelia nudge her classmate, point at him, and laugh.

When she caught my anything-but-kind-gaze, she blushed like a Maine lobster. After a few exchanged words with her friend and another look in my direction, they abandoned their post and scurried like away like rats on a sinking ship.

I should've told Jameson what Shelia had done. I didn't because I figured he'd forgotten about her.

How wrong I was.

CHAPTER TWENTY-THREE

AXEL

Six years ago

They met up again two years later at a party. Shelia, through her medical connections, learned my best friend had sold a patent for a transportable dialysis machine and it had netted him a sizeable chunk of change.

She came after my boy with dollar signs in her eyes and her tongue rolled out like a cash register drawer. Shelia sunk her claws in deep, taking Jameson's virginity and claiming his undying devotion on the same night.

I thought it would blow over, but no. The dumb-ass was cock-over-heels in love, and nothing I said against Shelia-the-opportunist would persuade him otherwise.

"Yes. I left to call her. She didn't answer." Jameson's defeated tone, as if he couldn't expect any better treatment, made my hatred for his boo rise in my chest like acid reflux. I clenched my lips and forbid my mouth from spewing out the loathing I felt for Shelia. To do so would only lead to an argument, and it was too damn early for all of that.

The bed springs squeaked. Jameson emerged from his cocoon of bedcovers and stood. I was bigger in width, but Jameson was taller. His long torso blocked the sunlight from the window by his bed.

Paying for It

Through bleary eyes, I watched him shuffle to his dresser. "You should know, Axel, especially after living together for four years that I'm not into screwing randoms." The drawer he yanked open squealed like an angry toddler. He rooted inside, upending his neatly folded socks.

I rolled out of bed, ignoring *my brother's* dig at my lifestyle along with his petulance. Reaching back, I gingerly touched my left shoulder blade. A random I'd had a few nights ago used her fingernails on me. The spot was still sore, but it was healing nicely. I should've known the trails she made were extensive, given the way she'd hissed and writhed while I was inside her.

No matter.

If Allison wanted to hook up—like she said she did— I'd make sure the lights were off and the room was dark. I didn't want her getting pissed and jumping out of bed after I'd worked so hard to get her there.

I leaned back and thought of Allison and the ways I would explore her tight body while Jameson continued to pout and take his anger out on his clothes.

Yeah, Allison was an excellent choice for my last few weeks at college. She was one of those shy types, eager to please, and low-maintenance. Trying to tame a Hellcat like the one I'd had a few nights ago would be too hard with graduation looming.

Jameson didn't have worries like mine. He'd been with the same woman for two completely faithful years.

At least on his part.

Paying for It

I wasn't sure about hers.

Shelia was off last night and she had *promised* to call Jameson. I heard her say so when I walked in on their phone conversation blasting from Jameson's phone speaker.

Why else would a girlfriend not call or text unless she was getting down and dirty with someone else?

The thought of my roommate, my best friend, *my brother* getting taken by a c*heating* money-grubbing ho' prompted me to get him to realize what a huge mistake he was making. "Look, I know you, Jameson," I said, my voice coming out raspy from too much talking and second-hand smoke. "I'm just wondering if you know the real Shelia."

Jameson's shoulders tensed as he picked out a neatly folded white undershirt and slung it over his arm. He turned to me, a mulish expression on his face. "I know her, asshole," he said, chucking a rolled up sock at my head. I batted it away with a flick of my hand. The balled sock spun to the edge of my bed and teeter-tottered for a few seconds before dropping to the floor.

Jameson walked towards the bathroom, picking up his sock on the way. "Look, I'm in love, Axel, and unlike you, I don't need to screw a million girls to run away from it." He threw me a look of half-pity, half-amusement before he closed the door.

If anyone else had given me a look like that, I wouldn't have hesitated to kick their ass. Instead, I sat on the edge of my bed, cooling my anger.

Paying for It

When Jameson turned on the shower, I got dressed. The water was still on when I left, slinging my red duffel over my shoulder and hanging my suit bag off my knuckles.

Jameson thought little of my hookups with weekly (okay, sometimes daily) randoms. He thought I should be more like him — a monogamous idiot in love.

And at one time I would have been with...

Shondra.

Just thinking her name made my heart beat faster. There wasn't a week that went by that I didn't wonder about my angel. Shondra had captured me in every sense of the word. I cherished my memories of her almost as much as those of my late mother. After meeting her (and even before) I'd never fallen for a girl as I had for her.

And I've told no one about her either.

After what happened my sophomore year with Tabitha Moore, I made it a fast rule never to discuss my sex life. If Jameson hadn't been there to smooth things over with Tabitha's parents and the administration, my future career would have crashed and burned before it started.

CHAPTER TWENTY-FOUR

AXEL

Six years ago

"Everyone is asleep, Axel," Allison whispered. My current favorite flavor splayed a tiny hand on my chest and started kneading a pec. I looked around at the others to make sure she just wasn't being eager.

Tony sat in the front seat. His head lolled against the window. Adam and Josh were in the second row of the van, lightly snoring. I gripped the edge of the seat and sneaked a peek at Mason. Curled up in the fetal position, dude was off to the races with an open mouth and REM-twitching eyes. Allison gave me a triumphant smile.

"See, I told you."

"What about the driver?"

She shifted closer so that her thigh rested on top of mine and her thin leg dangled between barley missing my sweet spot. "He's busy listening to his jams. He won't hear anything."

Our driver, an older man with frizzled, graying hair and a bulbous nose, was currently be-bopping to whatever genre old people liked.

"Yeah, okay. What do you want to do?" I had been sneakily playing with her breasts for the last thirty minutes. At first, it was quick tweaks and pinches as I talked and joked with the guys, then it progressed into full palm rubs under her halter top as my friends fell into dreamland.

"Well, since you asked..." She took my hand from her chest and guided it under her short skirt.

When my fingers found her, she gasped.

After taking care of Allison, I slept all the way to New York City, dead to the world. Mason punched my shoulder, his affectionate way to wake me. I came to raring to go. Easing Allison's head from my lap, I gently shook her awake.

"Hey, Allison, we're at the hotel."

"Wake up sunshine," Mason added. "You have an hour to get glammed up, and then we have to head down to the conference room for the lecture."

Allison sat up, groggily rubbing the sleep from her eyes. "Whaa?" she looked around, blinking. "Where are we?"

I couldn't stop my lips from drawing up with a smirk.

Yeah, I put it to her good. Knocked the awareness right out of her.

I brushed her hair from her forehead and tucked a bit behind her small ear.

"We're in New York. Come on, let's get you settled into your room. At the word *room*, Allison turned to me and smiled, promises of further fulfillment in her eyes.

Oh, yeah. I'm going to enjoy this trip.

Paying for It

Check-in was quick and efficient. Within fifteen minutes we were in the elevator, the members of our group getting off on various floors. Allison wanted to join me, but I held her at bay with the promise to get together this evening. I wanted some alone time and a shower—*without* distractions.

I scanned my key card. The double doors opened with a soft click. Through our dues, the organization we'd all joined, Business People of the U.S.A. (or BPUSA) paid for standard rooms for the conference and not much else. When I checked in, the clerk recognized my last name and upgraded me to a suite with a view over Central Park.

As I gazed over the green trees and kites floating in the wind, I wished I had someone special beside me to enjoy the view.

***

"So what are we going to do afterward?" Adam asked, rolling up his collar and threading the tie around his neck. Adam, on scholarship and a work program, was just as intelligent as Jameson and the most disadvantaged. The rest of us had money. Adam only had himself. I admired the shit out of him for making it on his own.

Josh slapped Adam's hands away and fixed his tie with deft fingers. When he finished, he smoothed down Adam's too big blazer in a motherly fashion. Adam rolled his eyes and grinned. "Hands off, queer."

Josh smiled at the barb. "Takes one to know one." Josh winked, then faux punched Adam in the stomach.

"You'll pay for that later," Adam muttered with cheeky promise.

Josh batted his lashes and cooed like a dove, "Oh, I hope so."

"Damn. Enough already," Tony said with a fake body shiver. "I'd hate to be in the room next to y'all tonight."

Under Adam's baleful glare, Josh looped an arm around Tony's shoulders, a sly grin on his lips. "Jealous?"

Tony shrugged him off, laughing. "You wish."

"What are you guys talking about?" Mason said, coming back from the restroom.

Josh gave him a broad flirtatious grin, ignoring the angry look on Adam's face. "I'm trying to recruit Tony—"

"We were talking about what we were going to do afterward," Adam interjected in an annoyed tone. Adam was a possessive boyfriend, and Josh loved to push him to his limits. I briefly wondered if I would be the same if I ever came to care about someone.

Probably not. I'd never come close to being in love. At least not since—"What do you want to do, Axel?" Mason asked.

Allison joined us with a murmured "good afternoon," looking downright tasty in her red halter dress and heels. When she met my eyes, she looked away, blushing.

My words were for my brothers, but my intense gaze was for her. "You guys do what you want. I'll be busy."

CHAPTER TWENTY-FIVE

SHONDRA

Six years ago

"He's here, Vegas. I saw him check-in with a bunch of guys and a girl." I didn't have to tell Vegas who he was. Vegas Shipley knew all of my secrets. We were best friends, sisters really. If anything good had come from the aftermath of what happened to me, moving next door to Vegas was it.

"Axel is there? In New York? With you? Are you serious?!"

"No. He isn't with me." Spiteful jealousy clouded my voice and chose my words, "He's hanging onto some basic bitch that is thinner than my thigh."

Vegas snorted her disbelief. "And? Nothing wrong with your size, your intelligence, or your looks. If Axel has any sense, he will at least talk to you."

Not by the way he has his arm around her.

The way his palm rested more on the swell of her ass than on the small of her back announced his possession. She was his.

"Don't think that's going to happen, Vee." And oh, how those words hurt. The numbing pain started in my heart and shut down every organ until settled in the tips of my toes.

My daydreams of meeting Axel again began differently and ended the same. the ending was the same. We finished what we'd started that day in the park—complete with marriage and two or three kids.

The fantasies of a fat chick.

Should be a damn book.

"Shondra, you'd better not give in to doubt. You know you're rockin' it, girl."

Yeah, right.

My it, my confidence, disappeared as soon as I saw Axel's broad shoulders in a muscle shirt and heard his deep voice. All that remained of me was an insecure and frightened girl of eight that was forcibly kissed by her drunk uncle.

What would Axel think of me now?

"Vegas, I've gained about twenty pounds since I saw Axel last."

My uncle, though dead these six years, still plagued me from the grave. All starting with the kiss he gave me in my mom's kitchen during a neighborhood barbecue when he thought no one was looking.

Well, Ms. Jenkins was. She came rushing from the bathroom and pulled him off of me with both hands. He shuffled his feet and hung his head under her verbal assault. I stood by with big eyes, uncertain of what was happening, yet feeling dirty and ashamed as if the fuss were all my fault.

Bastard got what he deserved. If I were a man, I'd piss on his grave.

Vegas brought me back to the present with another snort. "If Axel is a good man, he won't even care. And if he does, then he wasn't worth a damn anyway."

She has a point there.

"Also don't forget, you have a successful company, a mother...um...who loves and supports you, and of course..." she coughed like she was humble, "me." We broke out in muffled giggles at her bad acting skills.

Our laughter was cut off when Vegas' loud-ass stepmother's voice came through the phone. "Vegas? Where are you dammit."

I hated that woman with a purple passion. She berated Vegas for every little thing. My girl couldn't do right in her eyes no matter how hard she tried. It was a wonder Vegas had any confidence at all what from being shot down all the time.

"I'm sorry I'm not there, Vee," I said, trying to keep the sadness from my tone. Vegas usually came to our house when her dad was away. Under the guise of helping me with my business, she was protected from Tina, the bitchy witch, as well. "You know you can stay at our house till your dad gets back."

"I know, but she isn't very mean today," Vegas said with an overabundance of pep. She was trying to make it seem like she was okay. I knew she wasn't. How could she be, living with a woman like that? "Don't worry, okay? I can hold out till you get home, Sho. You just make sure you talk to your man."

My man. I wish.

"Vegas!" her stepmother screeched. "Dammit all to hell, if you don't answer me, Imma gonna slap you into next week."

"I have to go, Sho," Vegas whispered. "Good luck with your speech and call me tonight. If you can."

"I'll be all right, but if she touches you . . . "

My sister spoke with determination, "She won't."

"Vee—" I began, but she was already gone.

Vegas told me not to worry, but I did. Concern over her precarious home life and my shortcomings crept in, making my stomach growl. As always, when stress took over, I turned to food as a comfort. Luckily, the pizza guy I was waiting for in the lobby came through the sliding doors just as the elevator closed on Axel and his friends.

***

When I got to my room, sneaking down the hallway like I stole something in case Axel emerged, I texted Vegas to make sure she was okay. She replied right away, saying my mom had let her in and she was snooping through my drawers.

Her flippant message didn't fool me.

Things were bad at the Shipley House.

It burned me up that her father, weak-ass that he was, did nothing about how his wife treated his only child. Her dad seemed to care for her, albeit in an absent-minded affectionate way. Why didn't the man do anything?

When I asked Vegas, all she would say is that her dad loved the bitch he married and wouldn't hear a word against her.

Well, her dad and that thing were going to get an earful from me. If Vegas's shitty home life had progressed to such a level that Vee needed to escape to my house, then someone needed to intervene.

I sat cross-legged on the bed, my back against the headboard and the box of pizza warming my thighs. Zombies shuffled across the TV screen while Rick Grimes shouted directions at his crew. As I chewed, barely conscious of how much and what I ate, Rick's gravelly voice morphed into my uncle's. I dropped the slice I was holding as I relived that day in my mind.

CHAPTER TWENTY-SIX

SHONDRA

Twelve years ago

"Get up Shondra, and don't make me tell you twice."

Axel stood and moved closer to me. His knuckles were raw and bloody and his jaw, clenched. Duke lay prostrate on the ground, groaning. Axel had changed his face into a mashed up mess. Michael sat up slowly, holding his side. Afraid though I was, I smirked when I noted his afro was lumpy and missing a few patches. The Latino guy who was with them was now just a speck in the distance.

My uncle clapped his hand around my arm and hauled me all the way to my feet.

"Hey, wait a minute—" Axel growled.

Uncle Nassau pulled up his shirt, keeping a tight grip on me. A gun, its metal grip gleaming in the sunlight, rested sinisterly in the waistband of his pants.

"Is there going to be a problem?" Nassau challenged.

Axel looked unsure of what to do. His eyes darted between the gun, my uncle, and me. To keep him safe, I solved the puzzle for him.

"Axel it's okay. He's my uncle." Bile threatened to choke me at calling the scum a relation of mine.

Paying for It

Nassau looked Axel up and down, sizing him up. In a fair fight, Axel would have stomped my uncle's small frame into the ground. Nassau was huge to me at eight. He had intrigued then frightened me with his gleaming bald head, silver teeth, and stocky build. Now, even I had several inches on him. Only the gun he carried gave him a better advantage.

"Yeah, that's right," Nassau grinned his silver teeth gleaming, "You go sniff somewheres else, boy and not around my fourteen-year-old niece."

Bastard had his nerve. There was a twelve-year age difference between us when he came *sniffing* around me, not to mention blood.

Axel's face lost all color. He took a step back. "Shondra? You're only fourteen?

Nassau didn't wait for me to reply. He gave me just enough time to retrieve my bag then began to drag me away with him, deeper into the park.

I hazarded a look over my shoulder as I tripped along. Axel stood helpless, watching me. In that moment, I put everything he made me feel during our kiss into my gaze before Nassau jerked me forward.

"Eyes front, girl. You too big for me to carry ifin you was to trip and fall and hurt yo'self."

"Wh-where are y-you taking me?" I gulped. My heart was in my ears and my throat burned with fear. Eight-year-old me had taken over.

He didn't answer and I grew silent. Only the rustling of the leaves and the intermittent sound of laughter from the playground came between us. Just my luck, no one was around but the trees that stared down from an impossible height as the scene unfolded below them.

I tried to remain calm and think, but the image of Nassau's silver teeth kept coherent thoughts from entering my mind. When my uncle had kissed me those years ago, his mouth tasted of cigarettes, beer, and warm metal. His arm, strong against my back, had bent my spine so far, my feet had lifted from the floor.

This can't happen again.

I knew instinctively that Nassau wanted more than a kiss this time. It was in the way he licked his lips and eyed me like his last meal.

I'll be damned if I let this bastard get the jump on me.

"Where are you taking me?" I said in a firmer voice.

"You haven't forgotten our kiss, have you now?" He cackled when he saw my disgusted expression. "I want me some more of that, girl. In jail, I couldn't get no action except a few of them young boys and my hand." His laugh this time was full of sadistic evil, and my blood ran cold.

We entered my street. Nassau was taking me to my house to commit whatever heinous act he had planned.

Hell no.

He'd ruined my first kiss and the perception of all that was right and good. I couldn't let him be my first and ruin that as well. As he dragged me along. I mentally pictured all of the weapons we had—nothing but the knives in the kitchen. I then ran through the self-defense class I'd taken at school last week. The techniques the instructor had taught us allowed me to take care of Duke in the supply closet. I could use the same move on my uncle when he came at me.

Two houses to go.

I looked around for neighbors. No one was out doing their lawn, tending to their flowerbed, and even Ms. Jenkins wasn't on her porch. My mom was working at the diner and wouldn't be at home until after six.

My last external line of defense had been shut down. I had to save myself.

No problem.

We came up to our driveway. A beat-up hatchback that I wouldn't drive into battle stood where my mom usually parked her car. Thin tendrils of smoke wisped from under the hood.

"Is that your car?" An inane question to buy some time.

"Yeah. Piece of shit." Nassau hawked, spitting a glob at the passenger window. The spittle trailed down to pool at the edge of the door. "Don't ever borrow anything from a brother. Shit breaks down all the time."

Nassau pushed me inside my house. My eyes widened in the gloom. The surreal picture of my mom at the bottom of the stairs, a pool of blood under her head caused me to lose focus and start to hyperventilate.

I pulled from my uncle's grip and squatted next to her. My too-tight jeans strained around my belly. I checked for a pulse as Nassau peered at me from the doorway.

"Yeah, yo' moms came home early as a sooprise. She got one a'ight." He chuckled and I flinched at his undeniable mirth. Relief replaced my fear as I found Mom's heartbeat.

She would be okay. That was all I cared about. My knees knocked together as I rose from the floor.

"She'll be a'ight. I didn't killa. She my sis after—"

POP!

I punched that piece of shit straight in his mouth, cutting my knuckle on those damn teeth of his. I wanted him to go down, expected him to, but he was no lanky high school boy. This man had been in and out of prison since he was a teen. He could take more than a punch from me.

SLAP!

His backhanded was powerful. My head hit the paneled wall of the hallway creating a crack in the wood. A fountain of blood erupted from my nose. Stars invaded my vision, and the metallic taste of copper filled my mouth.

I refused to fall.

Instead, I shored myself up on rubbery legs only to see Nassau step over my mom and come after me.

I worked through the pain to fight for my mother. I stumbled down the hall to the kitchen, knocking pictures and the ceramic clock I painted when I was in the fifth-grade from the wall. The sound of broken glass and pottery rang in my ears. Grunts from Nassau synced in time to the rapid beating of my heart.

Paying for It

I rounded the corner into the kitchen when—

BOOM!

"Stop! Police!"

Red blossomed from the side of Nassau's head. He fell to his knees then crumpled over, his ass sticking up in the air. When I saw the profile of his glassy eye, I knew he was dead.

CHAPTER TWENTY-SEVEN

SHONDRA

Six years ago

I made my way downstairs, my heart beating a mile a minute at the free-wheeling of my mind. I had allowed myself to go back into that dark memory. Rocking like a little kid who didn't know how to cope.

If it hadn't been for Ms. Jenkins...

She'd heard noises coming from our house and watched as my uncle jog up the street in the park's direction. Ms. Jenkins rightly guessed he had been in search of me and she'd called the police. I had left a note for my mom after all...

Now... now besides the horrible memory of what happened to my uncle, I have to endure what will become a new one. The one where I run into Axel. It can't be one of the many that I envisioned. Not with his pretty, petite girl in tow.

Now... now besides the horrible memory of what happened to my uncle, I have to endure what will become a new one. The one where I run into Axel. It can't be one of the many that I envisioned. Not with his pretty, petite girl in tow.

Paying for It

What was the off-chance Axel would see me before I could prepare myself? How could I let him go after... *caring* for him for so long? And the question that frightened me the most was...

What if he'd forgotten about me altogether?

My eyes darted from left to right, searching for his tawny hair, his broad shoulders, and his beautiful eyes...

He's probably busy with his girl. I'm sure I'll see him soon enough. Too soon...

Just the *idea* of seeing Axel again had my heart racing and my hands turning clammy.

I wish—

A loud chortle startled me out of my thoughts. The reception had ended, and the lull before the speeches had begun. The people hanging outside the conference room spoke in quiet tones as they took their seats.

As a speaker, I fit the part in the clothes and shoes I'd bought at a Chicago boutique. The wraparound ice-blue dress I'd chosen was the same color as Axel's eyes. I didn't do it by coincidence. The color had always given me confidence in the past.

Now... it just seemed silly.

I wished I'd known Axel would be here so I could meet him on *my* terms. I need to get the word out on my business. That was why I came here.

Last September, when the BPUSA had asked me to be a speaker for their Young Leaders Summit-I jumped at the chance, happy to relate my struggles to people from all races and nationalities. The conference was also a prime opportunity to meet new people, and hopefully a few investors. I needed an increase in funding to grow into the next big thing.

And *nothing* was happening on my own.

I'd called the banks, I'd met with a few loan officers, and they all but laughed in my face.

Vegas had said my company was successful, and it was, but *only just*. Through my earnings, I paid the mortgage on our new house, Mom reduced her working hours to forty per week, and we paid cash for a used, but reliable car. After that, there wasn't much left over.

This conference was a golden opportunity for me to network, and I couldn't let a childhood... Hell, a *grown woman* crush, ruin my chances of elevating my business... or making a name for myself.

I drummed my fingers on the long table, lost in thought. After ten minutes, I grew frustrated. Why couldn't I be one of those trust-fund babies who had everything handed to them and not a care in the world? Worrying over my financial shortcomings had put circles under my eyes from all the sleepless nights.

And then there was Axel. I had no luck with him either. He had forgotten me. While I stayed on how good he looked—so strong and virile and so damn *big*...

Too much, Shondra!

I rubbed the space just under my collarbone where a dull ache had spread. Going for a distraction, I focused on the place setting. It was beautiful. A floral runner of

137

white roses, peonies, and hydrangeas ran on either side of the podium. The aroma from the roses, the only flowers with a scent, mixed well with the colognes and perfumes of the attendees. The plates, expensive bone china by the looks of it, had an ivory center that matched the tablecloth underneath, and the outer rim was a complement of the light-green fronds of the flowers. I placed a finger on my knife, running the pad down the Art déco style with a silver matte finish.

Gorgeous.

If I wanted to own such extravagant things one day, I'd have to get my mind off what was out of my reach and concentrate on what I could grasp. And I did just that by digging my pink note cards from my bag. A quick refresher of my speech would keep my mind from wandering where it shouldn't.

The chatter swelled as more tables filled with attendees. With Axel's entrance imminent, I hid behind my hair and kept my concentration on my cards. I didn't look up, even when the servers began placing a bread plate with a pat of butter and a hard roll next to each water glass. I did however smile at the one who served me. She smiled back.

On the outside, I probably seemed calm, on the inside I was screaming.

Why are you so agitated? Axel is just a man.

That was right. Axel was—just a man, here with another girl. Had I expected him to wait for me as I waited for him?

Dumb, Shondra. You're really dumb.

CHAPTER TWENTY-EIGHT

SHONDRA

Six years ago

Axel was nothing more than a built-up legend in my mind, a *myth*. Vegas and my therapist at the Victims of Crime Unit encouraged me to talk about him and what happened to my mom and uncle. They said it would be therapeutic.

They were right, but I had taken it *too* far. I had played up the good part of that day so often, Axel had achieved superhuman hero status in my mind.

He didn't deserve that title.

I was the one who'd kept my uncle at bay until the police arrived. No one had done that except *me*.

I was my hero.

And it was time to face reality. Axel Sexton had moved on, and so should I. I needed to let him go.

So struck by my epiphany, I barely noticed when a man sat in the chair beside me. He extended a long-fingered hand and said, "Hi, I'm William. William Rodgers." William had light-brown hair in a side-parted pompadour, a thin beard, and an amiable smile.

We clasped hands and shook. "I'm Shondra Williams."

139

Paying for It

He laughed. His ruler-straight teeth (The kind I would have killed for during my braces period) sparkled a shiny white. "We're connected," he said, directing his smiling brown eyes at me.

"Connected?" I asked, cocking my head sideways as if that would help me discover his meaning. "How?"

We can't be relatives. His skin is the same color as the tablecloth.

"Well, your last name is Williams, and my first name is William. We're connected."

Is that all? Humph. "It's a common name."

"Yeeeesss." He stretched the word out, transferring our conversation into a debate. "But to seated next to each other? At this exact point in time? With similar names? Sounds like fate to me." He gave me a sly grin.

I swiveled my lips to the side and shrugged. His smile grew wider and two dimples appeared in his angular cheeks.

Cute? Sure. But I refused to smile. Instead, I narrowed my eyes.

William continued, not backing down at my look of disdain or my refusal to answer. "I'm giving a speech on funding and finance and you ...?"

"On people of color in the workplace."

He leaned back in his chair with a smile wider than any crater on the moon. "Hmm. I can hardly wait to hear it." His liquid brown eyes bored into mine, causing a pleasant clench in my belly.

Paying for It

The stone on my chest slowly crumbled, and my confidence rushed back like a mighty river. It seemed all I needed to rise from the ashes was a bit of flirtation from a charismatic man.

"So... what do you think, Ms. Pretty Green Eyes?"

"About what, William?" I said primly, pursing my lips to keep from smiling at his compliment.

He scooted his chair closer. "Our meeting each other...here tonight...is it fate?"

I opened my mouth to give him a sassy rejoinder when a shrill laugh pierced through the low chatter of the crowd. Many heads, including mine, swiveled towards the entrance.

My heart seized, and my airways collapsed. Axel stood in the doorway, his arm around his girl's waist. She flipped her hair, preening under the male attention her loud giggle had garnered.

Axel's buddies waved him over from a table not fifty feet from me, right smack in the center of the room. He lifted his hand in a lazy greeting, then weaved toward them, leading his woman along by the hand.

Bile rose in my throat, choking me. Even after all this time, Axel affected me because (and damn did I hate to admit it) I was still *hungry* for him.

"Who is that?" William asked with genuine curiosity.

I shrugged and rubbed at the invisible weight on my chest that had come back with a vengeance. Must be the burden of unrequited love...

141

Paying for It

"Shondra, William prodded. "Who is that?"

"Um..."

Who is Axel, really? The guy you knew for five minutes and fell in love with after four.

"He is... he's a guy I used to know."

William assessed me with his gaze. "Hmm. How well did you know him?"

I rounded on him, my fortitude back in place. "That's none of your business."

William's head hung between his shoulders "Sorry, Shondra." The tone and gesture sounded so much like Axel's had that day, I sucked in a breath. It went unnoticed as William continued, "I didn't mean to overstep. Please accept my humble apology."

He looked so sweet; I bit back a smile, unable to stay miffed under his charm.

"I accept your apology, William."

He leaned in, his minty breath fanning my ear, "Thank you...you smell nice, what are you doing later?"

I peeked at Axel. He was twisting a lock of his girl's hair around his finger, laughing at something she said.

Yeah, I believed in fate. The kind that bit you in the ass and left you for dead.

William was cute. He was charming. He probably knew how to turn me out, but I wasn't about to fall for a handsome man who spoke charming lies and handed out false promises. Once was enough. Been there, done that, and I had the broken heart to prove it.

"I'm not doing anything afterward, William... except going to my room... alone."

My table mate threw back his head and laughed—a bit too loud for such a setting. When his chuckling tapered off, he said, "You're a fiery one, Shondra. You are indeed."

"Thank you, William. I'm glad you noticed."

Because Axel never had.

CHAPTER TWENTY-NINE

JAMESON

Six years ago

Dad's office was his sanctuary. Not that he needed it. Mom and he had a very giving, loving relationship. The kind I hoped, with the ring I held in my palm, would be mine.

Shelia had arrived two hours ago, full of chats and laughter. After an hour in her company, Mom still smiled, but the happiness at our news had faded from her eyes. Dad, his usual reserved self, said little one way or the other, yet he'd given me the blue velvet box that contained my Oma's wedding ring without hesitation.

One enormous obstacle averted.

"Jameson."

I closed the box on the round cut 5.2ct diamond and lifted my head.

My dad owned his expressions. I knew in an instant he wasn't pleased. With his elbows on the antique desk and his forearms standing straighter than the Queens's guard, he rested his chin on his knuckles. His intense gaze made my 6′ 5″ height shrink to that of an eight-year-old. "Your mom and I will ask you just once—don't do it."

"You're in good company, Dad. Axel also tried to get me to ditch Shelia before he left for the conference this morning."

Dad didn't smile. His lips didn't even twitch. Mom liked Axel, hell most women did. Dad never expressed an opinion one way or the other, but I knew he didn't care for him. Dad didn't care for swagger, and Axel had that in spades.

"How can you be so sure? You just met —"

"Please, son. Follow your heart."

I slumped in the chair. Before this, my parent's had questioned none of my decisions... except the time when I wanted German chocolate cake and coconut ice cream for my fifth birthday party. They thought with all that coconut, I'd be on the toilet for a week. Like an obedient son, I gave in and went for vanilla ice cream instead.

This... this isn't for a party. This is something a lot bigger. This is the rest of my life.
Instead of answering, I shifted my eyes to the frame above my dad's head. There, embroidered by my mom in navy blue on a cream background, were the words—*Ad usque fidelis.*

True to the end.

My parents met and married within a week when they were vacationing on the island of St. Tropez with friends. Mom was twenty, and Dad was two years shy of thirty. She was studying to be an interior designer in New York City, and he was just finishing up his residency at John Hopkins. They lived and worked in different states, came from different backgrounds, had different lives, and different friends. Only through constant communication, compromise, and understanding had they achieved the motto of the island.

Dad had insisted on adopting the phrase, and Mom, when relating how they'd met to anyone who would listen, said he'd stolen it. He didn't. He lived by it. The man was as faithful as I intended to be, unlike the other professionals in our affluent neighborhood.

Ninety percent of the men and women who lived in our gated community only saw their kids every other weekend. I always considered myself blessed to come from a two-parent household. That was why before I asked Dad for Oma's ring, I had to know if Shelia wanted kids. I wanted to give my children the love my parents had given me.

When I broached Shelia about the subject, she'd broken down in tears. How she'd cried spoke of her anguish. Through her sniffles, she reminded me of her home life. As the oldest, she was in charge of her three siblings while her parents partied in New York, skied in Aspen, and took summer trips to Europe. Shelia and her siblings received hand-me-down designer clothes and meager rations while her parents spent their money on trips to trips for two to Fiji and a two-seater Ferrari.

Growing up wealthy, but treated as poor, made Shelia hungry for better. She wanted a firm foot in the development of her career before she even thought about kids. Moved by her emotion, we reached a compromise. After ten years, we would talk about it again. We were young, and we had time.

Besides, I loved her enough to wait. The girls I had loved from afar were nothing compared to my fiancée. She—

What has she done? Has she encouraged you? Has she been there for you? Are you with her because she said 'yes'?

My inner voice had a point. I'd been out on two dates before Shelia. Once to the prom with a cousin (which didn't count) and the other with a girl who admired how I had handled the Tabitha Moore incident.

I'd forgotten her name, but she was a pretty girl: chestnut hair, large doe eyes, and a nice body, but her mind...there was nothing there...like no one was home. After finishing our coffees, I walked her to her dorm. She chatted about make up; I stayed silent. At the entrance, she offered herself to me. I refused, politely of course, and walked away as fast as my legs could carry me. Shelia was the only woman I'd met who I wanted to take the next step with. To be intimate with. Unlike Axel, I needed to feel a connection, a strong one, in order to take the plunge (no pun intended). Shelia was my first. My last. My forever. I turned my attention back to my stoic father, who patiently waited for my response. "I love her, Dad, and I've already asked her to marry me."
My father shook his head. His shoulders shrank under the dark blue Nike jacket he wore. With curly iron-gray hair, lined face, and pale skin, he had the whipcord body of a Tour de France participant. His deep blue eyes reflected his worry and Dad's Dutch accent, which grew stronger in times of stress, made my stomach churn with unease.

Paying for It

"*Je weet niet wat je doet. Je hebt met dit meisje een wolf in schaapskleren binnen gehaald.*"
I was bilingual, so I didn't mistake his meaning, but I didn't get it. In comparing Shelia to a wolf in sheep's clothing, Dad thought I was making a big mistake.

Until he was sixteen and moved to the US, Dad lived in the small traditional town of Marken in the north of the Netherlands. He grew up hearing and using *uitdrukkings*—idioms—to explain most of his thoughts. All he asked of me was to work hard, do my best, be true to myself, and honor my commitments.

As my parents lived by the motto, *True to the End*, I lived by it as well.

I'd proposed to Shelia. I couldn't... I wouldn't take the words back. Not only did I love her, but I'd come too far to change my mind. It was my duty to see our commitment through. Come hell or high water. Till death do us part.

CHAPTER THIRTY

AXEL

Six years ago...

Mason leaned over. His silver flask of Scotch jutted from the inside of his jacket pocket. "I knew you'd bang her. I told the guys that's why you were late."

Allison wasn't listening to us. She had her back to me, talking to Tony. He was babbling like an idiot about his family's stables in Kentucky. Allison was a horse fanatic, and Tony was trying to impress her. I shrugged it off. Tony could try his luck... once I finished with her, of course.

And it wouldn't be the first time.

Tony followed me around like a puppy begging for a treat from almost the first moment we met. Jameson and I met Tony and Adam when they were living across the hall from us freshman year. Adam hadn't met Josh then. In fact, we didn't even know he was gay until he began dating Josh two years ago. Dude didn't need to sweat it for so long, No one in our group cared about shit like that.

"Nah, man," I gave Mason a cool glance, warning him with my eyes to keep his fat mouth shut. "I just escorted her to the restroom."

Mason tipped back in his chair, clutching the shiny back legs with his thick fingers. "Why did it take you twenty minutes then?"

I mirrored him, tilting my head back so that the recessed lighting blinded me. "Poor girl needed my help. Claimed she had something in her eye."

Manson tipped forward with a *clunk,* whispering with his liquored-up breath, "What was in there? Your dick?"

I grinned toward the ceiling. "I never kiss and tell, so stop asking."

Mason pulled a hurt face, lip poking out and everything. "So you guys really aren't coming out with us then?"

My balls clenched as I thought of how good Allison's mouth felt on me. She was like a vacuum set on high. I wanted her to do me again before the conference was over.

Tonight was just the beginning for us.

I tipped my chair forward and sat straighter in the hard-as-hell stool. Sneaking a quick glance at Allison to make sure she was still occupied, I used my best Dracula voice to say, "Nooo, nooo my child. We'll be berry, berry busy tonight."

Mason guffawed, slapping his thigh.

Allison twisted in her chair to see what was so funny. She blushed when she caught my gaze.

Yep. Very busy indeed.

"If I ever do drag, I want to look like her," Josh's voice carried over to us from his seat on Mason's other side.

Paying for It

We both turned our heads to see whom he meant. I scoffed, expecting to see a celebrity from *Ru Paul's Drag Race*, not the elegant beauty seated at the long speaker's table. Her long hair partially covered her features as she cocked her head, listening to some douche chat in ear. From what I could see of her face, she was gorgeous. Almost as—

Fuck me, that's Shondra!

There was no mistaking that hair, those luscious lips, and the perfect symmetry of her face.

My angel.

"Axel, what's wrong, you look pale?" Allison's voice came out muffled. Almost as if she were speaking through a pile of sand. Mason had said something as well, but I couldn't make it out because of the roar in my ears.

Jealousy clouded my vision. I saw nothing but red.

Was that douche trying to pick her up? Was she... married?

I frantically searched her hand for a ring. My blood pressure lowered a few ticks when I determined she was free from encumbrances.

Someone clapped me on the back. I turned in a defensive move, a snarl escaping from the back of my throat.

"What the hell, dude," Tony said, stepping behind Mason. A furrow of concern had perched between his brows. "You spaced out for a minute, Axel. You scared us, dude."

151

Paying for It

I tore my gaze from Shondra to look at my friends. Tony was right. They were wearing the expressions of those who had just witnessed the aftermath of a deer getting hit by a truck.

Although Jameson had the coolest head of our group, I had the second... unless I was kicking someone's ass. My friends must have seen my ass-kicking face up close. From what I'd been told, it was pretty damn scary.

"Yeah." I faked a smile. "Yeah. I'm cool."

Far from it. I wanted to run up to the table, punch the fucker sitting next to Shondra in the throat, then carry her, bridal style, to my room.

It *would* happen. I just wasn't sure when.

CHAPTER THIRTY-ONE

SHONDRA

Six years ago

During her speech, Shondra roamed her eyes around the room. Once or twice, I swear they landed on me.

My face was more angular than it was at sixteen, and my hair was shorter, more of a buzz cut. I'd grown four more inches in height and gained almost twenty pounds of muscle. Still, I looked the same . . . or near enough.

But if she recognized me, she gave no sign. And until that moment, I never truly understood how Adam felt when Josh flirted with someone else.

I sure learned quickly.

A boiling heat engulfed me as I watched the fucker who'd kissed her hand smile at her from his seat. When she grinned at the audience during the pauses in her speech, I shot daggers in that direction. When people clapped, I made the loudest noise. When the crowd gave my angel a standing ovation, I whistled like I was at a football game.

Shondra sat back down, tossing her hair over her shoulder. That windbag next to her angled a puny-ass arm on the back of her chair. I nearly shot from my seat when his eyes met mine, sending me a secret challenge with a fuck-you-smile.

I gave him a tilt of my chin and a murderous, toothy grin.

That prick does not know what I'm capable of. He can't fathom how far I'll go.

I'd begun the morning from a point of *come what may and get laid along the way.* Now, I seriously considered a different future.

One that included Shondra Williams.

***

Mason was as dense as fuck.

With the speeches finished, I told him I wasn't feeling well. He gave me a blank look. I cursed him to hell. Any fool knew *not feeling well* was bro code for *I need you to care of the chick I came with so I can talk to another one.* I bypassed that fool and went to Adam and Josh. They got it on the first try, gathering up the others as I held my stomach and looked pitiful.

"Axel, do you want me to stay behind?" Allison placed a cool hand on my warm forehead.

I didn't have a temperature. My body registered heat because I *burned* for Shondra. My angel was no longer under the age of consent, and before the night was over, I planned on getting her consent to do many things to her person.

"No, Alli, you go ahead with the guys and have some fun. I'll see you in the morning." When she leaned in, I turned my head so she kissed my cheek instead of my lips. Perplexed, she opened her mouth to say something else.

Josh stepped in smoothly, looping his arm in hers as he steered her away. "I'll take care of you, honey," he said with a wink. "We can get into a lot of trouble."

Adam grunted. He reached out to push his boyfriend slightly with the flat of his hand. "Don't think so, Joshie."

Josh stopped short, glaring at Adam. "Don't push me, you damn brute."

"You know you love it, don't you, Joshie?"

Their banter became softer as they followed behind Mason, who had carved a path between tables and pushed back chairs like he was making his way through vines in the jungle.

Tony hung back, looking at me warily. He tried to hide his enthusiasm over my sudden illness with a forced frown. Tony probably figured that with me out of the picture, he had a fighting chance with Allison. "Hey Axel, um ... is it okay if I ask Alli…"

I gave my frat brother a sincere smile so he would relax. It was all good between us. "Don't sweat it, dude. I won't stand in your way if you want to make a move."

Tony bobbed his head in deference like an 18th-century servant in an English manor. The tension in his lanky build left him as quickly as my thoughts of hooking up with Allison had left me. From now on, it was Shondra or bust. There was no in between.

155

"Thanks, man," Tony blurted, striding to catch up to the rest. He clutched the back of a chair and turned, almost as an afterthought. "I hope you feel better."

I gave him a half-wave, silently wishing him well.

***

Mason texted me they were in the cab and headed toward a club. I stopped watching the show and joined Shondra's crowd of admirers. While I waited my turn, I scanned the room for the douche. I wanted to accept the silent challenge he'd thrown at me earlier, but he'd disappeared like the bitch he was.

Mofo was damn lucky.

After another ten minutes of tapping my feet, the crowd around Shondra thinned enough for her to notice me. I met her halfway, my heart galloping a three-quarter mile, and sweat rolling down my back like an errant ball on a steep hill.

She ignored my proffered hand and pulled me in for a hug instead. "Axel Sexton. So nice to see you."

I enveloped her with both my arms, squeezing tight. "Shondra Williams, likewise."

I sniffed her, my knees nearly buckling at the familiarity. Her scent was better than I remembered. Over the years, I went to several stores looking for a similar brand. Nothing smelled as good as hers. It was like… *home.*

We stayed holding onto each other until some dickweed coughed, bringing us down to earth. Shondra stepped back with an embarrassed grin.

156

"I didn't know—"

"I just wanted to say—"

"You first," I said.

Her smile left her eyes to grow tight around her mouth. "Where's your girlfriend?"

Hot damn! She's jealous. No wonder she didn't acknowledge me.

Maybe we could pick up right where we left off?

With that thought, *o*ur years apart melted away like ice in a glass of sun tea. "She's not my girl, Shondra. No one has been or will ever be except..."

"Except?"

I went for it, balls out, laying everything on the line with three simple words.

"Except for you."

CHAPTER THIRTY-TWO

SHONDRA

Six years ago

"Except for you."

I became lighter than air, a feather floating up to the ceiling.

"Ms. Williams," said the man who had cleared his throat. He had iron-gray hair and pink-tinged John Lennon glasses. "I just want to say what a mah-velous speech you gave..."

Axel's ice-blue eyes never left my face, no matter how many people congratulated me. The last person, an older gentleman, had become too long-winded for Axel. He snaked his muscular arm around my waist and said, "Sorry to interrupt, but we have an engagement."

I threw an apologetic look at the man as Axel spirited me away, and before I knew it, we were down the hall and at the bank of elevators.

"What floor?" Axel asked,

Floor? Was he coming to my room? Why? What did he expect?

I couldn't ask him. He would think I was crazy for my presumptions. Axel wasn't sixteen anymore. He was a

158

man, full-grown, and one who apparently had a way with women. If he knew I'd held on for him after all these years, waiting to give him the one thing I saved from all others, he'd probably laugh in my face.

"Um, twenty-one."

Axel chuckled over a private joke and pressed his thick thumb against the elevator button, lighting it up. The doors closed. We rose in silence. I was too keyed-up and nervous to speak, anyway. Instead, I entertained the questions that rose and fell in my mind.

How do I look? Do you ever think about me? What would you say if I told you I loved you?

I did. I really did. In less than two hours, I'd fallen for Axel like I'd known him all my life. When I told my therapist, she said it was understandable that I'd done so. The traumatic events of the day overshadowed by my feelings of the connection, the deep like I felt for Axel, and over time, those feeling had manifested into love.

Did he really feel the same?

"What's your room number?"

"Uh, what?"

"What's your room number, Shondra?"

He didn't call me angel...

"21012."

Axel nodded, more to himself than to me. "Not too far from the elevator, good."

Paying for It

Why was that good? What was he thinking?

Ask him, Shondra!

I can't.

I couldn't take it if Axel were to reject me after all those fantasies I had about him. No more than I could erase the image of my uncle, dead, with his unseeing eyes staring up at me.

I shuddered at the thought.

Axel pulled me in tighter to his side. "Are you cold?"

I shook my head. My hair made a whisper sound against the back of my dress. I shivered again.

Axel squeezed my waist as if I would disappear. The roll around my middle didn't seem to turn him off, on the contrary in fact. The look he gave me as he plucked the key card from my hand was full of something I couldn't believe.

He doesn't want me.

You're reading him wrong.

The click of the door swinging shut stung my ears, heating them up with some unknown emotion. I whirled around. Axel's intense gaze warmed me... even after all these years. I couldn't look away as there was no mistaking his look now. It was the same predatory look he had on his face when he looked at his girl.

All the good I was feeling, dissipated. I crossed my arms and got right to the point. "What do you want, Axel?"

160

Paying for It

He leaned against the door as if he had all the time in the world, casually tossing the key card onto the dresser situated under the TV. I broke our gaze for a moment to watch the plastic rectangle slide twice its length on the faux wood surface.

Axel loosened his tie, dragging at the knot as his smile widened. "What I want, Shondra," he said, jutting from the door to throw his tie on the bed, "is for you to pack a bag and spend the night with me."

I made excuses, edging my way away from him until I made it to the window.

He didn't buy any of them. He followed me and we stood side by side, watching the traffic below. I sighed at the beauty of the New York taxicabs making such a colorful backsplash on the gray pavement. They were like gold-colored fish in a cool, dark stream.

He moved closer, the thickest part of his bicep touching my shoulder. "My view is better. You can see Central Park."

"Axel..." I began, but my damn nerves got the better of me and I couldn't finish. How could I tell him I didn't want to end up like his girl whom he cast aside for something unfinished?

"I just want to talk, Shondra. That's all." He turned me around with the touch of his hand. Just like when I told him "never to lie to me" that day in the park, the earnestness in his gaze won me over.

That didn't mean he was off the hook. I moved away and said, "Won't you upset your girl by staying with me?"

Paying for It

He fired back with an agitated stance and narrowed eyes. "What about your guy?"

I swiveled my neck. "What guy?"

A tick in his jaw appeared. His biceps bulged as he crossed his arms. "The guy that was all over you. The asshole that sat next to you. Remember?"

I quickly thought of whom he meant. "You mean William?"

Axel tipped his head. "So that's the douche's name." He nodded as if to himself. "You were looking at him like a magical chest full of wishes. Did that fucker ask you out or something?"

Axel's obvious jealousy made me giddy. I had guys try to own me before—a turnoff to the tenth degree. With Axel, it was cute… and hot, but I wasn't about to let him know that. I didn't take shit from anyone, especially no man.

I swung my hair back and mirrored his stance. "Yes, he asked me out. I told him I was going to my room..." Here Axel bristled like a puffed up porcupine"... alone, Axel. So, don't give me that look."

Axel fumed, puffing out his kissable lips. It took him a few seconds before he dropped his arms to his sides. He then blushed, prettier than anyone I had ever seen. "You turned him down?"

I relaxed as well, giving him a big smile.

"I did." I poked him in the middle of his hard chest, pressing a dress-shirt button into his skin. "Axel Sexton, are you jealous?"

162

Paying for It

His muscular arms wrapped around me, crushing me to him. His spicy cologne tickled my nose. He brushed my hair aside and began nuzzling my neck with soft nibbles and slow sucks. A shiver went down my spine. He molded himself to me, letting me feel the length of his hard torso. When he came up for air, he whispered our fate in the shell of my ear, "Fuck yeah, I am."

CHAPTER THIRTY-THREE

AXEL

Six years ago

Damn, I'm comfortable.

We lay in bed, half-ass watching some TV show while making small talk. Well, she gabbed while I thought what a lucky bastard I was to have her wrapped in my arms.

We were in our pj's, T-shirts and thin cotton shorts—mine a pale gray, hers an over-sized blue shirt with black pants that came to her thick mid-thigh.

Her T-shirt alone was enough to keep me hot and bothered. As we talked, it kept slipping, exposing her smooth brown shoulder.

I didn't see a bra strap.

Hot damn.

I briefly wondered if Shondra had gone bra-less to tease the hell out of me because my dick hadn't gone completely soft since I saw her.

No matter.

I knew Shondra and I would seal the deal tonight. All that came before the deed was the foreplay. Shondra had come back into my life for a reason. She wasn't leaving this bed without concrete plans made for later… Hell, *for the future.* So, while her head rested on my chest, just

164

above my heart, I stroked the silky strands of her hair, and subtly pulled on her sleeve, hoping to see more skin. Shondra had yet to catch on to what I was doing because she hadn't swatted my hand away, only absentmindedly adjusted her collar when it sunk too low.

While she babbled on about her business, I thought of fate. Deep down, my conscious, my determination, *my soul,* had told me I would see her again. With all of those other girls, I'd just been biding my time. Sure, I learned a lot from each experience, and it was fun while it lasted, but from now on, everything that was in me would go to Shondra. The connection we shared in the park was back, even stronger than it was then. Shondra and I would last, I was sure of it.

As long as my father didn't interfere.

"... and soon, I'll be able to afford to hire a few employees. Maybe in a year or two."

"Why wait that long? I can help you." With plenty of money lying around, collecting interest, I could afford an investment in her... *our* future.

Shondra shot from my arms. With her hair spilling over her shoulder, she raised up on her knees to scrutinize me. Her T-shirt dipped, hinting at the swell of her breast.

I licked my lips at the view and *fuck* if I couldn't look away.

"Suuuuure thing, Axel." Her incredulous tone made me grin. "If you have a couple of hundred thousand dollars to give away, I sure could use it."

Paying for It

"Don't you know who I am, Shondra?" I couldn't blame her if she didn't. From birth, my father taught me to keep a low profile. I wasn't on social media, I didn't pose for pictures, and I rarely used my second last name unless someone asked for my ID.

Shondra folded her arms across her chest and cocked a perfect eyebrow. "Axel Sexton, are you some kinda rich boy?"

I leaned further back into the pillows and crossed my arms behind my head, flexing. My angel's eyes grew round with lust, just like I hoped they would.

"I'm Axel Sexton ... *Hammersmythe*." Just like Gates, Jobs, and Jordan, my family was a household name. Old money before the term even existed, we could trace our lineage back to the Pilgrims and a few centuries before. That was why I didn't sleep with underage girls, was overly cautious before, during, and after sex, and I *never* fought unless I was defending myself.

With shock evident in her expression, Shondra jumped up, looking at me in horror as if I'd picked my nose and ate my findings. "You're a ... no ..." She sat on the edge of the bed. Too far away for my liking. I moved to sit beside her, thigh to thigh.

"It's only money, Shondra. I'm still human."

With an inhuman amount of bank.

For the past thirty years, Dad made the top five of the Forbes one hundred every year. When I graduated law school and came into my inheritance, I'd make the list, too.

166

"Axel ... I never knew."

Shondra was still giving me the same wide-eyed look, and I cursed myself for springing my shit on her. I should have eased her into it like I wanted to ease into her body. To bring her back to our former camaraderie, I bumped her shoulder. Big mistake. Her top moved down far enough so I could gape at the valley between her breast. Right then, I became lost.

"Um, hey, are you okay?"

"Axel, this is all so much."

I'm losing her.

"Does the money matter so much?" I asked, fearing that it did.

She turned to look at me, searching my eyes for an answer to an unasked question. They must not have told her anything as she gave me a noncommittal reply.

"I-I don't know."

A simple answer, but not the one I wanted. Somehow, I'd have to *convince* Shondra of her place in my life.

I took her hand in mine. Same soft skin. That it still fit perfectly pleased me beyond measure. I met her eyes and held them. Ice-blue to her Kelly-green. "I looked for you," I said, rubbing my thumb along her knuckles.

She watched my movement for a second before looking up at me through her lashes. "Yes, I know. Duke told me years later." Her lips tugged into a reminiscent smile. "We've actually become good friends."

Paying for It

Jealousy burned me from the inside out. My stomach rolled while my jaw clenched in unfamiliar frustration.

She's friends... with that asshole?

Spitefully I asked, "Does he remember the beat down I gave him?"

Shondra frowned but kept her hand in mine. "We don't talk about that time, Axel. We've grown up and moved on from that day."

"Well, *I* haven't. If your uncle hadn't of taken you away, we'd still be together."

She laughed, a mirthless, disbelieving sound. "Axel, you don't seriously believe that."

Her doubt pissed me off. If she needed proof of my sincerity, I was all for giving it to her.

I rolled her on her back, caging her within my arms.

"Oh," she gasped when I molded myself on top of her, closing every gap so she felt *every inch* of what was hers.

"You told me never to lie to you, Shondra." I surged forward, and she moaned, pressing her hands into my ass to bring me closer. "*Now,* can't you tell how much I missed you?"

CHAPTER THIRTY-FOUR

SHONDRA

Six years ago

A knock on the door stopped him mid-suck.

"Fuck. I don't believe this," Axel said as he breathed against my breast.

Hovering above me, he cocked his head and listened. I squirmed beneath him, eager for more.

He chuckled. Lowering his head, he latched onto my nipple. I arched my back. The moan which came from the back of my throat nearly drowned out the flurry of harder, more insistent knocks.

"Axel, we know you're in there," said a deep muffled voice from the hallway.

"Maybe we should just go," said a Southern one.

"I wanna see if he's 'kay and *S-I'm* not gonna go until I do."

That was a drunken female.

His girl, I bet.

An older voice, one full of righteous indignation, floated to us, "You'd better, or I'll call the hotel management."

Paying for It

"Shit. Talk about timing." Without a word, Axel lifted from me, shrugged on a T-shirt and left, closing the door behind him.

The coolness that settled on me had more to do with his demeanor than his departure.

Does he think I'll lie here and wait while he goes to her?

Not this girl.

I eased up my panties and put my shorts back on, struggling with the button in the dark. After I fastened it, I patted the bed for my T-shirt, remembering how I'd giggled and blushed when a smiling Axel pulled it off me not ten minutes before.

I was no longer smiling. Far from it. The invisible self-doubt I carried around like the added weight to my body made a timely appearance. It cleared my vision and the fog in my brain. I may have stupidly saved myself for Axel, but he would not give up his lifestyle for me. He made that clear by leaving.

My hand touched upon a bunched up piece of fabric. When I lifted it, Axel's cologne drifted to my nose.

Terrific.

Axel was wearing my shirt.

I poked my head through the neck with my arms following seconds later. The tee circled my hips to rest on them like a vice.

The man wears fitted T-shirts. Wonderful.

Regardless of what I look like, I'm leaving.

Fully clothed except for shoes, I slipped toward the door and opened it a crack. I needed to see whom I was up against before I left the scene.

Two men, one with dark hair, the other with brownish-blond, had flung themselves on the couch like they were settling themselves in for a nice long chat. The petite girl Axel had come with draped around him like a second-skin. Her honey-blond hair hung in her face, hiding her beauty. Her head rested on his chest like it belonged there. If she had stood up straight, she would barely reach his chin, and widthwise, she was less than half his size.

I'm an Amazon compared to her.

No wonder Axel found this girl attractive. I was tall and wide, a fighter and a schemer, while she was the epitome of delicate femininity. The kind who made guys feel big and strong enough to conquer the world. I couldn't compete against *his* damsel in distress. I was a fool for even trying, especially because he had left me as soon as she came calling.

"Where are Adam and Josh?" Axel asked those lounging on the couch. I zeroed in on how he tightened his grip on *his girl's* waist while she all but purred into his pec.

The dark-haired guy waved an arm like he was conducting an orchestra. "Probably gettin' down to business in their room. They were already in the elevator before we helped Allison from the van."

"Axel, why you didn't go?" his girl said, booze dripping from her voice. "We missed you... *I* missed you." She stood on her toes, trying to reach his lips. Axel saved himself from my immediate wrath by lifting his head out of her reach. *Alli* gave up with a huff and a perfect pink pout that poked out her lips.

The dark-haired man tilted his head, and a devilish smirk rode his voice. "Allison insisted we check up on you, man."

Axel looked down at her with affection. My heart seized up and turned to stone.

Go, Shondra, while you still can.

Damn straight. He can keep my shirt.

Ignoring the brick resting on my chest, I left the door open so their voices could reach me while I began the silent hunt for my belongings.

"You missed a great time at the club, dude."

"Why? What happened?" Axel asked. The curiosity in his tone hurt me more than it had a right to. Seems he was more interested in their story than finishing up what we started.

I berated myself as only I could do: Here I am, hunting around like a fool for my shit in the dark. I'm so stupid.

You should've known better, Shondra.

I had hoped Axel was different. His words and actions suggested me he was, but he was like all the others. Axel had only wanted one thing, and tonight, I had almost given it to him.

What a damn mistake that would have been.

Why don't you leave while you still have some dignity?

Excellent advice.

I hurried to the bathroom to get my toothbrush.

WHAM!

Pain flared in my hip bone and traveled up to stomach and down my leg. In my haste to run away, my hip had collided with a chair, nearly toppling it over. Blessed with quick reflexes, I caught the stool just in time. But I could not stop the hot tears that formed in the corner of my eyes.

I let them fall as I heard Axel say, "Sorry, I missed the evening." His indifference spoke louder than his touches had. I cried—big, sloppy, makeup-ruining tears. My throat clogged with the stifled sobs that racked my frame. I sat on the edge of the bed that was still warm from our bodies and let years of pent-up misery rise and overflow from my swollen eyes.

Over my crying I heard one guy say, "... wasn't even the best part. Adam nearly leveled a guy over Josh. We had to hold him back and everything."

"That's nothing new," Axel said dismissively. "I'll never understand why Adam gets so pissed."

But you had over me. Was that a lie?

"Whasss 'bout me, Axel?" Allison asked. "Why won't you kiss me? You liked it when I sucked—"

Axel cut her off from voicing what I surely would have done had we continued. "Mason, Tony, take Allison to her room."

173

Paying for It

That was my cue. As soon as they left, I was gone. With trembling fingers, I rose from the bed, wiping at my tears. I gathered up my bag and waited by the door, praying for my courage to join me soon.

"Axel, I wanna stay with you," *his girl* said, tapping her small hand lightly on his chest. "You *promised*." I hated the whine in her voice, but I could understand it. *I had been whimpering and begging Axel just minutes ago, my own damn self.*

"Here, Tony, take her. You too, Mason."

The brownish-blond guy jumped up and removed Allison's remaining tentacles from around Axel. Allison sagged against and he struggled with keeping her upright.

Axel narrowed his eyes at the slighter man and growled a warning, "Just put her to bed, dude. Nothing else."

I'm not the only one he gets jealous over.

Tony gave him a sour look in response, but wisely held his tongue against Axel's intimidating glower.

"I'll make sure she gets there safe," Mason said, clapping Axel on the back. He took one of Allison's arms and lopped it about his neck. Tony's face straightened to give his helper a grateful grin. "We'll text you when we're headed down for breakfast."

Axel opened the door. Mason turned to him with a sly smile and jerked his head in the direction of the bedroom. "Give me the details later."

Axel's laugh, directed at me…at us and what we'd shared, chilled me. "As I told you, I never kiss and tell."

CHAPTER THIRTY-FIVE

AXEL

Six years ago

To put an end to what I was doing to Shondra caused me physical pain, but I had to reign in those idiots from causing trouble. Jameson usually took care of our group of misfits. *Me* included.

Time and time again, my roommate, *my brother*, had stopped me from wreaking havoc, bringing me down from my adrenaline high in that calm-ass way of his. His stoic expression, paired with his tempered voice, worked magic to keep the peace, rescuing us from situations that our asininity landed us in. Now the duty fell on me since he wasn't around.

I left Shondra without a word, afraid if I spoke, I'd let my friends wind up in jail. It was no accident that I grabbed her shirt. I wanted her with me.

As soon as I opened the door, Mason deposited Allison in my arms. I was forced to hold her drunk-ass when he and Tony settled their asses on the couch. As they proceeded to talk up a storm, I played along so they wouldn't get curious. They would bother the shit out of Shondra if they barged into the bedroom and I wasn't having that. I wanted to keep her to myself.

Paying for It

I did my best to look interested in what they said and hold up Allison, who at that point was killing my arm. The guilt at touching another woman was weighing me down. I ached to get back to Shondra and complete our reunion.

"Sorry I missed the evening."

Sorry, you are screwing mine up is more like it.

"You missed the fireworks, man," Tony said, "There were a few fights you would've been in the middle of for sure." His mouth grew thin as he stared at *his desire* in my arms. "I had to fight them off of Allison." He lifted his chin to give me a triumphant smile.

Big fuckdy whoop. I couldn't give a damn.

Mason scoffed and rolled his eyes. "You shoved a drunk prick on his ass, but that wasn't even the best part. Adam nearly leveled a guy over Josh. We had to hold him back and everything."

It was my turn to scoff. "That's nothing new. I'll never understand why Adam gets so pissed."

Ah, but I do. I dug my hand into Allison's side as I thought about that windbag and Shondra. Only in the midst of a beatdown on some unfortunate prick had I ever gotten so angry. Now, all it took was a kiss on the back of my angel's hand.

Allison came to life, twitching in my arms to look up at me with her unfocused eyes. "Whasss 'bout me, Axel?"

What fucking about you?

Paying for It

I gave her a look that would freeze the sun. She turned petulant. "Why won't you kiss me? You liked it when I sucked—"

I cut off her whine with a command, "Mason, Tony, take Allison to her room."

Mason, obtuse as they came, didn't move. Tony smirked. I bet the fucker knew I had special someone waiting and that was why he was digging in his heels. It was his passive aggressive way to make me suffer because Allison had rejected him.

I'm getting tired of this shit.

"Axel, I wanna stay with you. You promised." Alli tapped her hand on my chest, and I just managed not to cringe at her touch.

How could I have wanted her this morning?

"Here Tony, take her." I pushed her into Tony's arms as I gave Mason a pointed look. "You too, Mason."

Tony's hand placement on Allison's ass was unnecessary. I gave him a look that told him to back off and spoke in plain words so there was no mistake, "Just put her to bed, dude. Nothing else."

Tony's mouth worked like he wanted to give me lip. He wouldn't. He knew better than to try me- especially now. My patience was at an end. These assholes had taken up enough time.

"I'll make sure she gets there safe." Mason clapped me on the back then shored up Allison's other side. Her head hung limply between her propped up shoulders. I hoped they would get her to the room before she hurled.

177

Or maybe not.

I hurriedly ushered them to the door, glad to see the back of them. They were halfway through when Mason, the ass, had to turn and piss me off even more. "We'll text you when we're headed down for breakfast." His head jerk toward the bedroom let me know he had been fucking with me all along. "You'll have to give me the details later."

I had to laugh thinking of all the hell I was going to give him when I got him alone. My boot to his neck would be the least of his worries. "As I told you, I never kiss and tell."

CHAPTER THIRTY-SIX

AXEL

Six years ago

Friend free, nothing was going to stop us.

Except for Shondra herself.

Bag packed, eyes puffy, my gray shirt wet with her tears.

WTF?

The depths of hell yawned before me. My heart plunged through my feet. The lost souls that waited in purgatory feasted on my organ as I noted the sadness in her eyes.

"What's wrong, Shondra?"

I walked toward her. She moved around the couch—away from me.

You fucked up, Axel. You should've let them knock.

I counter moved. Shondra changed direction so we wouldn't meet. I threw everything I was feeling for her into my gaze. She waited for me with a transfixed expression.

When I was an inch away, she shook her head and held her palm out to stop my approach. "I'm going to my room, Axel. This was a mistake."

Like hell it was.

Paying for It

"Shondra, my friends just wanted to see if I was okay. I
pretended I was sick earlier so ... they ... my friends ...
they ..." I couldn't continue. Her expression had changed
from sad to downright livid. Smoke came from her
nostrils and ears. She threw her bag down so hard it
bounced an inch or two.

"I figured as much." She pushed me in the chest. I
stumbled back, surprised at her strength. "You couldn't
tell them you wanted to talk to a friend." She tossed her
hair, and it fell over her shoulder in a dark wave.
"Noooo." She swiveled her neck and *tsk-ed* behind her
teeth. "You had to lie and say you were sick." She
snatched up her bag, heading for the door.

I clutched her arm as if it were a life jacket and swung
her around. The momentum toppled us onto the couch,
me on top. She struggled, fighting to be free.

I pinned her arms above her head, and still, she
managed to rock me. I rode the wave, relishing in the feel
of her while I had the chance. Anger and lust fought for
dominance on her face. I prayed for the lust to win even
as I bent my head and tried to soothe her with sweet
words. I was no Jameson, but I had some skills.

She fell still, no longer trying to buck me off. I lifted my
head from her ear, expecting to see her passion reignited.
I was wrong. I rose when my brain registered the
unbridled fear on her beautiful features—eyes large and
wild while her mouth set in a silent scream. Shondra
scrambled to the end of the couch, pulled her legs up to
her chin, and began to rock.

"He tried to own me that day. He hurt me. Nearly killed
my mamma. You or any man won't own me."

Paying for It

As I hid my balled fist behind my back, I forced myself to speak calmly, "Who, Shondra?"

She dipped her head forward and spoke to her knees, "My uncle."

"What did he do?" Dread boiled my insides, charring them in a flash of understanding.

I wanted to go after her that day, but when *he* threatened me, lifting up his sweatshirt to show me his gun, I didn't follow. Not because I was scared for myself, but for her. She seemed resigned to go with him, but the longing that flashed in her eyes as she turned to leave, haunted me ever since.

The next day, Mom put me on lock-down because some man got killed in the neighborhood. Sneaking out was a no go because my aunt and uncle had some sort of robbery prevention device on their windows and only they had access to the keys.

Finally, when the old folks went to visit some relative, I stayed behind, playing sick. I walked the hood for hours with no luck. My quest took me past a doughy woman who eyed me suspiciously from her porch and a house with yellow police tape on the front. When I saw Duke with his busted lip and split mouth, glare at me from his front door, I flipped him the finger and walked back to my aunt and uncle's home with a heavy heart and lead-filled feet. My parents and I left the next day back to Vermont.

I hadn't been back to Chicago since.

Hindsight was 20/20. I went back to the day in the park when her uncle came to get her. Her eyes had grown

181

large in her head when he held her by the arm, licking his crusty lips like he was digging into his last meal. My sixteen-year-old mind hadn't understood, but my twenty-two-year-old one did. A perversion of desire had been on her uncle's face, and right now, I had acted no better.

"Please, tell me, angel. I can help you."

I wasn't sure what cracked her wall. Maybe it was the "please," the "angel" or perhaps it was the distance I forced myself to keep, but she started talking. Her voice, choked with tears, made it hard to understand everything she told me, but I understood enough of the picture to wish her uncle were still alive so I could rip out his throat and shit down his neck.

After she finished, I wanted to say a million things to heal her. I seized on one that had the most value. "I'd give all that I'm worth, Shrondra, even my damn soul, to go back to that day and do things differently."

She came back to me then.

She lifted her head and peeked from under her wet lashes. I inched closer, wanting to help. Shondra lowered her legs, and without a word, folded herself into me.

I shivered when her lips moved against my skin. Shondra dug in deeper, sucking. For the duration, I hardly breathed. She could mark me up a thousand times, and I wouldn't care.

To hell what my father thinks.

She released me with a nibble, giggling as she traced an outline of her love-bite. "I'm sorry. I got carried away."

Paying for It

I shook my head. "It's me who's sorry. I should never have answered that damn—"

She placed a finger against my lips. "Kiss me, Axel. Like you did in the park."

Shit. I have much more finesse than that.

I planned to erase her uncle's sick shit and replace it with a memory we would talk about into our old age.

I laid my mouth against hers, tilting my head at the perfect angle as I breathed against her lips in a gentle caress. I dipped in and away, then moved back so she could meet my eyes and gauge the depth of my feelings. She nodded, inching her head closer.

I moved back in with a hint of tongue. Shondra moaned. I delved deeper as she roamed her hands along my sides, squeezing and kneading.

Our mouths still connected, I pressed her into the back of the couch as I fisted my hand in her hair. She rubbed my back, releasing the perfume on her shirt. The subtle notes affected me, drawing out my control. I picked her up against her protests and once in the bedroom, I placed her gently on the bed.

I pulled her top over my head and balling it, took a deep breath before I tossed it into a chair. When she did the same with my shirt, her heavy brown globes heaving with her inhale, I shucked my shorts and tanks in record time. I yanked the rest of her clothes off, panties and all. I was in too much of a hurry to peel them off with my teeth.

I was ready, and I wasn't waiting.

183

CHAPTER THIRTY-SEVEN

SHONDRA

Six years ago

The pain hadn't compared to the pleasure. Axel had been gentle to the point of exquisite torture, the caressing, the teasing, the ... *sucking*. As he moved inside of me, my thoughts of inadequacy, which plagued me every waking moment, disappeared. It became about us ... *him*, and how good he made me feel.

I lay on his chest, listening to his heartbeat while snuggled into his embrace. Axel rained kisses on the top of my head every so often, making me so treasured... so relaxed, my eyes fluttered closed.

I shouldn't fall asleep. I should get up and wash off the stickiness—

We hadn't used a condom. We hadn't used ...

My heart galloped in my chest as fear rode my veins. I sat up straight, knocking his hand away. Axel startled from his reclining pose, his eyes wide and wary.

"We didn't use a condom, Axel."

Paying for It

He relaxed into the propped up pillows, his arm at the ready to welcome me back to his side. "Relax, angel. Whatever happens, happens."

I gave him an incredulous stare. His arm curled around my shoulders, tugging, and it took everything in me to resist. "Axel, don't play. How can you say you're going to step up if the time comes?"

I couldn't say the word: *pregnant.* To do so would be a jinx.

Axel leveled his eyes at me. My worry faltered under his determined glare. "How could you believe I would let you raise our child alone?"

I let the sheet fall from me as I twisted to look at him, trying to judge his sincerity. Instead of looking at my boobs, which he had feasted on like a starving man, he kept his eyes on my face, a hard tick to his jaw.

"Is that what you think of me even now?" With a disgusted look, he threw back the bedclothes and stood. Between his strong shoulders lay an expanse of tense energy crisscrossed by scratches I hadn't inflicted.

They kept me from calling out to him.

Axel marched to the bathroom, all post-sex afterglow gone. "I'm going to take a shower."

I didn't follow. Instead, I lay in my bed of indecision, wondering if I should save myself the heartache I *thought* would happen. How could I, considering the world we lived in, that Axel and I would last the test of time?

Paying for It

Doubt, like the tiptoeing of a cat, crept into my mind. Every damn day I wondered if I was good enough. If I deserved love.

Just like my mama.

Two years ago, my mom revealed my uncle had abused her. He'd started from the time she was twelve. When Nassau was sixteen and my mom was fourteen, my grandmother had walked in on them.

Nassau landed in jail. Mom had gotten an abortion.

At eighteen, the prison board saw fit to release Nassau from prison, but his victim wasn't so lucky. The shame, the pain, and the stigma of her abuse followed her, weighing on her so heavily, she walked around like a ghost most of the time.

Would that be me?

If I didn't take my chances.... if I let doubt hold me back, it would. Axel and I had met again for a reason, and I'd be a fool to let him get away.

The shower kicked on and I waited a few beats before joining him.

The bathroom was enormous with brown and cream swirled marble and bright white porcelain sinks. I'd be lying if I hadn't thought about Axel and me sitting in the tub built for three, but that was for later. A more pressing issue was at hand.

My shower cap lay packed in my bag and the complimentary one was too small for my hair. I bit my lip with my final decision. If it were between saving my hair or saving my man, Axel would win every time.

186

Paying for It

I slipped into the cabin. Axel had his hands on the wall, propping himself up as his head hung between his shoulders. Water cascaded over his muscled form, the drops clinging to his skin like moss on a redwood tree.

"Axel, I'm sorry."

He didn't change his stance, not for a few moments at least. Unease crept in, billowing into my nerves like the steam. He pressed a button to change the water pressure into a mist and then moved, lightning fast, to gather me in his arms. He rested his chin on my increasingly damp hair as he spoke, "Don't doubt me, Shondra. I'm a man of my word."

I leaned back, looking into his ice-blue eyes. They were a soft, inviting blue that let me know everything was A-Okay. He bent his head for a kiss and when his lips met mine; I seized them with an eager passion, moving my fingers along the scratches from another woman's hands.

It was in me to move on, *to trust*, but I had to *know*.

Blinking water from my eyes, I tilted my head up. "Who are these from, Axel?"

Axel didn't fake me out with half-assed excuses and little white lies, he looked me in the eye and told me the truth. "They're from a girl I fucked a few days ago. She got carried away, I guess." He smoothed away the hair that clung to my forehead, and I noticed that his tall frame blocked out most of the cabin light. "I'm done with her ... with all of them. There is only you."

As water ran in a rainfall, steaming us up... making us wetter, he waited silently while I—judge and jury—

debated his case in my mind. It only took half a second to bring in the verdict.

"Then give it to me like you gave it to her."

Axel's devastating smile grew as he pushed me against the wall.

***

"Do you have everything?" he asked for the third time.

"Yes, I do." I had only unpacked my toothbrush and a change of clothes. Axel insisted on keeping my shirt, half-ass promising to give it back when we met in D.C. three weeks' from now.

The hours without him would be hell on earth, but I had my hands full with the business and working out a solution for Vegas. I counted on the days flying by at an insane speed.

Axel's phoned beeped in his pocket for the umpteenth time. We stayed in his room, agreeing to say goodbye here instead of in the lobby under the prying eyes of hotel guests, his friends, *and* his former fling...

Trust. I was going to trust him until I didn't.

Axel agitatedly ran a hand over his buzzed hair. "I've got to go." He looked at me with mournful eyes. "Fuck, I hate this." He pulled me to him, his growing excitement pressing into my belly.

I stroked him. He groaned. "Save that for me, big man." I slipped from his arms and left his room with a heavy heart, aching for one more kiss. As the elevator's doors closed, a thrill ran through me when our eyes met and we exchanged a million promises between us.

CHAPTER THIRTY-EIGHT

VEGAS

Six years ago

I took a quick peek in the hallway mirror. The swelling on my face had gone down in the day and a half she'd been away, but the bruise around my eye was still noticeable. Tina had let loose this time, marking me up in a fit of rage. She usually had more control, delivering her slaps with more sting than bite, but a store had declined her credit card during a shopping spree with friends.

Arriving at the Williams's with the clothes on my back, my hair a mess, and blood dripping from my nose, Shondra's mother made a lackluster threat to call the police. I asked her not to, with my hands clasped and tears streaming down my face. Daddy would face trouble, and I loved him too much for that to happen.

A car pulled up in the driveway... sooner than I'd expected. Shondra was home from the conference. She came in, bounding like a puppy in search of a treat. Seeing me, she skidded on the hallway tiles, her suitcase falling to the floor and her mouth dropping to catch it.

Shondra's mother dumped her car keys in her bag and clasped her daughter's arm in a weak grip. "Go easy," her mother said in her toneless voice. "She has been through enough and doesn't need a lecture." After giving Shondra a reassuring pat, she shuffled to the kitchen. The woman didn't like confrontation, and deep down, I knew that was why she hadn't called the cops on Tina.

Main reason no one got involved, teachers included. Who wanted to deal with the hassle?

"What the fuck happened, Vee? Did that bitch—"

"*Shondra*," Ms. Williams's admonishing voice cut through her tirade. My abuse was okay, but she didn't allow cursing.

"Sorry, Mamma," Shondra said, pulling me down the hall. Her long strides had me stumbling after her. Reaching her bedroom, she closed the door, shutting off her curses from her mother's ears. "This shit has to stop, Vee. Today, it's going to end."

I sat on her bed, brushing the straightened part of my hair over the damaged part of my face. I had been busy fixing my hair when Shondra called from the hotel. After the Wife turned me loose, I had run from the house with it half-done. "My dad is home. She won't touch me when he is there and—"

"Forget it, Vee. He won't do shit about your eye, just like he did nothing about your busted lip a few months ago, and the welts on your legs after Christmas. I don't even want to think what happened to you before we moved next door."

I didn't either, as it had been hell on earth. The Wife didn't strike out often, but when she did, she went for the gold. On the times my dad would come home and see my injuries, by default we didn't discuss them. He wouldn't go against her. The one time he did, she had struck out at

191

him harder than she ever had me. He'd missed two days of work, waiting for the swelling to go down enough for him to return.

Shondra sucked the back of her teeth and went to the window. Our houses were on a cul-de-sac, and the view from her bedroom was of our driveway. Against my silent plea that my dad had *somehow* gone into work, both cars sat in the sun.

Not good.

Shondra was through the front door before I even thought of moving, fear rooting me to the spot. Shondra, an adult, could do what she wanted, but at sixteen, I was still a minor and subject to my father's rule...my *step-mother's* rule. I could stay here for the weekend, but not forever. The Wife made it clear that would never happen... *at least* not without some compensation...

My feet started moving while my brain played catch up. I nearly collided with her mother, who was also hot on Shondra's heels. *My sister* respected her mom, and listened to her in all things, but in this, there would be no stopping her. All we could do was watch the spectacle unfold.

The wind had warm fingers, and they threaded through my half-done hair. Worry over my friend had me panting up the drive as though I'd been running a thousand miles rather than a few dozen feet.

Entering the open screen door, Shondra's raised voice greeted us.

"... father are you to let your bitch beat your child."

Paying for It

Dad stood with his balding head bowed, and his hands clasped one over the other. He wouldn't answer Sho's questions. There wasn't a need. The Wife did all the talking, *all the time.*

"Listen, Shondra," The Wife said, her mouth a snarl and her mean eyes snapped on me, "you only see the good side of this ungrateful child. All she does is stay in her room, sealed off from everyone, doing who knows what." The Wife's eyes slid to Shondra while Dad kept his on the floor. "Princess Vegas does nothing around here except eat, shit, and give me mouth. I'm sick of it."

Shondra made a lunging motion. Ms. Williams and I sprang forward, each grabbing a shoulder before things got out of hand. The Wife scampered to the man who would always take her side.

If Shondra had smacked her down, The Wife wouldn't hesitate to file charges. She'd ruin my girl's life with a phone call, and the bitch would smile as she punched in the numbers. The irony was so great, hysterical laughter puffed from my lips. I disguised it as grunts of effort. Shondra, her neck jutting over her chest, had dragged us a good foot forward.

"You're a lying piece of shit. When he's gone, you work Vegas like a field hand, and you know it." She wiggled in our grasp, and my arms strained with the effort to hold her back.

"Don't do it, Sho." I said in an effort to deescalate the situation. "She isn't worth it. Please, Sho. Please."

Paying for It

With one last ugly look at my Tina, she shook our hands off, making it look easy. "Vegas, get your books and some clothes, you'll stay with us."

The Wife didn't say a word. Not then, at least. But her later actions had us paying for that day for a long time.

CHAPTER THIRTY-NINE

SHONDRA

Six years ago

Between the two of us, Vegas and I rearranged my room by pushing my desk/makeup table to a far corner and dragging my old twin bed from the basement. The bed sheets were in a box next to it and I put them in the wash to get rid of the stale smell. Once they'd dried, I'd hang them on the line. There was nothing better than sun-and-wind dried sheets. I'd been trying to recreate the smell forever.

While we were straightening up, Vegas asked about Axel. I'd shushed her right away. At twenty, I could vote and almost drink, but I wasn't quite ready for my mom to overhear I was no longer a virgin.

Vee bided her time, though, throwing me smirks when she caught me drifting off... remembering.

Axel had been so powerful... so strong. I couldn't help but clench as I thought back on how he'd felt inside of me... his harsh breath in my ear. My own cries. His low growls.

I'd drifted back to that night more than I should have, and Vegas took note. As soon as Mom left, her car pulling out of the driveway, Vegas dropped what she was doing and demanded the tea.

"So," she said, fixing me with a bemused glare, "tell me the good stuff."

My insecurity rose to the surface. It still boggled my mind Axel had taken an interest in me. How could I convey that anomaly to someone else? So, I avoided her question to gather my wits. "This situation is only temporary, Vee. Once I have a minute to fix up the sewing room, you can move in there."

Vegas whined like she was four, "Come on, Sho. You've made me wait forever." I sat on my bed across the room while she bounced on her unmade mattress. Her straightened hair had come loose from her braid while her twists had slowly unraveled. Chile had that 3C hair.

I pursed my lips and shook my head, putting up a token of resistance, "You're too young, Vee." Sometimes I'd forget about our age difference because Vegas had a double helping of brains and more common sense than the average human.

"So you did it? What was it like?" Never one to be a jealous bitch, Vee's face brightened with happiness. Of all the nights we had talked about Axel, she knew what he meant to me and what it felt like to be in...

Love?

Lust?

Hmm.

Lust was definitely there. However, love...

I'd know for sure when I met him in D.C.

Paying for It

Axel had an internship there as a glorified errand boy for a congressional representative. The position, arranged by his father almost as soon as he was born (was how he put it) was highly prestigious and—

Vegas waved her hands, grinning. "Earth to Shondra."

"Come sit here." I tapped my foot on the floor space in front of me. "I'll do your hair." My new burgeoning sex life would be easier to talk about if I couldn't see her expression. "Get the wide-tooth comb—no, not the silver one, that snags. The purple one."

Vegas sat between my thighs, her head coming to my stomach. As I picked apart the mostly unraveled braid, I confessed my nocturnal activities.

"Yes, we had sex."

Vegas squealed and turned, her hair slipping from my hands. "What was it like? Did he live up to your expecta — Why am I even asking that, you haven't stopped smiling except for..." She angled away, facing front, but I'd already marked the sadness in her eyes.

I grew angry all over again. A helpless rage that scorched my throat and tore at my heart.

Since I wasn't legal, I couldn't help Vegas through the courts like I wanted. The lawyers I'd contacted in the past had all but laughed in my face at my promise to pay in installments. My mom, bless her, also couldn't help financially or emotionally.

After my uncle died, Mom confessed he'd molested her a handful of times before my grandmother found out and sent her to live with an aunt. The reason Mom was so detached fell into place after that. She relived my uncle's deeds the same as I did.

Although Mom wasn't the hugging or kissing type, she worked inhuman hours to make sure I had everything I needed. That, and her constant reminders of how proud she was of me proved her love.

If I were a mom, I'd be the same way.

Pregnant...

"We didn't use a condom, Vee."

Vegas whipped around, her curls eschew and pointing in all directions. "Oh, Sho." Her upturned eyes were enormous with worry. "If... if you are, um, pregnant, I'll move back. I'll..."

"Don't worry about it." I smiled while my stomach flopped like a fish in a net. Vegas moving home wasn't an option. I loved her too much to allow the Witch to subjugate her.

Besides, I was too young to have a child.

"If I am, I'll be fine. I mean, I should be, anyway. My period is due to start within a couple of days."

Vegas gave me a skeptical look with both eyebrows high on her forehead. "Shondra, you know your periods are irregular. How can you be so sure?"

Again, the girl was too smart.

"Turn around," I said, pressing lightly on her back. I didn't want to see the trust in her eyes.

When she reluctantly complied, I started combing through the smoothed side of her hair. "If I don't start in a week or two, I'll take a test."

Vegas relaxed her shoulders. "If you are… you'll let me know?"

I combed her hair for a moment before I lied to her, "Yes, I'll let you know."

CHAPTER FOURTY

AXEL

Six years ago

"Hang up, Axel," Shondra said with an amused huff.

"Why?" I lay in bed with a hand on my resurrected morning wood. Just hearing her voice had me ready.

"It's nearly seven-twenty, big man. I have a meeting at eight-fifteen."

"With who?" Better not be with that Duke.

Duke owned a gym, and Shondra worked out there sometimes. She went more miss than hit, but I bet on the days she showed, he was there busy ogling what was mine. However, I trusted Shondra implicitly. His ass was another story.

"A contact I met at the conference."

I relaxed, but I was still curious. "What kind of contact?"

"A woman who wants to invest in my company."

Shondra had refused my offer for monetary help, saying she wanted to do it on her own. Not that I had too much to give her after all. Dad had the money I'd inherit after I graduated locked up tighter than a medieval chastity belt.

Paying for It

He gave me a monthly sum to live on, paid everything associated with my studies, and that was about it.

"What percentage does she want?"

"I don't know. That's why we're meeting."

"You'll talk to me before signing anything, right?" I wouldn't take my first course of contract law until my second year, but I knew enough to find the loopholes. At least in that way, I could contribute.

"Yes, as always."

"Okay, stop rolling your eyes. I get it."

She giggled, and I smiled at the beautiful sound. "You know me too well, Axel."

"Not as much as I will when you come to D.C."

"Hmm," she purred, smacking her lips.

I couldn't help but stir down south as the seductive noise went straight to my cock. "I hope that's a promise."

The desire I felt for her deepened my voice, "You can count on it, Shondra."

"Ah. Axel, *stop*."

I smiled again, glad that she heard me loud and clear. "I will when you hang up."

"You're impossible. Goodbye, Axel." She ended the call, pretending she was mad. Didn't worry me. She would call tonight, as usual, with a smile in her sweet voice.

Our days worked around each other. I'd call her before my workout in the morning and she'd call me when she finished work, usually after nine. I never thought I'd ever want to talk to someone so damn much. My high lasted all damn day.

I guess it was a good thing Jameson wasn't here to listen in on my calls. He'd left for his parents while I was at the conference. When I talked to him after I returned, he told me he wouldn't come back before graduation. He didn't say, but I suspected he went down there to introduce Shelia to his parents and talk his dad into giving him his great-grandmother's ring.

What a fucking mistake.

And I probably wasn't the only one who thought that way.

Jameson's dad, a general practitioner with a small practice in a middle-class suburb of Chicago, was a no-nonsense guy who shot his opinions straight from the hip. That was the Dutch in him, I supposed. If he couldn't talk sense into his son about marrying so young, especially to a someone as obviously greedy as Shelia, then no one could.

I'd kill to be a fly on the wall when Hendrik Thijssen got a load of Shelia and her gold digging antics. My bet was that he'd rip her a new one.

Funny how I used to laugh at Jameson for being head over heels for Shelia. Two weeks ago, I wouldn't have even thought it was possible for me to feel that depth of emotion. But after connecting with Shondra again, my world had done a 180, flipped upside down, and entered a parallel universe, one where I felt an all-consuming love for another person. Whatever Shondra wanted, I would

202

do—including giving up the life my parents had planned for me.

Well... at least I'd seriously consider it.

Thinking of the future, I stared at the patterns of sunshine on the floor and walls. Only the rattle of my alarm at 7:30 stirred me for present duties. I had woken earlier than normal and called Shondra right away, wanting to hear her voice.

I silenced the chime, scrambled off the bed, dressed, and then headed out the door in under ten minutes. My normal workout was an hour and a half, but I'd increased it to two. I needed stamina for my angel's visit.

Half way to the gym, the salty tang of sea in the air, my phone chimed with a familiar, but infrequent ringtone. I laid my bag on the concrete of the sidewalk, dug the device from my shorts, and answered on the third ring. "Hey, Dad."

"How's it going, son?"

"Can't complain." I expected he knew that. Dad was anything but "out of touch", especially since he had me followed. The first time I'd spotted a man following me, I thought he was a kidnapper. Hell, I was only eight.

I'd run home from my friend Billy's house, heart in my throat. Later that night, as I stood trembling in my mom's arms, Dad explained the way of a rich-man's world.

"Axel, you've seen Blake and Kaitlynne's bodyguards, right?" I nodded. Blake and Kate were the senator's kids.

I nodded my head, my cheek rubbing against my mom's housedress. She alternated between patting my hair and my shoulder, and the heavy weight of her arm comforted me.

Dad smiled and said, "Well, you are important too. More so, because you are mine."

I shrugged, confused. "But we aren't important... I mean, we don't help run the government."

"We will...you will, they have promised me. All you have to do is stay safe and keep yourself clean."

I thought Dad was talking about taking a shower on the regular and not riding my bike without a helmet. The older I became, the more I realized what doors the name Hammersmythe opened... and the doors the name could close. Tabitha had found that out to her peril.

Dad lets out a chuckle that was fake as fuck. "Did you have something to complain about?"

"Nope, not in the least."

I could go easy on him and give him the information he had called for, but he had soured the high Shondra had given me.

"So... I saw you canceled your graduation trip to Europe."

I had a two-week trip planned before I started my internship. I gave up that shit for time with Shondra. "Yeah, I did. I want to head on down to D.C. the Sunday after graduation."

As I waited for Dad's reply, a group of girls passed me on the sidewalk. They headed toward the gym with their pastel bags and matching water bottles. When they noticed me, they started whispering. One of them, bolder than the rest, looked me up and down, an explicit invitation in her eyes. I turned my back, hoping she wouldn't bring up the intense few days we shared my freshman year, especially since I was off the market and more than happy to be so.

"Now, Axel. Why do you want to head down two weeks early?"

I could practically smell his curiosity over the phone. I'd been to Europe more than a few times, but never alone. And with the jet at my disposal, I had girls lined up from Amsterdam to Zurich. Two weeks of self-indulgence and then it was off to D.C. to do a summer internship for my Congressman before I started law school in the fall.

"I just don't want to go. No big mystery, Dad." I turned at the soft sound of my name. The girl stood there, apparently waiting for me. Her light brown hair blew in the breeze and her skin, the color of bronze, looked polished in the sun. As pretty as she was, she didn't have *nuthin'* on Shondra.

Dad's easy chuckle brought me back to the conversation. I didn't take his laughter at face value. He'd dig until he knew about my angel, and if she saw her as an obstacle to my plans, he would find some way to end it. I had to tell him what Shondra meant to me on my own terms, and not in the middle of campus with a past fuck listening to every word.

I lowered my voice, hoping it wouldn't carry across to the random with the breeze. "When you come in on Friday, we'll go out to dinner and I'll explain."

Paying for It

"Everything?" My dad sounded genuinely surprised, leading me to believe that he *knew* something.

If he wasn't telling, then neither was I.

"Everything," I said as I crossed my fingers.

CHAPTER FOURTY-ONE

SHONDRA

Six years ago

The examining room was cold and impersonal with its scuffed grey paint, hard stools, and lack of decoration. Only the doctor's diploma hung crookedly on a bare wall. Above that was a picture of the last president. The blinds in the window had turned a tobacco yellow, and they swung back and forth with the force of the air-conditioner. Puffs of dust particles few into the air with every pass of the oscillating ceiling fan.

I switched the position of my legs for the umpteenth time. I'd been waiting for only ten minutes, but the wooden chair was uncomfortable despite my natural cushion. At least I had Vegas's text to distract me from the news I was waiting for.

Vegas: U lmk ASAP

Me: np

Vegas: ?

I had bought Vegas a smart phone since she didn't have one. The Witch had forbidden it. Vee had quickly caught on to the text shortcuts but she didn't know all of them yet, hence her question.

Me: np=No problem.

Paying for It

Vegas: KK/BOL

Vegas: Teacher's coming GTG

Vee's phone was a luxurious necessity. Vegas needed to contact me in case of trouble.

And I didn't doubt it would happen.

Vegas's step-monster had lawyered up, angling for a payoff. Her attorney, a man with a thick Texas twang, hinted that for a five-figure settlement, "for costs associated with rearing the child for the past eight years," her legal guardians would sign over their rights.

It always came down to money. Shit made the world go 'round.

A rush of cold air along with the doctor's entry shifted my mind on other worries. In a wrinkled hand dotted with age spots, he carried the results of my tests.

Doc sat down with a huff, eyeing me with slight disdain and a curled lip. He was a big man. Not in height, but in width.

Well, for the price, I couldn't expect Dr. Dreamy. I was at one of the last remaining "free clinics" and the eighty-dollar fee was in my price range. Government budget cuts had raised prices and dwindled sites. I'd spent an hour on the way, and with the one-hour back, I already wasted my day.

For the inconvenience and the coin I'd paid, the building should've been a palace. One could wish. When I arrived at the strip mall location, there was one lone protestor holding a poster against abortion. I averted my eyes at the graphic image, but not in time to stop the bile rising in my throat. At reception, I didn't receive a smile, how you doing, or kiss my ass from any employee and the Doc was proving he had an attitude as well.

"Well, Mrs. Williams?" Doc looked down at the paperwork and gave me a fake apologetic smile, "Oh, it's still Miss, correct?"

Ol' dude's slight wasn't lost on me. I was probably just another stereotypical statistic to him. Young, unmarried, and uneducated. One in the hundreds he sees in a week.

I held myself back at his slight smirk, but my thighs remained tense in case I had to spring across the desk and slap him down for his shade.

Doc became all business when he caught my thunderous expression, his grin disappearing into the fold of his mouth. "Well, I have your results back." Drawing out the suspense, he paused like Maury before he announced a guest's DNA results.

I used to watch that show, yelling along with the audience who was right and who was wrong, laughing at the antics of the participants when the test came out in their favor. Then they showed the faces of the kids. The innocents. And the picture became clear.

Regardless of the outcome, the man walked away free while the woman sat condemned. She became the primary caretaker of the child, and often ended up with a man who didn't trust her, or in the worst case, one who was happy to leave her.

That was not the life for me. If the test came back positive, no one but God and I would ever know. Bringing a child into the world required a sound mind along with stability. I had neither. I had no home training on how to be a mother. My mom, a closed-off ghost of a woman, floated through the house on silent feet, head down and mouth closed. She hadn't taught me how to succeed at life as she wasn't living it.

Then there was Axel. Not that I disbelieved him when he said he would take care of me, he would …until it all became too much and he wanted out. Just like Vegas's dad. Just like my mom. And probably just like me.

Besides, changing diapers, helping with homework, running to music lessons wouldn't allow me to be in charge like I needed to. My business was the one thing that soothed my soul, if only for a few hours.

Thank heaven the worry wasn't my concern.

"Ms. Williams… you're negative for STDs and the pregnancy test." The doctor gave me a stern look from his watery hazel eyes. "I hope you will take heed from your… reprieve and no longer have unprotected sex." He raised his eyebrows as he looked down at the paper. "I can write you a prescription for birth control, but you really should do something about your weight as it only adds complications."

Two digs for the price of one. He fully expected to see me in here again with a swollen belly and a sad tale. That's why I hated going to the damn doctor. Each one that I'd ever been to always nagged me about my weight. Almost as if they took it as a personal affront that I was big. Instead of concrete solutions, they thought all I needed to do was drop the fork and push away from the table.

Paying for It

If it were so easy.

My dead uncle Nassau still invaded my thoughts after all this time. He'd pop up when I was most vulnerable, and I could only drive him away by my favorite foods. Until I found another way to deal with him, I'd continue to go to my best source of comfort.

The doctor droned on about what pill he recommended and how I should use them. I caught his lecture hit and miss as a delayed wave of relief washed over me. I wasn't pregnant after all. I should feel like I was walking on clouds, but way deep down, I was sad.

***

The mail was heavier than normal. I paid all of our bills online, so it surprised me that an envelope in my name came in the mail. The outside was creamy and thick, and it smelled of prestige and money. The crisp, uncirculated kind.

I dropped the folders haphazardly on the kitchen table, and one rather gracefully fluttered to the floor. Taking a knife from the drawer, I carefully slipped it between the sealed folds. I already knew I'd keep it forever, no matter how we turned out.

Pride burst through my chest as I gazed at the beautiful invitation. I would never graduate from anyone's college (who could afford it?) but my man was graduating from Harvard.

The crest was on the outside, raised from the paper of course. I traced it and the lettering with my fingertip for about ten minutes before I read his note. Although, I told Axel he should have the day to be about his family and his friends; I didn't want any confrontations when he introduced me to his friends... Or truth be told, his former women.

That's in the past, Shondra.

I knew Axel wasn't a saint. He had learned his skills from the girls before me, and I'd thanked each one. Perhaps someone would thank me one day because if (I refused to think about when) we broke up, he'd be right back in the saddle ready to ride again. And there was nothing I could do to stop it.

I grimaced at my thoughts and unfolded the note Axel had written.

My Angel,

Too bad I can't change your mind about coming, you stubborn girl. I want you to have this, anyway.

I'll be thinking of you and will see you in D.C.

Big Man

Enclosed was a ticket to his commencement exercises. Axel was inviting his aunt and uncle from Chicago and his father.

It wouldn't go to waste. I decided then and there to attend.

CHAPTER FOURTY-TWO

AXEL

Six years ago

The restaurant was easy to find. Made of glass and brick it overlooked the harbor and boasted the freshest seafood the East Coast offered—with prices to match.

It wasn't my kind place. I was more at home in a burgers and fries' establishment. I dressed for the occasion in dark gray dress pants, a light-blue Oxford, and thousand-dollar shoes imported from Italy.

Dad was already there. Seated in a quiet alcove away from curious stares and the hum of other patrons, he sipped his wine while he waited for me. He was in the uniform of the ultra-wealthy with a dark blue jacket white shirt and black dress pants. Dad stood as I approached, sticking out his hand.

As a child I had to look way, way up to meet his eyes, now he was almost level with mine. His snow white hair went well with the deep tan he'd gotten during his trip to the Caribbean where he had taken his current fling. After Mom passed, he waited a year out of respect before taking up with a bevy of bimbos who had more dollar signs in their eyes than brain cells in their heads.

I wondered if the latest one would get upset when she realized Dad wasn't the marrying kind. The last one, a former model with a floundering career in fashion, had threatened to make a stink in the tabloids after Dad had called it quits. Once he turned his pack of lawyers loose on her she quieted down quick enough.

We shook hands firmly, like the men we were, and sat down. The last time we'd hugged was after Mom's funeral and we hadn't said "I love you" since I broke my wrist falling from a swing in the third grade.

"I've ordered for us. Hope that's okay," Dad said with a genial smile.

I shrugged. I couldn't care less what I ate. After our convo it would probably sit like a brick in my stomach, anyway. Dad had called this meeting for a reason — to discuss Shondra. It was a given he'd had Shondra investigated, and those he employed, were adept at discovering the grimiest dirt.

I wasn't angry he'd done so. There was too much at stake for us to lose. But I knew Shondra, and nothing he'd found out would change my mind about her.

While I played with my napkin, taking my time to unfold it, Dad watched me with his deep blue eyes full of intelligence and keen understanding. When he turned the wattage on full blast, it hit his victim like a hot lamp, making them babble. I'd been in on a few meetings when Dad had done so, it was cringe-worthy to witness.

I vowed to hold my own. Before I could get started, the server came to our table. With a grand flourish, he announced our appetizer of lobster bisque and shards of garlic bread.

Paying for It

I'd never heard of shards of bread before, but I wouldn't know how to describe the wisps of crunchy, garlicky, buttery goodness as anything else. I took one in my mouth, surprised to find it was almost as good as sucking on Shondra.

Almost.

"So, Axel," Dad said, lifting a spoon of bisque to his mouth. "Tell me about your girlfriend."

I finished chewing the bread, wiped my greasy fingertips on the napkin then met his eyes. "Why don't you tell me what you know and I'll fill in the details."

He smiled, recognizing my tactic of revealing only what I needed to.

Not my fault if he'd taught me his tricks.

Dad started out by saying I made an excellent choice in Shondra. A strong, independent woman with her own company, that was an up and comer. He would even consider investing himself had circumstances been different...

A thing about my dad—he only extended nepotism (without expecting something in return) as far as me.

While he lauded Shondra's accomplishments, I continued to eat the shards and slowly drain the soup from the bowl, silently waiting for the hammer to come down.

It never did.

We finished dinner, dessert, and coffee all without an ultimatum. Not even a hint.

However, I wasn't at ease. I sat in a DEFCON 4 holding pattern—Code Red all the way.

Dad, lulling me with non-confrontational talk and praise of my angel, had gathered more intel from than all his investigators put together. How could those outsiders know the depth of my feelings? Only I could relay that, and I had through my smiles as I recounted how Shondra, without a degree, challenged my intellect. Then there was the light of pride that shone on my face as I told him about her business and how she had started it with little more than ambition and the drive to succeed. And when Dad promised to send some investors her way, I couldn't keep back the relief and happiness in my eyes.

I knew I was in love, and now he knew it as well.

By my actions, Dad had let me reveal my poker hand even as he kept his hidden. Just like that time when I was ten, and he brought me to a Christmas party at the company's headquarters.

One of his VP's had come up to him, blathering how good business had been during the year and his role in helping it along. The man was red in the face with drink and his cocktail kept sloshing around in his glass as he talked.

Dad had smiled and nodded, even clapping the man on the back as he laughed at one of his quips. When the executive left Dad turned to me, his eyes flat and hard. "I'm going to fire that asshole after the New Year."

My mouth flew open with surprise. By the way my Dad had acted, I thought he and the VP were the best of buds. "Why're you gonna do that, Dad?"

216

Paying for It

Dad's eyes fell into slits and his mouth a ventriloquist's line, "That man there, son, is a piece of shit bully."

By that time in my life, I'd beaten more than a few bullies into the concrete simply because they existed, so I nodded, accepting the fact without question. What I didn't know was that the VP had been criticizing my mom, telling anyone who would listen about how grossly fat she was.

I found out that little tidbit when his son, a mean looking beefy bastard with a thick neck, roided arms and chicken legs, confronted me years later during halftime at a Harvard football game. We exchanged words. He threw out a challenge, and I accepted. We then went off campus to avoid security and the involvement of the cops.

In the parking lot of a nearby Denny's, we settled our differences. It took only two punches to lay him out cold on the mist covered ground. His girlfriend, a thin, crack looking ho' in leopard print pants and some shiny pink bomber jacket, screamed at the top of her lungs to, "Get up and finish the job," as mascara covered tears ran down her face.

Luckily Jameson was there, talking me down, keeping me from inflicting more damage on the bastard other than a broken jaw and nose.

Dad settled scores. I did too. It would be something to see which one of us came out on top.

***

The day of graduation began with a bang of thunder. The clouds poured its oppression, and somehow, the doom and gloom had seeped its way into our room.

217

Paying for It

Jameson paced the floor, fiddling with his glasses and fidgeting with his hair, twirling lock after lock between his fingers. Every so often, he would take a peek at me. I laid in bed, pretending to be asleep.

I already knew what he was going to say before it came out of his mouth and I didn't want to hear it, so I pretended to be asleep while I watched him through my lashes, hoping he would turn his back so I could sprint to the bathroom. On the day of our graduation, all the hard work behind us, I wanted to avoid telling Jameson he had made the first step in throwing his life away...

"I'm getting married, Axel."

I let out a weighted sigh and opened my eyes. Jameson was a sensitive soul. He wrote poetry. He laughed at cartoons until he cried. And when the TV news reported on some sick shit, Jameson would leave the room.

Marrying a woman like Shelia would kill him. Either literally or figuratively. "So, you're really going to do it?'

Jameson stopped combing his hair in the mirror and faced me. Faced my disappointment. Squaring his shoulders, he said, "Yes, I am."

Nothing I could say would stop him in his trajectory of hurt. All I could do is support him and be there when he crashed and burned. "Well, I wish you all the luck in the world." I muttered a prayer for him under my breath, hoping God took care of foolish men.

CHAPTER FOURTY-THREE

JAMESON

Six years ago

Axel and I weren't in the same disciplines. He was in Arts and Humanities. I was in engineering. We graduated at different times, but too close together to see each other walk across the stage. He'd miss my speech, but he'd seen me practice it a few times, so we were all good.

Axel ignored Shelia and she him when we found her under the awning of our house, shaking out her umbrella. We parted ways after a man hug and a "see you later."

I turned to Shelia. She was breathtaking, even when she masked her dislike of my brother with a sunny smile. Yes, Shelia's personality wasn't the best, I didn't care. Growing up in neglect made her harder... tougher than most. I admired her perseverance. Her spirit. I loved her enough to forgive the way she viewed life through cynical glasses.

I had to. We were getting married, for better or for worse.

I took her hand in mine. She smiled up at me. The weather reporter predicted the day would clear, and despite the downpour that pattered the awning and soaked the grass, Shelia wore a backless summer dress with tiny daisies on a white background. Men, some my age, some a lot older, and some with their hand around their wife's waist, looked on in admiration at us.

At her.

Yeah, I was a lucky man.

And yes, I also ignored the way she glanced at those men who watched her every move.

***

AXEL

Six years ago

Before I left the dorm with Jameson, I tried calling Shondra. All my calls went straight to voicemail. I figured they would. Against my protests, she insisted the day be about me, my friends, and family.

"We have ten days in D.C., Axel," she'd gently chided in that no nonsense voice of hers. "Just you and me. Take this time to be with your friends and father, and I promise, for the next ten days you'll see so much of me, you'll be happy to put me on the plane back to Chicago."

"Not fucking likely, Shondra," I'd answered, slightly hurt that she thought I would rejoice at her leaving.

I should have heeded her words as little did I know, Shondra had predicted our future.

***

That night, in the midst of my third party at yet another frat house, I called her. It was close to two in the

220

morning; I was on my second drink (Drunks make mistakes, son. We can't afford mistakes) and fed up with fending off girls which circled me like sharks in a frenzy.

It had started with the one eavesdropping on my conversation with my dad while I was on the way to the gym a week ago, and the randoms hadn't let up since. It was if they could smell I was off the market, but still they wanted a taste.

Not this guy.

Shondra answered on the second ring, her voice sultry with sleep. "Axel, we agreed—"

"You agreed, I didn't. Not really anyway." A blonde approached at ten o'clock while a rainbow haired chick approached at two. I gave them my back, hoping they would take a hint.

"Yes, I know, but I didn't want you to have to babysit me while your friends—"

"If they're really my friends, they would understand." Jameson would, and maybe Mason. Adam and Josh would certainly understand. Tony, on the other hand, would give me hell and probably try to steal Shondra away.

As if the prick could.

"Maybe," she said with doubt lacing her voice, "but I didn't want you to worry about me."

"Shondra--" I shrugged away from the blonde that clasped my bicep, "when will you realize I worry about you all the time? Your happiness is mine. Nothing will change that."

221

Paying for It

Not even my father.

"Axel, that's some serious words. I hope you mean them."

"I do, angel. I do."

She grew silent, thinking in that way of hers that reminded me of that day in the park. I imagined her luscious lips pursed, swung to the side in contemplation. Her unlined forehead lowered over her arched eyebrows. Her beautiful green eyes staring off into the distance.

I let her have her moment as I watched rainbow and blonde push each other into the start of a cat fight. I backed away and let the show unfold until the noise of the bystanders drowned out Shondra's words.

When the fight erupted in full swing, I had to shout, "Hold on. Let me get outside."

I made my way through the crowd even as bodies of those trying to get the best filming angle tried to push me forward. I soldiered through, trying to hold my temper in. Finally, I made it out the door.

The balmy air hit me, fresher than inside, but sticky. This type of weather made me ache for an all-night session filled with sweat, shudders, and lots of moans.

Fuck. Shondra should be here now, with me.

"Shondra... damn. I need you--"

"I'm here," she said in an excited rush, "not too far from campus. I rented an Airbnb room from a couple that—"

The details of why, when and how could wait. As soon as I had her in my arms, I was going to make use of the night air and her warm body, right there in my car.

"Text me the address, Shondra."

"I already did," she said before laughing in that way that made my balls tighten with expected release.

Google Maps told me it would take fifteen minutes to reach her.

"Pack your stuff. I'll be there in ten... and Shondra?"

"Yes, Axel?"

"Don't make me wait."

I hung up, already halfway to my car. Shondra in town was an unexpected, yet highly welcome surprise. As I walked the last few steps, a casual passerby would undoubtedly mistake my smile for something sinister. They would be wrong. I was thinking of nothing more than giving out several commands and having them obeyed.

Chiefly: lift, squeeze, more, and right there.

CHAPTER FOURTY-FOUR

SHONDRA

Six years ago

Axel had given me a ticket to the afternoon exercises. The one where they called his name and handed him his diploma.

I barely made it.

My plan was to fly into Boston in the early morning and have a leisurely breakfast at a place recommended by Trip Advisor. From there, I'd drop my bags off at my Airbnb, freshen up, and then take an Uber to the ceremony.

It didn't happen.

In the morning, there was a two-hour flight delay because of heavy rain. The water from the skies came down in sheets and everyone clapped when the wheels hit the tarmac. I checked my watch, hurrying toward the cab stand. There was no time for a leisurely breakfast, so I asked the cab driver to drop me off at the Airbnb.

He was quiet and so was I, worry fueling my anxiety. A pain lanced through my chest at the thought of not making it on time. I tried to push it from my mind by focusing on the sights of Boston. I didn't review what landmarks I should look for. With too much work and too little sleep, only excitement kept my eyes open.

Same with the day before I left, Vegas had kept me up most of the night chattering about what I should do and see with Axel while I was in D.C.

I didn't tell her, but I would spend the first few days in bed. I wanted Axel like a triple layer chocolate cake after giving up sweets for Lent. He had turned me out, flipped me over, and done it again. And again.

And once more after that.

Axel made me feel like a woman should... cherished and adored. As for feeling loved? I hoped so. Dreamed so—

A honk from the driver pulled me from my thoughts. The guy must have been a native. He took me down side streets at breakneck speed, missing most of the delays on Google Maps. After he unloaded my bag onto the sidewalk, I gave him a generous tip and accepted his, "Thanks, miss," with a smile.

What I gained time wise with the ride, I lost it in picking up the key (per instructions) from the renter's neighbor.

The woman, a retiree with seemingly a lot of time on her hands, gabbed the entire time. I couldn't get a word in edge wise. She led me to my digs, talking the whole way.

Being in the basement, the studio had little light, but there was a lot of room. Since it was only for one night, I couldn't complain. In the morning, I'd call Axel and let him know I was in town.

Paying for It

After unpacking only what I needed for my brief stay, I put on a dark blue wrap around dress and black pumps. My hair refused to lie straight, what with all the humidity, so I did it up in a bun during the Uber ride to Axel's graduation. I finished just as the driver pulled up to the closest entrance. I scrambled out with a "thank you" and headed up the walk.

The rain had let up while I was unpacking, leaving in its wake a briny sea scent and the tangy air swirled dark-blue fabric against my knees. I checked the campus map for the umpteenth time. I couldn't for the life of me recognize one building. With time ticking, I had to pull two people aside and ask directions.

Out of breath, and with my makeup half sweated away, I arrived at the correct venue. The security guy wanted to not only check my bag but get my number. I held up a palm to forestall his ass. "I'm here to see my boyfriend graduate."

He gave me an affable wink and smile, causing me to feel slightly guilty at being so abrupt. "Go ahead on, girl," he said.

My mouth lifted in a small grin to show there were no hard feelings, and on I walked. The closer I came to the entrance of the Malkin Athletic Center, where Axel... my boyfriend was graduating, the wider my smile became. I didn't give Axel the title of boyfriend because I believed it was true; I gave it to him for lack of a better term.

Sure, Shondra. Sure.

Well, he was that in my mind, even though he hadn't said so himself.

226

Paying for It

Maybe he will in D.C.?

Yeah, maybe...

Entering the building, the powerful air-conditioning cooled me down and when my sight adjusted from the brightness of outside; I searched for a spot where I could see the stage but stay out of sight. I found the perfect spot behind two men who resembled tanks on legs.

I stood behind them, rocking back and forth on my heels as a nervous anticipation bubbled in my belly. Fifteen minutes later, peeking around broad shoulders and muscled arms, I heard Axel's name called.

He jumped from his seat to deafening applause.

I will never forget how the moment struck me as surreal. Every detail was amplified, blown up out of proportion. Axel's blond hair was a glowing field of wheat under his cap, his teeth, a searchlight, and his ice-blue eyes burned a hole in my heart from nearly sixty feet away.

He was a summer day at the beach. A perfect view of the Milky Way. He was my everything.

And I was in love with Axel Sexton Hammersmythe.

He high-fived the people as he made his way back to his seat, his grin as broad as he was and just as sunny. His head dipped and bobbed, talking to those around him, and I refused to let jealousy ruin the day if a girl captured his attention...no matter how long they spoke.

Just before the ceremony wrapped up, I left, sticking to my plan original plan even as my heart begged Axel to turnaround and catch me. Out into the brightness once more, I shielded my eyes until they adjusted and caught sight of...a man staring at me from behind a pillar. He looked vaguely familiar with his clean-shaven face and light-brown hair styled into a pompadour.

Was that... William? He'd had a beard at the conference, but without it... that still could be him...

What was his last name, anyway?

Roberts? Reid? Romero?

That was it. Romero.

Was it?

The niggle in my mind told me "Romero" wasn't a bingo.

I'll ask him then.

I strode forward, my pumps kicking up dew and splattering my stockings with moisture.

Before I could get close, a group of loud-talking graduates with their caps in their hands swirled around him, swallowing his frame in their midst. My eyes couldn't keep up with all the movement and William, whatever his last name was, had disappeared.

CHAPTER FOURTY-FIVE

SHONDRA

Six years ago

We didn't fit. Axel's length and my girth didn't make for back seat lovin'.

It wasn't for lacking of trying. We switched positions, shifting our bodies this way and that, until we could both move, our low moans coating the BMW's windows until the glass was as slick as our torsos.

Axel surged forward, his angular face a mask of pure pleasure. I half-closed my eyes, reveling in the sensation of our union. When Axel pulled back, my leg that had wrapped around his middle, bunched and flexed in the worst cramp of my twenty-year-old existence.

I let out a loud yelp. A neighborhood dog answered back.

Axel pulled away, concern coating his voice, "What is it, angel?"

"A cramp," I whimpered, disengaging my hand from the seat belt to rub the sore muscle.

Axel brushed my hand away with impatient fingers. His magic touch soon had the pain dissipating, but not the embarrassment. He was probably used to much thinner girls being able to fit perfectly in the back of his car while

I sprawled halfway on the floorboard and halfway on the seat.

After one final rub, Axel lifted his rear to pull up his shorts.

And thus the act ended.

"Better?" he asked as I scrambled up into a sitting position.

"Yes, I'm fine." But I wasn't. The demons whispered in my ear, making me rethink what I was doing with someone like him. Axel had it all at the end of his fingertips while every day I stumbled through the muck of Vegas's situation, Mom's depression, and the vicious cycle of food cravings inside my head. It was nigh impossible to fill the hole inside of me. Even with the attention of someone like Axel.

I was sure the next ten days spent in his company would make the outside world cease to exist. That was a given. But at the end of my trip to paradise, I'd go back to the same ol' bump and grind with no buffer to fall back on. Axel would start his internship, meet some hot bitch, and forget all about me and my wagon load of problems.

"What is it, Shondra?" Axel's ice-blue eyes glowed silver in the streetlight. I shifted mine to the window and the blurry view outside, gathering my thoughts.

Axel and I hadn't even said a proper 'hello' before we'd fallen into a tangle of hands, fingers, and legs. I wanted to tell him I was on the pill, had started it that morning in fact, but I didn't get a chance. Axel only let me speak a mangled, "Hey," before he was on me.

Now that our passion had faded, I started thinking. Maybe sex was all I was to him—something different from the norm. A box he could tick before he settled down in the suburbs with 2.3 kids and a wisp thin wife who was the president of the PTA.

The noise of a passing car made me suddenly aware of our surroundings. We were in the house's driveway I'd paid over a hundred dollars for. Money I could have used to help Vegas.

Two days before I left, the witch next door had a court summons delivered to our house. A scruffy-looking guy on a bike had handed me the papers with a shit-eating grin and a "you've been served." Mom was at work and Vegas was at school, so I stuffed the summons into my overnight bag with no witnesses. Dealing with the witch will be my burden to bear, and perhaps Axel's if he looked them over...

"Haha," Uncle Nassau said in my mind. "Do you really think some rich white boy is going to help yo' big ass?"

The voice was right. I was in way over my head.

"Axel, what're we doing?" Losing money was something I could ill afford. It made my voice resentful— more towards myself than anyone else. I was the fool, not Axel. He was just getting what I'd freely offered.

When moments ticked by and he hadn't responded, I turned to face him. If I expected to see answers, a clue to what he was thinking it wasn't happening. His face was granite with silver agate for eyes. His lush lips hid under a thin, hard line.

"You won't accept my love because you don't love yourself, Shondra, and that fucking pisses me off to no end."

If there were any words that I'd expected him to say, those weren't it. The wind left my lungs as his face softened under my shocked gaze.

"I don't know what to do, what to say, to get you to trust me," Axel said, scuffing the back of his short hair in an impatient gesture. "My mom had the same issues with my dad. I'd see it in her eyes every time a slimmer woman talked to him. He never cheated and had no desire to, but Mom would still go quiet, retreating to the shadows to watch as she struggled with jealousy and doubt." Axel's eyes burned and his voice lowered with pain and regret. "Eventually, she let it consume her." He rubbed his palms on his shorts, and turned to the window, hiding his anguish from me, and I barely made out his next words. "She left me and Dad because she couldn't love herself. Don't do that to me, angel. I couldn't take it."

A damn of emotions: happiness, joy, relief welled in me. The weight of the future, the fear of the unknown, broke free from my chest and left through a cracked window. Those heartfelt words broke down all my walls and laid them to rubble.

When I turned his face towards mine and our lips met, and we molded into one.

From then on, we fit perfectly.

ACT THREE
~ There are some days
when life hits you harder
than you ever thought it would.

CHAPTER FOURTY-SIX

VEGAS

Present day

"Who are you?"

Disappointment made my belly clench, and I tried not to let the sigh in my throat come out from my mouth. He asked me that question each time a bad day was on the horizon.

And those days were occurring more and more often.

"I'm Vegas, Daddy. Your daughter."

The parent I loved scrunched up his lips and turned his head to the window near his bed. "Tina and I never had kids."

He remembers that bitch, but not me.

Chill, Vegas. He can't help it.

Daddy's doctor said that Alzheimer's patients remembered some people's names, but not others. I knew this, even so, it cut deep.

My childhood all over again.

"Hey, Ms. Shipley." Oscar, a wiry man with bronze skin, goatee, and dark hair, sauntered into the room with my dad's meal tray. He wore the standard hospital green scrubs, but put his own flair for it with a bright neon-pink undershirt.

Paying for It

Oscar set the food on the rolling table and gave me a hug. With a squeeze of sympathy, he headed toward the window and opened the blinds. On a sunny day, the view of the gardens was breathtaking, what with the rolling hills and majestic trees. It was the one thing Daddy remembered to look forward to.

A child-like smile hovered on my dad's lips. His rheumy eyes lit up with pleasure as he gazed out the window and into the fields beyond. The room cost... a lot, but he deserved a nice place after the hole Tina had stuck him in.

I settled on the chair at the end of my father's bed, waiting for Oscar to feed the man who could no longer do it himself. If I tried, Daddy would get upset. He was wary of people he didn't know, and today, he included me in that group.

Last time I'd visited my dad was a good day. We'd talked about his travels, and he asked after his granddaughter. The "good days" were the ones I would remember long after he passed. Not the ones with suspicious side-eyes or sullen silences.

It was a given my visits would decrease once I started my residency the next week, but to ease my mind, Shondra promised to visit on the days I couldn't.

Daddy always liked Shondra, even though she gave him hell that one time.

My best friend had been there when no one else was. She'd not only helped me find Daddy, but six years ago, she'd given up her future for me.

I owed her more than I could say.

Paying for It

Daddy began coughing, breaking me out of my thoughts. Oscar settled him down with soothing strokes and a few sips of water from a glass on his tray.

"How has he been, Oscar?"

Oscar cracked open the window. The breeze whistled through the blinds, chasing away the stale aroma of hospital disinfectant and sour despair. Oscar gave me an empathetic smile. "Same. No real change."

I nodded, staying silent while Oscar made his preparations.

"I'm going to raise you up a little more, Mr. Shipley, so you can have your lunch."

Daddy nodded once in response, keeping his eyes on the window.

Oscar took the remote from my father's lap and pressed a serious of buttons. The bed lifted and elongated like a snake in the sun. He chewed the meal of warmed tomato soup and small pieces of soft bread slower than a cow chewing cud, and the bib around my dad's neck did an outstanding job of catching the food his mouth didn't.

"Now, Mr. Shipley, open wide." My father clamped down on the spoon and released it. A dribble of red traveled from his mouth to his chin as his throat worked to get the rest down. Oscar took a napkin and wiped at Daddy's vacant, grinning face. "There you go. Very good."

To see the man once so proud and robust reduced to a child put an unsettling ache in my heart, the pain

236

attacking me like an ultra-sharp sword. Oscar made a show of focusing on my father while I hurriedly wiped at my tears.

***

The drive to the North Shore and the Bakers' mansion took an hour, and I was ten minutes late for my meet up with Shondra. At a stoplight, I took a few moments and erased the remnants of my crying jag. Applying a thin coat of concealer under my eyes and fresh foundation on my cheeks did the trick. It wouldn't do to meet Jae with a tear-streaked face. He would think it was because of him.

Be strong, Vegas.

Confidence straightened my spine. I sat taller in my seat...until I compared my small Korean sedan with the Mercedes, BMW's, and Italian Stallions lined up and down the street. The valet, to his credit, didn't lift his nose when I gave him the keys. He only smiled and wished me a pleasant day.

Would it be?

Time would tell.

The fountain on the horseshoe drive splashed merrily, and its sound ushered me into the cool hallway. A few people lingered in the foyer and although none gave me welcoming glances, they didn't snub me either. Summoning my earlier courage, I lifted my chin a notch and walked further into the mansion, searching space after space and room after room.

There was no sign of Shondra, only people I didn't recognize.

Paying for It

Ignoring the rather loud clacking of my heels on the creamy marble floor, I continued to look for my best friend. I didn't mind looking...it was more admiring, really. The Bakers' home contained tons of sunlight and many feet of expensive flooring. Paintings from modern artists graced the ivory walls, and the opulent antique furnishings rounded out the upscale décor.

Like Shondra, the Bakers' could afford it. They owned a chemical company similar in size and profit to Dow. Since Shondra's cosmetic company was more or less in the same industry, one phone call was all it took to receive our invites via a via.

My girl knew everybody.

I exited from a living room and turned into an empty corridor. I passed a room, intent on searching the expansive lawn, when a voice and a familiar name stopped me in my tracks.

"Who was that woman you were talking to, Axel?"

Axel? Not Shondra's Axel?

I peeked through the crack of the half-closed door, bobbing and weaving my head to get a better look. I arched and lowered my neck, but could only see part of Axel's face and the brownish-blond mop of a shorter guy halfway blocking my view.

It was Axel.

I recognized him from the picture Shondra had taken that time she stayed with him in D.C. The other guy I didn't know.

Axel answered the question with a sneer in his tone, "The big one? She is nothing but a leftover, Tony."

Tony made a scoffing sound from the back of his throat. "Why? Did she turn you down?"

Shondra hadn't 'turned him down', but she sure did mess him up.

"Let's just say I know her," Axel said with a tone so bitter, he looked as if each word caused him physical pain. "Or at least I thought I did, and that fat bitch is bad news."

Axel had cause to be angry. I had told Shondra a million times she couldn't fault him for his animosity, but that didn't give him the right to call my sister out of her name.

I started forward, intent on confronting Shondra's estranged love when a hand circled my waist, pulling me back.

"I didn't think you were the kind to listen at keyholes, Vegas."

CHAPTER FOURTY-SEVEN

JAMESON

Present day

"I didn't think you were the kind to listen at keyholes, Vegas."

She leaned into me and I held her close, not wanting to let go. It had been two years since we stood flush like this, and the feel of her body against mine had me instantly hard. That hadn't happened with Shelia since a month after we married.

"Jae," she whispered in her melodious voice. She slid her palms down the back of my hands and held them. We stayed like that for a moment before she turned to look at me with wary eyes. "Jae, I need to tell you something."

She could tell me anything as long as it wasn't "goodbye."

"What is it, Vegas?" I tightened my grip. "No need to look so scared." I was sure she wanted to talk about her fiancé. She didn't need to worry. I knew everything Adam and Josh's investigation firm could find.

Terence Kovack was a month shy of forty and had a doctorate in poly sci. Within reason, he could afford the finer things in life. If one of his relatives weren't commanders in the military, they, in some capacity,

240

served the people—mainly in politics. By all accounts, Terence was a good guy who had an excellent chance of becoming mayor—given his competition was a womanizer and a cheat.

All unproven, of course.

Terence's sainthood wouldn't stop me from pursuing Vegas, though. Once Shelia was out of the way, I intended to do just that.

Vegas stepped back and grabbed my hand, leading me from the hallway. "Can we go someplace private? What I have to say..." She stopped, peering around my back. My spine stiffened. If Shelia were the person approaching, we were in for a world of hurt. My ex would make it her mission to destroy Vegas. I couldn't have that, no matter how or if our relationship progressed.

"Vegas, girl, I've been looking all over for you. I—" Shondra scolded, only stopping when I turned around.

I looked at Vegas in askance. "So you two are ... friends?"

There was something rotten in Denmark.

The longer I thought about it, the more skeptical I became. Why would her good friend, the person she lived with, come on to me? It made little sense.

Vegas, with a smile full of trust, pulled her roommate close. "Shondra, this is Jameson."

Shondra failed to meet my scrutiny, instead she focused her eyes at a point past my shoulder.

Well, if she won't tell, I will.

"We already met earlier. Right, Shondra?"

Without meeting my expression, or denying my accusation, her gaze turned uneasy.

I wanted to tell Vegas everything, but Shondra beat me to it, rushing her words out like a swollen river, "I used the perfume on him, Vee. I wanted to make sure he was legit."

Vegas stopped smiling, and her mouth flew open. Her eyes took on a haunted look. "What happened?" She peered at us in horror, her hand covering her mouth as she backed away.

"Nothing happened," Shondra and I said at the same time, looking at each other for confirmation. I was innocent, yet I felt tainted just the same. Second hand guilt oozed from me like Play-Doh from a can.

Vegas rounded on her friend. "Shondra, why would you do that?"

We all spun on our heels when Axel boomed, "Yeah, Shondra? Why would you do that ... again?"

CHAPTER FOURTY-EIGHT

AXEL

Present day

Shondra spotted me as soon as I stepped into the hallway and her beautiful green eyes, sharp with intelligence, watched me from over Jameson's shoulder.

"What's going on?" Tony whispered. He stood behind me, not daring to peek his head out of the doorway in case he got hit in the crossfire.

"The day of reckoning is happening, dude." I leaned against the doorjamb, arms crossed with a smile full of teeth. Shondra's parlor grew ashy with worry, and she bit the plump bottom lip I'd kissed a thousand times.

Yeah, I ached for her still. But I'd crossed the thin line of love and hate that night in December when she played me for a fool. Bitch brought me low... lower than when she left me in DC six years ago. I hadn't gotten over it. I doubt if I ever would.

"I used the perfume on him, Vee. I wanted to make sure he was legit."

Shondra's confession got me moving, Tony trailing behind. I was ready to jump in the conversation with both feet. The world needed to know just what a fake that woman really was.

243

Paying for It

The woman next to Shondra covered her mouth, and
with unsteady legs, backed closer to Jameson. Poor
woman looked like she was about to collapse. I identified
with that feeling all too well. That was me after Shondra
revealed how she'd duped me. Only in my case, we were
in bed. After her revelation, I'd laid there in shock, my
heart beating in my throat as my world crumbled around
me.

Shondra, tears streaming down her face, had begged my
forgiveness. I didn't give it. Why should I? In our twelve
odd years of knowing each other, she'd done what she
wanted and broke my heart not once, not twice, but
thrice. December was the last straw. And now she was
trying to screw Jameson over? Not on my watch.
Jameson had been through enough with that bitch of an
ex, Sheila.

"Shondra, why would you do that?"

"Yeah, Shondra." I said, my long strides closing the gap
between her and I, determined to expose my ex-lover for
the liar and cheat that she was. "Why would you do
that… again?" When all eyes turned to me, I took the
floor and didn't let go 'cause her deception needed to
end.

Right here and right now.

"Will you tell them, Shondra, or shall I?"

The look of hurt she threw me made me livid. I balled
my hands into fists as an icy heat invaded my limbs. How
dare she play the victim when she'd caused me nothing
but pain? I was never one for controlling my temper, so I
let all the frustration, the anger, and the heartache pour

244

from my lips like poison from a vile. "She bamboozled you, bro, just like she did me."

Jameson, confusion on his face, looked at her friend for confirmation. The woman nodded, shifting her eyes to the floor.

Jameson frowned and his dark eyes sunk in his head, giving him a haunted look. It didn't take a brain surgeon to guess my buddy cared for this woman deeply. The guy didn't do one-night stands. When he fell, he fell *all the way*.

Jameson rubbed a hand down his face and left it clinging to his chin. "What did she do, Vegas?"

I didn't give her the chance to answer. I didn't trust Shondra or her friend to tell my boy the truth. "This one here," I said, pointing to Shondra with a finger full of righteous rage, "developed some kind of love potion. Something to do with pheromones." I tapped my finger to my chin, trying to come up with the names she had rattled off that day: my sight had closed to a pinpoint and a clanging had pounded in my ears. "Estrogen and Copulus, or some shit like that. She used that crap on me in December. I was in so deep, I almost proposed to her ass."

"Estratetraenol and Copulins, Axel," Shondra mumbled, her eyes averted from mine. She didn't want to look at me because she knew she was in the wrong. Just like her friend, whose head hung between her slight shoulders like a fifty-pound bowling ball.

I whirled on Shondra and snarled, "Who gives a fu—"

CHAPTER FOURTY-NINE

AXEL

Present day

"Hold on a minute." Tony, who had no business in the conversation, interrupted my tirade. He inserted his lanky ass between Shondra and me, shielding her like some white knight. "Whatever she's done, she seems sorry for it."

I let out a derisive snort. "Sorry doesn't even cover what she is." I turned to Jameson and physically pulled him away from another damn mistake. "Jameson, any friend of Shondra's has to be tainted as well. They're in it together."

The woman—Vegas—snapped her head up, scorching me with burning eyes. "I knew nothing about her using the perfume." Her countenance softened as she turned to Jameson. "I didn't, Jae. Please believe me."

Jameson shook his head. He looked like he'd just walked through hot coals and his feet had blistered. "I always wondered why I fell for you so quickly. I-I knew there had to be *something...*"

Shondra stared at me blankly. I gave her a triumphant smile. She wouldn't be fooling anyone else soon. Turning my back, I pulled Jameson further down the hall. He stumbled along, shaking his head in disbelief. "Bro, you'd best cut all ties before you—"

"Before he does what?" Shelia, that ball-busting blonde, came from around the corner. Her icy presence put a pall over those present, and the hallway became as frosty and as still as a snowy night. Even the overhead lights flickered.

Whatever Vegas had or hadn't done to Jameson, I wouldn't wish a broke-dick dog to face the wrath of Sheila. She made ruining lives an art not even my father could match.

Her latest victim was an eighteen-year-old valet. The poor bastard worked for his cousin, a hotel owner, and *still* he had gotten fired because Shelia had slept with the owner and then threatened to tell his wife. Jameson said it was because the valet had slammed her coat in the car door.

What would the hag do if Vegas had slept with Jameson?

I shuddered internally at the thought.

Jameson shrugged from my grasp. With a pale face, he spun the situation so that it involved no one else. "Axel suggested I cut off a supplier who wanted to raise his price mid-contract, remember? I told you about it last week?" He smiled and reached out to touch her shoulder, rubbing it in a lover-like caress. I nearly gagged at the display of affection. It cost him a lot to pretend to care.

Vegas took in a sharp breath. Shelia's eyes flickered in that direction, and after a quick intake of the scene, she lazered her blues onto Jameson. "I'm surprised you're

247

bringing up that subject here, darling." She tipped her head to the trio behind me. "Won't your friends be curious?"

Jameson made his face impassive as he looked over his shoulder at Vegas, Shondra, and Tony. He shrugged, giving Shelia an innocent smile. "They're no friends of mine."

Vegas started forward, but Tony, finally not clueless for once, held her back by stepping in her way while Shondra took her arm.

Shelia smiled like a jackal. "Then if you're ready, let's go. We have to meet the Lamberts at seven for dinner and I'll barely have time enough to change as it is."

Jameson tucked Shelia's arm under his, and without a backward glance, turned the corner. Half a beat went by before an anguished sound, that of a heartbreaking, echoed in the hallway. Vegas did her best to muffle her cries behind the knuckles of her hand, but was having little luck. Looking perplexed, Tony shifted from one foot to the other, wanting to help but was unsure how.

"Please take her outside to get some air?" Shondra asked Tony, gently placing Vegas in his arms. "I need to talk to Axel for a moment."

I scoffed. There wasn't a damn thing I wanted to hear from her, so I turned on my heel and was almost to the door when Shondra's voice, calm on top and defeated underneath, stopped me.

"Why do you hate me so much?"

I nearly caved. Hurting her made me hate myself, and hating myself made me want to strike out at the object that caused me pain. I held grudges, I couldn't help it. It was the anger in me, stemming from my mother's death, which fueled my passion in the courtroom...and the bedroom.

Shondra had hurt me, no doubt. Not since the death of my mother from a heart attack when I was seventeen had I felt the bone jarring, teeth clenching pain she'd inflicted on me over the years. I didn't know it at the time, but I'd only *glimpsed* the surface of my abject misery. In the months to come, agony would become an old friend, following me around like a homeless drunk begging for change.

But that was later, and this was now. I stood silently, forcing down the flame of lust, which surfaced automatically when I was near her, and replaced them with scorn. "You know what you did was wrong, Shondra. You took away my free will and made me fall for you all over again—not by working for my affections, but by some cheap magician parlor trick."

"It was the only way I saw to get close to you. You were always parading your women in front of me and—"

Wrath made me step to her and with my chest, push her against the wall. I kept the contact between us even as my body betrayed me with a want, *a need* of her so strong, I could barely concentrate on what I was saying.

I took her chin between my fingers, forcing her to look me in the eye while daring her to deny what I was about to say, "Like you haven't been screwing every man you've come in contact with." Except for this party,

249

Shondra had never been without a date. She even took Duke to a function once. I left as soon as I saw them together, took my date home, and fucked her like there was no tomorrow, trying to erase the image.

Shondra gave me a small, sad smile. Her words came out as soft and as quiet as a kitten on the stairs, right before it changed into a lion and pounced on my balls. "There's been only you, Axel. Since we split up in D.C... since the night of your graduation, there has been only you."

CHAPTER FIFTY

SHONDRA

Present day

"There's been only you, Axel. Since we split up in D.C... since the night of your graduation, there has been only you."

Axel stepped back, his face registering shock at my confession. I couldn't let the embarrassment of telling him my secret stop me, so I gathered up my burgeoning courage and kept going.

"There has been only you because you were right. I couldn't love anyone properly until I learned to love myself." I let out a self-depreciating giggle that grated the inside of my throat. Loving myself was once an impossible dream, but through patience, understanding and *forgiveness* it was becoming a reality. "I started going to a therapy after our... *incident* in December. My therapist helped me realize how much I've hurt you over the years, and I'm sorry, Axel. I truly am... for everything."

Axel let out a grunt. I took it as one of surprise instead of disbelief even as his upper lip curled over his teeth and he crossed those enormous arms over his chest.

"You already apologized when you told me what you'd done. What makes this one any different?"

Paying for It

The need to tug his arms loose was overwhelming. I wanted to break down his wall of skepticism so bad; it was a physical pain. In the split second that my hand shot out to do so, Axel moved further away and I embraced cold air. To play it off, I wrapped my arms around my middle.

I could do that now.

Starting a month ago, I'd been working out faithfully three times a week come hell or high water. Duke helped train me and my assistant, who Duke dated, was my encouragement-slash-exercise buddy. Each pound I shed was less of a physical burden on my body and a mental drain on my mind. In the mirror, I saw *the real me* and I liked it.

Now, I had to shed the weight of my past.

Letting go of Axel was long overdue. His actions in dealing with Vegas made it all the easier.

I took a deep breath. What I had to say was hard… harsh even, but in order to heal completely, I needed to face my fears. Lifting a brow, I swung my hair back. Axel needed to see all of my face so he wouldn't misinterpret what I had to say or what I was feeling.

"Axel, this apology is different because it's the last one you'll ever hear."

Axel's mouth made a perfect sweet "O". He dropped his arms and worry marched across his brow like weary soldiers heading towards yet another battle.

"What do you mean, Shondra?" He took a step forward, and I took two back, my butt brushing up against the

252

wall. If he had touched me, who knew what I might have said? I wasn't ready to confess the secret that I, along with two other people, had kept for six years. No one else ever had to know, but my therapist was too damn good. After months of buildup, she had set off a trigger within me, and in between choking tears and body tremors, I told her the tale. It had been ugly, but the utter relief I felt afterward more than made up for the soul wrenching cry during.

I bypassed Axel's question so I could say what I needed to and leave before he wrenched something from me he had no business hearing. "What I *mean* is, I'm done waiting for something that will never happen. I kept the hope of us alive through your fiancée, your name calling—" Axel flushed red and took his eyes from mine for a moment before switching them back, the blue filled with regret.

"Shondra—" Axel began, but I couldn't let him finish. *I* had to say what I needed to first. Otherwise, I'd keep him on his golden pedestal for many more years to come.

"Axel, I get why you felt the need to call me… "*Damn this hurt,* "the names that you did. Fat-ass Bitch and the like. I heard about them from several of our acquaintances."

His lips trembled, and he ran a hand through his longish hair.

Damn, do I wish I could feel those fingers on me...in me, one last time.

Stay strong, Shondra!

Paying for It

Axel came from a family of settling scores. He'd wanted to hurt me as I'd hurt him. I could forgive all of his disparaging comments as I loved him. *And* I always would, but that didn't mean I would carry a torch for him for the rest of my life. It was time to move on... without him.

I patted him on the arm to shore up my words. The last time I would permit myself to touch him with the love I *still* felt.

From this day forward, I'll keep my hands to myself and my mind on the future.

With that thought, I provided my closure. "And even though you may not care, I forgive you for everything you said."

With amnesty given, I let my anger loose.

Anger at the injustice of the world. Anger at what happened because I trusted too much. And last but not least, an anger for a man, who I convinced myself in that moment, cared so little about me.

"Though what I can't forgive... what I *won't* forgive is you squashing the hopes of my sister. "

Axel opened his mouth to protest, but I cut him off.

"Vee needed to tell Jae... *something,* and now she'll never get the chance. You've ruined that with your dislike of *me.* Vee had nothing to do with any perfume, and you knew that. Like I told you back in December, it only works with my natural scent, and only if the person is attracted to me, yet you still had to stick your nose in and mess up her life."

Paying for It

"Damn it, Shondra, why did you have to use it on Jameson, then?" Axel and I stood toe to toe, both of us angry and frustrated. "Why did you try it on *my brother*? Were you trying to hurt me some more?" His ice-blue eyes undressed me and hated on me at the same time.

Hot. So damn hot.

Axel wasn't mad I used the perfume, he was mad that I used it on *his brother.*

Damn!

I wanted to distance myself from him, but with those smoldering looks, Axel kept pulling me back in...

And my fury grew white hot under his sexual scrutiny.

"This day wasn't about *you*, Axel." I poked him in the chest, forgetting my newly minted rule in the height of my acrimony. Axel gave me a wolfish grin, which I tried damn hard to ignore even as my finger sank into a hard pec. "I didn't even know you would be here—"

Axel grabbed my hand and pushed it behind my back. He pressed me against the wall so that I couldn't wiggle it—let alone the rest of my body. His mouth travelled in a downward descent and was mere millimeters from mine when I fluttered my eyes closed and lifted my chin.

"Um, sorry."

My lids sprang open. The guy who I'd asked to take care of Vegas was in the doorway, flickering his eyes between Axel and me. "Your friend wants to leave." He half turned and gestured with his thumb behind him to point the way. "I came here with a colleague, so I offered to drive her car if you... um, if you..." His voice died under Axel's glare.

I seized the opportunity the interruption provided to escape what was fast becoming a sexually charged argument. "That's fine. I'm ready to leave."

The guy nodded and hightailed it in the direction he'd come from.

Axel let out a growl when I slipped past him, jutting out a hand to grab me.

But all he embraced was cold air.

CHAPTER FIFTY-ONE

SHONDRA

Six years ago

The universe was created in seven days. My world was destroyed on the eighth.

While in D.C., Axel and I established a pattern. After he returned, showered and shaved from his early morning workouts in his gym room, we laid in his big four-poster bed until nine, discussing everything that was going on in the world—including our plans for the future.

Some of Axel's talk, like transferring his law studies to UChicago Law instead of going to Harvard, made me pause. True, it would be the optimal solution for us as I had my business firmly entrenched in the Windy City, and there was Vee and Mom to consider. Axel didn't say much about his dad, but from what I gathered he saw him for a few weeks in the summer and at Christmas, so I didn't worry about taking him further away from that connection.

Nevertheless, I tried to talk him out of it, saying we could see each other every other month instead of him giving up his plans. UCLS was an influential school, no doubt, but Harvard...wasn't it known throughout the universe?

Paying for It

Silently, while he spoke of the pros and cons of moving, I thought of how to come up with the money for flights to New York every other month. Axel offered to pay for them, even going as far as sending a jet. He quickly recanted when he saw the appalled look on my face. If he put a ring on it, I'd happily accept what gifts gave me, but until then, I wasn't anyone's gold-digger.

Besides, the longer Axel talked with no concrete action, I eventually forgot my initial unease and accepted his plans as wistful thinking. We could dream, couldn't we?

After our morning talk, we'd go to brunch, or I'd cook. He refused to help, preferring to watch me from a stool at the granite island, his gaze focused and intense on every move I made. While he did the dishes and puttered around, I'd carve out a few hours for work. My company didn't run itself, and I had neglected it more than I should have in coming here. Axel understood and gave me space when I needed it. Not too much, though. Usually after an hour, he sought me out, bringing me a cup of tea or a can of soda. His deliveries always came with a touch or caress, and his soft expression and wide smile let me know he was proud of me.

Most afternoons, we alternated between going to a park or driving to see a film (anything but action). Then it was *home* for a *nap* filled with a lot of laughing, teasing and *sweating*. Later, if we stirred ourselves from bed, Axel would make us a sandwich or an omelet and we would watch a Netflix or Amazon Prime movie from his flat screen pop up TV.

Truth was, we never finished a single movie. But *hey*, I didn't complain. Axel usually made the first move by gathering me close, touching his lips to mine... and while the screen flashed with light and noise, we made our own productions.

***

The days flew by, and I had seen none of the sights. I couldn't leave without seeing the Smithsonian- especially the African American Museum. I still didn't know if I'd come back to D.C.

The weather made it possible two days before I had to head back to Chicago. The sun had disappeared behind the dark clouds rolling on the horizon. My remaining days had rain in the forecast (via a smiling weather reporter on the news).

It was a sign of things to come.

Axel had a morning appointment with the congressional representative to discuss his duties for his internship. I'd go to the African American Museum, look around, and he would text me when he was at the entrance.

In bed, my legs tangled in the sheets from where he had left me, I watched him get dressed. There was nothing more erotic than watching my man pull on his pants and slip a starched shirt over his broad shoulders, his six-pack flexing when the material touched his abs. When he ran a hand down his stomach, dipped it in his tanks and adjusted himself, I stifled a groan.

Remembering just how good he'd given it to me that morning, all rough and demanding with harsh commands and my hair wrapped around his fist, my hand fell between my thighs, searching. To stop myself until he left, I crossed my legs.

Paying for It

Axel strutted to the bed, smirking as he noted my movement. He knew *exactly* what I had planned.

"I have a few minutes, you know."

At my nod, he carefully lifted the shirt over his head and placed it on the wing-backed chair by the bed. He lowered his pants, and I flipped back the covers, uncrossing my legs and laying myself bare... without shame.

CHAPTER FIFTY-TWO

SHONDRA

Six years ago

Axel left in a flurry of blue suit and shiny black shoes. I hopped out of bed, took a shower, slapped on some makeup and forty-five minutes later, I was ready, just in time to answer the door. The driver of the car Axel hired stood at the threshold. A reserved older man with fading blond hair, he greeted me perfunctory with an impassive face, his black coat lifting at the corners in the increasing wind.

"Best hurry, miss. It will rain soon." So focused was I on his slight English accent, I didn't register that I had company waiting for me in the back seat.

"Hello, Shondra Williams. It's damn good to see you again."

Rain came down from the flat gray sky. Fat drops of water that resembled heartbreak's tears. From behind me, the driver made an impatient sound in his throat.

"Get in, Shondra. You're getting wetter by the second, and I'm sure you wouldn't want to meet Mr. Hammersmythe looking ragged, would you?"

The inclement weather pushed me forward, and as I fell into the seat beside him, I finally remembered his name.

261

Paying for It

William. William Rodgers.

As William gazed at me, I could only stare back at him with my mouth ajar.

He broke the silence when we entered the expressway, headed towards the Potomac, "You saw me at Axel's graduation, didn't you?"

I nodded, still unable to speak.

"Yes, those pretty green eyes see a lot, I bet," he said more to himself than to me. When he continued, his voice was stronger. "We were there, Mr. Hammersmythe and I, watching the golden boy achieve yet another crowning moment.

The pique in William's voice scared me, but curiosity prompted me to ask, "Do you work for Axel's father?"

William's eyes glazed over before he turned his head. I didn't need to see the bitterness on his face as it was clear in his voice.

"I do as a matter of fact." He plucked at his pant leg, adjusting it over his knee so the material fell in a smooth line. "Some people don't get everything handed to them. Some people have to work for the what they want."

I let out a derisive sound. "Do you mean Axel? Because I know for a fact, he's not like that. He works hard at—"

"Hard at fucking whatever he can and ruining whatever's decent. Yes, I know *all* about Axel." William let out a laugh so scathing, the driver glanced at him in the rear-view mirror and chills went down my spine.

I silently seethed at the slander against my man while William rolled up the divider to keep our conversation private. Once shut, he spoke again, tearing at my confidence with his words.

"You've probably only seen the good side of him, Shondra." He patted my knee once and withdrew his hand.

I hated to admit it, but there was something so familiar about his touch, I couldn't bring it in me to recoil.

"The stories I could tell you of how many girls he has carelessly tossed aside—"

"I don't want to hear about it!" I covered my ears like a six-year-old and closed my eyes as if that would stop his comments, shaking my head so fast my hair wiped in my face. No one could guarantee the future, not even Axel with his devotion to my body and his love of my mind. If Axel had made concrete plans to do something about our future, I would have laughed at William trying to feed my insecurities, but Axel *hadn't*.

And William used this to his advantage.

"Come on, Shondra. You must be curious about the others, right?"

I was, but he would never know. William had lost all my good faith when he'd started in on Axel.

"Just tell me one thing: what's this meeting about? Why did Axel's father send you to get me?"

Probably to tell you off for daring to date his son, was my immediate thought.

Since Mr. Hammersmythe had his baby boy's internship arranged, he probably had a girl in mind for him to marry. A woman with a pedigree finer than mine could ever hope to be. *Like stays with like,* was the saying, and I was as far removed from the likeness of Axel and his ilk as I could get.

William grinned as he watched the demons take hold and *wrassel* the trust Axel had built up within me.

"Mr. Hammersmythe wants to meet the lil' darling that's so special to his son. Since we'd made contact before, he sent me in his stead." He shrugged, a nice lifting of lean shoulders. "Mr. Hammersmythe thought it best to meet you on neutral territory rather than using his key to the house… and break in on you two fucking."

I bristled at his language. Only Axel could use that word around me, as when he said it, he made me hotter than the fires of hell. I refused to tolerate it from anyone else, and I didn't hesitate to let the errand boy know.

"You don't have to be so crass, William."

This time his laugh was full of sinister glee.

"You want to talk about crass? Your boyfriend is crass. Did you know he got a girl pregnant? And when she told him about the baby, he laughed in her face and said it couldn't possibly be his? He outed her in front of all his friends, flat out refusing to have anything to do with her or the baby."

"Stop it, William, just stop it. Axel would have told me—"

He cut me off with another laugh. "Yeah, he'll probably tell you when you end up the same way. I hope you made him glove up before you two fu—*made love.*"

I ignored his sarcasm to wonder if maybe I'd dodged a bullet the first time Axel and I were together, only to get caught this time.

Shit!

I forgot to take my pill again this morning.

Since I'd been in D.C. I'd forgotten to take it more than a few times. I also wasn't clear on what the doctor had advised on making up the missed pills...

Uh, oh.

Sweat pooled under my arms and my heart rate doubled.

Would Axel's promise hold true? The one to take care of the child? Or would he run like my sperm donor when Mom told him the news about me?

That thought banished the worry from my mind and allowed anger to take its place. I resented the hell out of the man who helped create me. Mom never told me anything about him, except he'd floated away on the wind when she'd told him she was pregnant.

If that piece of shit had just stuck around maybe what happened to me when I was eight wouldn't have occurred.

I blamed him as much as myself.

"Tell me you were careful, Shondra. I wouldn't want you see you humiliated when Axel shows his true colors."

I straightened up in my seat. I wasn't a weak bitch who cried and asked the heavens "W*hy me.*" At least not in front of people.

"It doesn't matter what we were. I don't believe you."

Axel had promised never to lie to me, good or bad, and I trusted in his promise.

William shrugged his shoulders and turned to the window. The car ate up the miles, and the silence stretched between us while I grew lost in my thoughts of Axel.

We arrived at the meeting place, a restaurant with a view of the river. William came around the car and opened the door. He stuck a hand out; I ignored it and stood, brushing past him like I knew where I was going. His words halted me in my tracks.

"Look up the tragedy of Tabitha Moore when you have a chance. There's a Facebook page made by her parents. It doesn't say Axel's name specifically, it can't because they signed an NDA in order to settle, but those that know him will recognize the signs."

William passed me and led the way into the restaurant while I shambled behind, my faith in Axel, cracking at the corners.

And yeah, I was dead scared to meet his father.

Axel had spoken sparingly about him, but I knew enough from what he had told me: *"If he ever contacts you, and he probably will at some point, watch what you say. He remembers everything and will use your words against you."*

266

It seemed Axel's father was exploiting people's weaknesses. I wouldn't give him any ammunition. My plan was simple: I would say "yes" and "no" and try to look intelligent.

A smiling hostess in a black dress told us Mr. Hammersmythe was waiting even before we opened our mouths. She beckoned us forward, and I glanced around as we followed her into the bowels of the restaurant. Since it was early, few people were dining. If I had come under better circumstances, I would have admired the linen tablecloths, matching napkins, and shiny silverware and the small flower arrangements.

In short, the place oozed money.

I probably can't afford a glass of water in a place like this.

The hostess halted at the entrance of a private room."Mr. Hammersmythe would like you to go in when you're ready." William squeezed my arm in commiseration, whispered, "Good luck," and walked away with the peaches and cream hostess, already chatting her up.

I had to enter the lion's den alone.

CHAPTER FIFTY-THREE

SHONDRA

Six years ago

Axel's father looked up from his magazine at my entry. He laid down his copy of *Psychology Today* and rose to meet me. Given the circumstances, I was unsure of the protocol on how to greet him, so I stood silent... waiting.

He grabbed me in a hug. Not one of those one armed ones, but a true fatherly one with arms around me and a soft pat on the back. Brief and to the point, the action made me feel comfortable...safe even.

What stranger would hug a person only to tell them off?

"Shondra Williams," he said, releasing me from his grip, but not from the sheer power which exuded from his person. It oozed from every pore, scenting the surrounding air with wealth and privilege.

I didn't let my awe control the situation. Instead, I studied him as he held me at arm's length. At one time he must have mirrored his son in size. Now his arms hung close to his body while Axel's, due to muscle mass, stood away from him.

He was shorter than his son by a negligible amount. Only a couple of inches at most. His hair, a halo of thick fullness, might've been the same dark blonde as Axel's at one time, but now it was mostly white.

And there, the similarities ended.

Mr. Hammersmythe, or Paul as he directed me to call him, had brown eyes that didn't need to be ice blue to be intimidating. The intensity he projected into them was more than enough to make anyone self-conscious, and nervous, and awestruck...

Yep, I was all three.

"Sit, sit," he said after getting the "Call me Paul" and the "I've heard so much about you out" the way.

I did as he asked, praying the delicate chair wouldn't creak, or worse, break under my weight.

Paul undoubtedly weighed more than me, but I knew the chair wouldn't dare spill his ass on the ground like it would mine. Unlike me, he belonged here.

While he stirred more sugar in his tea, I admired the decor. From the burnished mahogany wood and expensive works of art on the walls, everything, like the chair, spoke against me. The words they said, like *interloper* and *fraud*, whispered from every knickknack and burnished wooden floorboard. I wasn't used to *better* growing up and Axel had never taken me to places such as this. He preferred to go to sports bars or undiscovered diners.

Yep. That's all he took you to. I bet his other girls received the red carpet treatment and trips to the Hamptons.

"Shondra," Paul said, snapping me back to attention, "are you comfortable here? We can go somewhere else if you like?"

I was too busy trying to bolster my confidence to let his keen observation skills worry me.

They should have.

"No, no. Here is fine," I said, adding a smile that I was sure didn't reach my eyes. It wasn't fine. *I* wasn't fine. Not at all. Despite Paul's fatherly concern, and his soft demeanor, the fear and doubt William had started on the ride over grew like a bad debt.

And I had a feeling... payment was due.

"Are you interested in the human mind, Shondra?" Paul asked with a twinkle in his eye.

Of all the questions he could have asked me, I wasn't expecting that. It threw me for a loop. I stammered, trying to hold my guard up as I searched my mind of the right answer. "Uh, well, yeah, sure."

"Then you should read this article. It's about a psychologist, Dr. Kamara." I eyeballed the black-and-white picture of a thin man with a bushy black moustache and a bald head. His dark eyes were impossibly full in his narrow face. "This Dr. Kamara uses hypnotism to cure people. From what it says here..." he tapped a page with a thick finger, "with only a few sessions, he reprogrammed a person's mind to fight of dementia, amnesia, and even psychosis. They are calling his methods a medical anomaly."

Paying for It

"Oh. Wow. Interesting." What the hell does that have to do with Axel and me?

Paul laughed. "I ordered you a cup of Earl Grey. I understand that is your favorite."

"Yes. Yes, it is. I hope you remembered the milk."

Paul laughed again, an indulgent sound. "Yes, yes, of course."

Before getting down to the 'real business,' Paul asked about my thoughts on D.C.

I replied that any city I didn't stick out in was a wonderful city.

Here he laughed for a good minute and had to wipe at the corners of his eyes. I didn't join in. Growing up in Chicago, I knew never to let my guard down when dealing with strangers. Paul tore through my reservations when he started telling me stories of Axel as a little boy. All too soon, I was giggling, then chuckling, then out right laughing at what a handful my man was. The way Paul told it, Axel was always the tough guy, the big man in town...

Until his mother died.

Paul took a sip of tea, rattling the cup as he placed it back in its saucer. "Axel retreated into himself that summer Majorie died. He barely came out of his room except to work out or eat. Majorie's death hit him hard...it hit us *both* hard."

He fiddled with his spoon, tapping it on the edge of his newest cup of brew. Between us we had drunk at least a gallon of tea and eaten a field of finger sandwiches.

271

By that time, I felt as relaxed with Paul as I was with Vegas, no longer wondering about Williams's dire warnings or if meeting Axel's father on my own wasn't such a good idea. I should've been on the lookout for some sort of trick, but he'd pulled me into complacency by excellent food and enjoyable conversation.

And that was when Paul struck.

He blindsided me with sound reasoning and played on my love for his son until all I could do was sit there and let his words take hold, twisting and turning everything I knew to be right into what was wrong.

Paul's gaze was steady as he chiseled at my heart. "You're a remarkable woman, Shondra. I'm not only impressed by your business acumen, but your wit and your beauty. You're the full package, and one day, I hope to welcome you into the family."

CHAPTER FIFTY-FOUR

SHONDRA

Six years ago

I experienced only half a second of pure joy before he snatched it from me with his next words, "That day is not now, though... nor soon."

My mouth flopped open and my tea stained tongue grew drier than a homemade crouton.

"I'm sorry. W-what did you say?"

Surely I must've heard him wrong. He'd hugged me. We broke bread together. He said I was smart...

"Shondra, you're a distraction Axel doesn't need right now. Did you know he's been making plans to move to Chicago and go to law school there? Do you realize what will happen if he does?"

I shook my head, trying to process where he was going.

"All that Majorie and I planned for him will fall apart. I can't have that." Paul shook his head as if shaking off the worry. "I won't let him cast aside his mother's hopes and dreams. I'll disinherit him first."

I chuckled as his threat sounded like a bad *Lifetime* movie. His granite like expression made my disbelieving sounds die in my throat while ice water replaced my blood. "Uh, I'm sorry. I thought you were joking."

"I never joke, Shondra. Life is too short to play games."

His eyes burned into mine, and the potency of his gaze had me stumbling over my words, "Um...well, um, I don't have that much influence over Axel. We've talked about his moving ... um, sure, but that's as far as it has gone. If it helps, I don't think he should move either."

Paul gave me a 'you're so clueless look' as he shook his head at my naivety. "He's made several calls to law schools in Chicago, and he's sent feelers out to my contacts about part-time jobs. He's as serious as I've seen him, Shondra, and he always follows through on his plans." Paul leaned forward in his chair. "I understand that you, through your friend, have a heavy custody issue. I could make all that go away." He gave me a seal-the-deal-smile. "How does that sound?"

I couldn't tell how anything sounded. I hadn't told Axel the entire story about Vegas. To my shame, we'd barely glanced at the court documents before my foot carelessly shoved them off the bed and onto the floor when Axel rolled on top of me.

"I can open doors for you that no one else can. You can work a lifetime and never achieve the greatness you are capable of. Let me help you with your court case... your company. All you have to do is let Axel go until law school is over. He'll be in Chicago after that, anyway. Axel has a job waiting for him with a friend of mine... and if he follows my plan, he'll be set for life. Don't you want that for him? Don't you want him to achieve his mother's dreams?"

Paying for It

On that day, I learned what genuine power was. At the snap of his fingers, Paul could cure me of my one biggest worry… in exchange for giving up my one greatest love.

Later, I applauded myself for being able to speak through the pain that had settled like a viper in my heart. It struck repeatedly, filling my lungs with poison and making it difficult to breathe.

His father, who cared… one who worked hard to give him the very best, was asking me to love his son enough to let him go. What I would have given to have a father do that for me. How could I take it away from Axel?

I nodded, more to convince myself than anyone. Even my demons. "I only want the best for Axel, Paul. He is my world."

I took a shuddery breath and convinced myself I was doing the right thing. Vegas would be safe. She had no one else to rely on, and it was up to me to do what I could to ensure her safety and happiness. My girl had saved me after my uncle's death by talking me down from my nightmares, believing in me and my business with every breath she uttered...

It was my time to save her. Axel would stay in his proper rank and file, going to Harvard as he should, and afterward, he would inherit his billions and marry a pretty, confident wife while I would… I would *somehow* carry on, as I had for all my life.

Alone, and dependent only on myself.

Paul breathed a sigh of relief and the intensity of his gaze grew softer. "I like you Shondra, now more than ever." He patted my hand once with his large one before finishing his tea. I didn't find the gesture as condescending as I should have; it was more comforting instead.

His cup didn't rattle this time as he set it down. "I hope you and Axel will find each other again, as I don't think he could do any better. Anyone who would cast aside their happiness… to sacrifice it like you have… is someone who has my admiration… and gratitude."

It was a done deal then. I'd given Axel up with minimal fuss.

That was the outside appearance. Inside, I was a whirling dervish of emotions. The demons were working overtime filling my head with:

Cast aside . . .

Like me . . .

It will happen . . . eventually.

You don't deserve him.

Fat. . .

Tainted. . .

Insecure . . .

You won't accept my love because you don't love yourself. . .

He's right. I don't . . .

The truth was staring me right in the face. Axel was better off without me bringing him down.

***

Paying for It

I'd ridden back on my own, and I was grateful for it. I didn't believe William's accusations when he first said them, but the silent ride home had me thinking... *wondering.*

Axel peeked from the front window. I exited the car, and he was there in the doorway...on the sidewalk... taking my hand. The car drove away just as the front door clicked shut.

And there in the hallway, we had it out.

"Axel, tell me about Tabitha. The girl you got pregnant and rejected."

His face, a healthy tan, went ghost white, and his hand on my arm tightened to an uncomfortable level. "Who told you about her?"

I pointedly gazed at his grip on my arm. He dropped his hand, balling it into a fist. "Does it matter who told me?" My voice raised with each question. "Is it true? Did you do it? Did you leave a girl to raise your child on her own?"

He leaned against the wall and let out a deep sigh, eyes to the ground. "Do you believe I would do something like that?"

"I don't . . . I didn't . . . I don't know." Confusion rode me hard. Why wasn't he asking about where I was or who I was with? It seemed he already knew...

"What did my father do to you, Shondra?"

So he knew.

Paying for It

He folded his arms across his chest—his go-to defensive move. "You're already gone, aren't you?"

The strangeness of the entire day caved in on me. All I could say was, "Axel, I agreed you should focus on your future—"

"You're my future, Shondra."

If he had moved from the wall, unfolded his arms, and held me, I might have reneged on my promise to his father, but he didn't. In fact, his whole demeanor, despite his declaration, was as cold as a barren tundra. He didn't lift a finger to change my mind. That coupled with the fact that he skipped my question about Tabitha wasn't lost on me.

"Axel, tell me what happened... *please*." It was my last ditch effort to save us, and Axel used it to create a chasm that would take years to close.

He looked at me for a long moment. So long that sweat broke out under my arms and my heart ran the Indy 500 in my chest.

"If you have to ask, if you have to *know*, then we might as well end it here." He pushed from the wall, took my suitcase from the hall closet and deposited it at my feet. "I'll get you on the red-eye or an earlier flight if I can."

Stinging tears blurred his retreat. I packed quickly, throwing items without a care or method into my suitcase. I had to leave as quickly as possible, only then would I start to heal.

How wrong I was. I'd *never* get over what could've been, and I would pay for it in heartache, and... in blood.

Paying for It

***

Axel changed my flight to one going out that evening. He'd also done some trick with miles or points and upgraded me to first class. I knew nothing about it until the bored-looking agent with micro braids, handed me my boarding pass and told me I should have stood in the premium line.

Axel hadn't taken me to the airport. Didn't even offer. Instead, he called me a cab. We didn't hug goodbye, didn't even say the words. He stood at a distance, sculpted from stone. I stood awkwardly in the bright hallway, waiting for him to say *stay*, or *see you around, something*— *anything* which told me we weren't over.

Nothing. No sign. No regret. No *feeling*.

For him, we were done.

For me, it was more complicated than that.

Three weeks later, I found out that I was pregnant.

CHAPTER FIFTY-FIVE

VEGAS

Present day

For all of a minute I was livid at Shondra for what she'd pulled. How could she have subjected Jae to such a test? Once Tony took me outside and I could breathe the fresh air, my mind became clear. Sho had done what she did to protect me. She didn't want me to suffer like she had with a man who went after anything in a short skirt. A man who'd blighted her name every chance he had.

After she came back from dropping Tony off, we had a long talk.

I met her at the door and the first words out of her mouth were, "Vee, I'm so sorry. I wanted to make sure he didn't hurt you and Kae..." She patted my baby girl on her back as she lay with her head over my shoulder. Kae giggled, her little body twisting in my arms at the sound of her Auntie's voice. Shondra clicked her tongue, smiling at Kae.

I brought her back on topic. We needed to put the day past us. "Did Jae try anything? What did he say?"

Shondra reluctantly took her eyes from my daughter to meet mine. "All he said was that he was married... but he never mentioned love, Vee. He doesn't give a da-darn about that heifer he is with. I'm sure of that." Her confident expression turned pleading, "Now, if Jae had

280

gone after me, I never would've taken it further. You know that, right?"

"I know, Sho." I handed her Kae, who whimpered in my arms. Once she was in Shondra's, baby girl was all smiles again.

The little imp.

Kae knew what was what. Sho spoiled her rotten while I didn't put up with her nonsense—the burden of being a mother. Mothers received all the flack and very little of the glory.

That got me to thinking what kind of father would Jae make? Would he retreat into the shadows while his wife decided my daughter's upbringing like my dad did, or would he stand up for his child and welcome her into his home? I prayed for the latter rather than expect the former in my effort to keep the faith.

Shondra switched Kae to her other hip. Her worried brow spoke of her need to decipher my thoughts. "So, are we good?" she asked.

"Of course we are, Sho. You were just trying to get the lay of the land." We'd discussed things enough as far as I was concerned. My sister did what she thought was right. I couldn't fault her for that.

We headed to the kitchen with Kae babbling about her day in her Auntie's ear. Sho humored her by saying, "Uh, huh," at the right moments.

Shondra sat Kae in her high chair, content to talk to my daughter instead of me. That was fine, but only after I asked my burning question.

281

"What did you and Axel talk about?"

Shondra harrumphed, rolling her eyes. "What happened between us. I apologized, and he rejected it, but *this time,* he knows it's final." Sho stood up, taking a shuddery breath. "I'm done with him, Vee. I can't wait for him to decide. I've waited too long already."

Sho wasn't lying about that.

Ever since Axel moved to Chicago three years ago, Sho had given him every chance to put a ring on it. Axel chose instead to keep her at a distance. When Sho used the perfume as a last resort, he went ballistic. Axel, a walking wall of testosterone, had a predictable reaction to what Sho had done. It was never wise to emasculate a man like Axel. He wasn't the type and my sister learned that to her detriment.

***

"You'll do fine, baby. Stop worrying." Terrence leaned over the gearshift and gave me a light kiss on the lips. "*I'm* the one that should be worried. Think of all the stuff I have to do." To stop any more intimacy between us, he rattled off his schedule. He didn't have to bother. I wasn't asking for *more.* Jae was on my mind.

What would Jae think of me when I told him about Kae? Would he hear me out or go off the deep end—spouting threats of custody and involving lawyers?

The thought of going to court turned my blood cold, and I shivered despite the heat circulating in the car. No matter what the outcome, Jae and I would work things out. He would know about his daughter. Of that, I had no doubt.

Paying for It

When, though? That was the question.

As I looked into Terence's already distant eyes, I vowed it would be sooner rather than later.

"You'll still be able to pick me up?" I asked with my hand on the lock. "I'll be off by five o'clock."

"Yeah, yeah. Sure, sure. You'd better go. I'm practically blocking the entrance here."

As if to prove his words, a sleek silver Audi came zooming up to park in front of us, the driver stepping hard on the brake.

An involuntary gasp escaped me when I saw the passenger open their door.

Terrence took notice. "Who is that? Is that him?"

I'd told Terrence I would work under Shelia Caldwell Thijssen, Jae's wife. We discussed the scenarios in which I would run into him: maybe in the cafeteria, maybe at the front desk as he waited for his wife, maybe in the parking lot, but *never* on the first day.

My heart clenched as I watched him help his wife from the car, taking the keys from her slim fingers. The diamond ring I coveted for all that it represented winked in the sun. He gave her an air kiss on the cheek. I grinned, noting that it was much drier than the one Terrance had given me.

Jae's phone rang. He put it to his ear as he slipped in the car and shut the door, cutting off his wife mid-sentence. Her profile turned into a hard mask as she banged on the window with force enough to make it shatter.

Jae ignored her and continued talking. Shelia gave up with a stamp of her foot. With a glare in our direction, which I quickly shielded my face from, she disappeared into the sliding doors with a jerk of her powder blue skirt.

"Damn, that was cold," Terrance said with a chuckle. "I don't know about you, but they won't get my vote for couple of the year."

***

Five other residents rounded out my group of four men and two women, and we all came from different nationalities and backgrounds. Thankfully, no one had an ego or God-complex like at my other hospital. It was a refreshing and welcome change.

Three of the six, including me, had also transferred in from other residencies—all POC's. At the start of the day, our glances asked if we were tokens. Not so. St Vincent's was a melting pot and had even had a spread in several magazines that herald its diversity. Besides being a teaching hospital for doctors around the world, there were POC's in all levels of the administration. By the time our orientation finished and we headed over to receive our pagers and rotations, I was on cloud nine.

I loved my workplace.

The staff that I'd met were friendly with everyone giving us words of encouragement or helpful tips. St. Vincent's also had state-of-the-art equipment and a streamlined process in place that made paperwork a breeze.

The good feeling ended when I Shelia introduced herself.

Paying for It

She greeted our group with a bright smile. "My name is Shelia Caldwell and I'll be your go-to person should you have questions or need guidance." Her deep blue eyes flickered to each of us, stopping longer than was necessary when she reached me.

I found nothing friendly in her gaze as it lingered, in fact I saw a challenge. The Wife used to look at me the same way, and in the end, look what happened to *her*— pushed in front of an 'L' train for running her mouth.

I would never dream of going so far. But *no one* would get in my way of pursuing Jae. So...

Challenge met and accepted, bitch.

CHAPTER FIFTY-SIX

AXEL

Present day

For the tenth time that day, my finger hovered over Shondra's number. It was the same one. I had called and hung up more than a few times when I first moved to Chicago, blocking my number so she wouldn't know it was me.

That all stopped after I saw her at a party with Duke. At the time, I thought she had moved on, and it took me until that night to do so as well.

It had been a month since she told me I was her one and only. A month since I lost that title for good. She was dating Tony, and I had it on good authority (from Adam and Josh) he was taking her to Paris.

I threw my phone on the bed and let my body follow. Gazing up at the ceiling. I revisited the thousands of recriminations I'd been telling myself since the Bakers' party.

You should have told her about Tabitha, my mind admonishes me. You shouldn't have let her go that time in D.C. She gave you the chance you had been waiting for in December, and what did you do? You got angry...

On and on the thoughts turned and twisted and scurried around in my mind like rats in a maze.

Back in D.C., during those long talks in bed, Shondra and I had discussed going to Europe after I graduated from law school. She wanted to walk over the bridges that spanned the Seine. I said we should visit a terraced café and drink coffee while we watch life unfold on the cobblestoned streets. We both agreed to search for Jim Morrison's grave...

Funny how life bit me in the ass.

I'd talked to Tabitha (another woman I'd treated poorly) about Paris too. To please her parents, she was going for a degree in business, but art was her passion. What better place to explore artistic shit than in Paris?

She wanted me to take her there. I didn't say yay or nay. I never did with randoms...until I finished with them. Then it was nay all the way.

However, Tabitha hadn't taken no for an answer.

***

AXEL

Revisiting the past

Tabitha's small hand was fingernail deep into my Harvard sweater. We stood in the hallway that led to the common room. Students milled around us, their voices almost drowning out my former random's low whine of a whisper.

"Axel, are you listening? I said I was pregnant. What are we going to do?"

I planned to meet up with Jameson and the other guys for lunch, and I was already late. My course had run past the house because of a heated discussion between a couple of students. I only stayed because the girl I had been eyeing had been involved, otherwise, I would have sneaked out.

Trying to catch my breath from running full tilt, I didn't answer Tabitha right away. When I did, my voice was harsh, and a lot louder than it needed to be. "Tabitha, you're lying. And if you aren't, you need to go on Maury, because I am not the father."

Yeah, I was flippant as hell, especially with such a subject, but if she thought to trap me, she had the wrong prick on the right day. There was only one woman I had entertained thoughts of as the mother of my children and Tabitha Moore wasn't the one.

I shook loose of her grip and continued down the hall. Tabitha followed, close on my heels. "Axel...please."

I whirled on her. "What, Tabitha. What do you want from me?" I shouldn't have shouted at her, but fuck was I pissed. I slept with her for a week and used condoms I knew hadn't broken. How could she accuse me?

Jameson came around the corner. His tall, gangly stature, somehow calming me down. "What's going on, Axel?" He flicked his eyes between a blushing Tabitha and a scowling me.

I waited for her to spout her lies, and when she didn't, I took over. "She says, she's pregnant. She says," I pointed a finger in her direction, "that I'm the baby daddy. I'm not."

Several students had stopped to listen, and the titters started behind raised hands covering gossiping mouths.

"Let's take this outside, to get some privacy, shall we?" Jameson held out a long arm, pointing the way towards the outside doors.

The guys joined us out on the grounds: Tony, Mason, Adam, and his friend, Josh. Only later would we find out that they were more than friends at this point.

My glares kept other students from getting to close as I relayed to the rest what Tabitha had accused me of. Tony lowered his head, but the rest looked on in disbelief. Adam was the first to speak up. "Axel...uh, you are always so careful, how could you slip up?"

In the past, I'd bragged about my conquests, going into as much detail as the others would allow, which in truth, wasn't very much, but the one thing I would always specify was that I'd gloved up before I plunged in.

"Yeah, I know...she's got me mixed up with someone else."

Tabitha had been silently weeping at that point. At my words, she broke out into sobs. Jameson held her, promising her it would be okay. I didn't feel one way or another about it. I just felt disgusted (in myself) and numb (about the situation) and I felt that way for a while... until I finally learned the truth.

CHAPTER FIFTY-SEVEN

JAMESON

Present day

The group of college kids made the bar seem more crowded than it was. Their tinkling laughter and loud guffaws occupied the small space and made the somewhat somber area come alive.

There were plenty of empty seats at the bar top and the tables beyond. Instead, I waited until *my* stool became available.

The stool I'd sat on when Vegas had tapped me on the shoulder.

A woman, blond with an athletic body—Shelia's carbon copy—occupied my seat. I ordered a drink and retreated to the shadows, sipping my martini slowly until she left. I hoped it would be before Axel arrived. He'd give me hell if he caught me waiting for a chair when any old one would do.

What could I say? My unique rules of conformity made me a creature of habit. I gravitated to places that held fond memories and avoided those that maimed my spirit. Shelia had made many a place I'd held dear off limits in her quest to destroy our relationship.

It was a tragedy in two acts.

Paying for It

The lakeshore hosted our first fight shortly after our honeymoon—a real verbal knockdown drag-out over her, finally coming clean and admitting she'd laughed at "my goofiness" when I'd asked her out the first time. Apparently, she could only tell the truth *after* I'd put a ring on it.

It was the beginning of the end.

Then there was The Art Institute fundraiser where I, along with a group of our mutual friends who were helping me look for her, caught my then wife and her resident doctor in a compromising position.

The final curtain.

Needless to say, I didn't go back to those tainted places, no matter how much I missed them. The city I loved had grown smaller because of it.

Pity, that.

The *Near* Shelia drained her drink, threw some money on the bar. She hopped from her seat, tapping furiously on the keys of her phone. At the door, she nearly collided with Axel who'd finally shown up. He steadied her with an outstretched arm.

Winding through the crowd of kids, I watched Axel and Near Shelia interact on my way to the bar. She looked up from her phone and blushed under Axel's gaze. The woman tucked a few strands of hair behind her ear and spoke a few words. She then tilted her head towards the door. Axel looked around, saw me, and jerked a thumb in my direction. I settled in her still warm chair while her dark eyes swept over me appreciatively. She bent towards Axel, her pink glossed lips moving in consonants and vowels. He laughed at whatever she'd said. I was the first time I'd heard him do so in several weeks.

A genuine miracle.

Look-a-like Shelia stared after him a moment, her face resigned. Turning, she once again she focused on her phone, the keys suffering under her wrath as she walked out the door.

"What was that all about?" I asked. Axel shifted onto the stool on my right and eyed the drink in my hand.

"A martini night, huh? I'm going for something harder than that." He motioned to the bartender, two fingers in the air. Once his double of Scotch was in his hand, he answered my question. "She wanted to know if I was meeting someone. I told her I had a date with my partner and let her draw her own conclusions." He drained his glass, leaving the two cubes of ice with no liquid to cool. "I had to laugh when she said, 'All the hot ones are gay.'"

"Well, I know I'm hot, but you look like shit, Axel."

"I've been working from home, you prick, and why the fuck I need to make myself pretty to have my weekly drink with you is beyond my comprehension." He pulled at his oversized gray hoodie and matching sweatpants with a hole at the knee. Then signaled for a refill for himself and another drink for me.

It looked like we were going to have one of those nights. I indulged occasionally, but with Axel it was becoming routine.

Yeah, my brother had been steadily going downhill. He always gave a variation of the same excuse of why he'd

292

show up looking like he slept on the streets instead of the billionaire he'd become. Still ripped... but those that gave him a cursory glance wouldn't know by looking at him. His face was gaunt . . . hollow, as if all the life had slipped from his features and dissipated into the air. The chinstrap beard had grown over the last month and had become a mass of scraggly hair.

I didn't need to address his fall from grace, I already knew the reason — Shondra Williams.

We'd met up the day after the Bakers' party with the aim to confess our secrets. In this very bar on the stool I considered mine, I told him all about Vegas, and he laid out his tale of Shondra. By the time finished our heart to heart, a nearly empty bottle of Glenlivet stood between us.

Since the Bakers', Axel hadn't seen Sho at any party, soirée or function, and the poor bastard was beside himself. Axel could've easily gotten his fix by going to her office, but he was too afraid of rejection—just like me.

I'd wrestled with myself on whether or not to contact Vee when I learned she worked with Shelia. I was on the phone with Axel, Shelia banging on the window to give me further instructions I didn't care to hear when I glanced in my rearview mirror. Vee's feline eyes locked on mine and the world tilted.

A moment later she rushed from the car. Her dark blue scrubs, the kind the residents wore, filtered through my brain. She worked at St. Vincent's, *the same hospital as Shelia.*

Paying for It

I called the front desk, pretending to be an administrator, and asked where Vee worked. Utter terror gripped me when the girl on the other end chirped rather cheerily that Vee worked under my ex.

Shelia would ruin Vee for even *looking* in my direction. I shuddered to think what she would do if she learned we slept together.

It didn't bear thinking about.

So, I kept my distance from Vegas even though I watched her being dropped off by her fiancé. They days I didn't take Shelia, I went all the same, hiding in my car, perched over the steering wheel hoping to catch a better glimpse of her. I turned my head when Terrance kissed her cheek, my heart hammering in my chest, fist clenched.

Axel and I were both afraid of facing the music of our actions. I'd shut Vee down when she was trying to prove her innocence while Axel deprecated Shondra at every turn. We let our women down in every way imaginable, and in our reckoning, we didn't deserve a second chance.

Besides, Vee was with her fiancé, and Shondra was dating Tony. The information had come via many a mutual friend that things were getting serious.

The bartender, a tall African American with a perfect fade and a winsome smile, broke off his convo with an attractive co-ed to collect our glasses. "Another round?"

I nodded, but Axel said, "I want to try something else." He tapped his chin. "George. Give me a—hey do you have those little umbrellas?" At George's nod, Axel said, "Then give me Piña colada with a pink umbrella and keep them coming." Axel slapped a hundred on the wooden bar top, making the guy next to me jump. George laughed and made the bill disappear before it settled.

According to Axel, a Piña colada was Shondra's favorite drink. On the night of our confessions, Axel said he often caught her at parties, twirling the umbrella from her drink as her eyes rested on him.

"So, what's new in your world, Jameson?"

"Shelia is off to a conference until Sunday."

Axel lifted a brow, "And?"

CHAPTER FIFTY-EIGHT

JAMESON

Present day

"And Vegas is off for the entire weekend."

Axel took a long slurp of his drink, twirling the umbrella between his thumb and forefinger in quick bursts. He set his drink down and rubbed his mouth with the back of his hand. The guy on my left scoffed at Axel's lack of manners.

We ignored him.

"How do you know this?" Axel asked, eyeing the guy behind my shoulder.

"Last week I had dinner with a supplier at Piccolo's— that new restaurant in South Loop, and I ran into Tony and Shondra." Axel, his jaw tight, folded his arms across his chest and returned his eyes to mine. "She took me to the side, apologized, and told me Vee had nothing to do—"

"How did she look? Was she happy?" Axel's gaze was like coming from a darkened room into bright sunlight. The intensity was so blinding, I looked away.

"Um. Yeah. She looked great, actually. . .healthy. . . and yes, happy." Shondra had lost weight and the fitted clothes she'd worn that night stressed her new figure, making even more eyes follow in her wake.

Paying for It

As Tony hovered a respectful distance away, and my supplier busied himself by chatting up a hostess, I asked Shondra about Vee. She didn't answer, only pulled a card from her purse and wrote something on the back—Vee's schedule for the week and her direct phone number. When Shondra pulled me in for a hug, she whispered I should call her girl without delay.

I did as I was told, speaking to Vegas the next day and . . . well, her *enthusiasm* was legendary, giving me hope.

Since she was at work where Shelia could pop up like an unwanted blemish, we stayed on the phone only long enough for her to accept my apology and agree to meet here, on Thursday, after her work finished.

I booked the same hotel room . . . *just in case.*

In twenty-four hours my life would begin, and my goal for this evening was to set Axel on the path to *his* new start.

"She's happy, huh?"

I nodded. Shondra's smile had been brilliant when Tony wrapped an arm around her waist, and she'd melted into him when he led her away. However, there was no hiding the sadness in her eyes.

Telling Axel Shondra still carried a torch for him wouldn't do my boy any good. He had to think she was out of his reach. Only then would he get up off his raggedy ass and work for what was his.

Pride was a terrible thing.

"Happy? Damn . . . *fuck.*" Axel slammed both fists on the bar top, making the glasses near us rattle.

Paying for It

"Hey, dude. Watch it, will you?" The guy to my left was a good seven years Axel's junior and nearly matched him in body size. His date, a co-ed with a monstrous designer bag weighing down her lap, opened her pink duck-lips into an elongated oval.

I stood as Axel did, stopping him by placing my hands on his tense shoulders. "Don't do this, Axel."

"Yeah, don't do this, *Axhole,*" mimicked the guy behind me. His girl tittered snidely.

I ignored everyone who had stopped to gape, and began my routine of calming him, which had halted more than one of Axel's infamous beat downs. "Ignore the prick and focus on the future. Your dad would be pissed—"

"Yeah, son. Don't upset, *daddy,*" bleated the man.

"Wrong reason, Jameson. He's the reason I'm in this mess." Axel made as if to move around me. I held him back, but just barely. Axel was a couple of inches shorter, but I hadn't his muscle mass, nor was I as quick. "Axel, listen—"

Determination and a sort of eagerness filled out the hollows of his face. His eyes took on a fanatical glow. "You really need to move, Jameson 'cause I don't want to take you down as well."

I'd always been able to calm Axel enough to where he'd listen to what I had to say. Not this time. He was way beyond buying what I was selling... and it was then I realized Axel had been itching for a fight all along.

Crappy clothes, a girlie drink, and another hot-head were all it took, I suppose.

It took me a second longer to step back. Maybe Axel needed this to snap out of his funk. We all had our crutches and fighting was Axel's.

"Axel, if you're going to do this, let's take it out—"

The loud prick moved from his chair, pushing me aside so hard my back slammed into the bar. "Let him at me, dude. With that foo-foo drink he was slurping down, what harm could he do?" The fool then pushed Axel in his chest, hard.

The idiot should have run the other way when he saw Axel didn't move a millimeter, but only smiled at the assault.

My blood ran cold at the fire behind my boy's chilly grin.

A half second later, all hell broke loose.

ACT FOUR
~With true love
sacrifice and pain
are inevitable.

CHAPTER FIFTY-NINE

SHONDRA

Six years ago

I closed the toilet seat and sat on it. It was the third time I'd thrown up that day. I'd read about morning sickness, and I was one of the lucky ones to start at five weeks. Who knew how long it would continue?

Till you end it tomorrow.

I wasn't mother material. I had a business to run and things to do. That was why I made an appointment at the clinic for the next day at noon. I hated to leave work after I neglected it so much while I was with... *him*, but if I didn't get my... matter taken care of... I wasn't sure if I ever would. I really didn't—

"Shondra?" My assistant called through the door. "Are you okay?"

"Yeah, Deja," I responded weakly. "I'll be out in a minute." It took more like ten before I rose from the throne, my hand over my mouth in case I had another urge to spew more of my breakfast.

Thankfully, I didn't.

At the sink, I washed my hands and brushed my teeth. Using a capful of mouthwash to rid my breath of any traces of half-digested egg and ham burrito. I had a meeting with a possible new investor and funky breath just wouldn't fly.

True to his word, not only did Mr. Hammersmythe take care of Vee's custody problem, he sent me people who were genuinely interested in my brand. I had met with four so far. They all wanted various percentages of my company in exchange for their money, time and expertise. I had done my research on all of them and the one I wanted to work with the most was the one I would meet with in...

Ten minutes!

With one last look in the mirror — not a pretty picture with circles under my eyes and worry scrunching my brow—I opened the door and flipped off the light, ready to face the day.

The woman who walked into my conference room (which doubled as the break room in other times) was heavily pregnant. Judging by the way her beige cotton shirt draped over bowling ball stomach, I'd say at least eight months.

She was famous enough to where I was sure I heard she was expecting, but with everything going on in my own life, I didn't remember the facts of others. Just those in my immediate circle, and barely that.

I blew out an annoyed breath.

Since I found out an egg of mine had been fertilized, *her type* was all I saw. Women with bellies both big and small... round or drooping. Babies in strollers, pushed by women with wide smiles and sunglasses, happily chatting about their bundles of joy...

Paying for It

"Sorry, I'm late. Things are getting difficult these days." She fluttered her hands and rolled her eyes. "I just discovered this morning I couldn't fit behind the wheel and had to wait for my husband's driver to return from dropping him off." She brushed back her Senegalese twists, pushed up her silver tortoiseshell glasses, and met me halfway to shake my hand.

As we sat, Deja came in pushing the catering cart. "What can I get for...Oh!" I glanced up to find my assistant's face had gone a few shades lighter than her normal sienna. "You know," Deja said, more flustered than I have ever seen her, "when your secretary called to schedule the meeting, I didn't put two and two together...*you* are Ms. Malcom. Ms. *Randy* Malcom."

Ms. Randy laughed. "Did you think I was a man? The name Randy throws people off, I'll admit."

Deja had regained her color and her checks had flushed a darker shade or red. "No, ma'am." Deja, a petite woman with a small frame, shook her head reverently, her chin nearly brushing her chest and her large brown eyes round with awe. "Your clothing line is..." She placed a hand to her throat and fangirled like it was her only duty. "There are no words."

Deja wasn't the only one intimidated. I was that and more.

Randy Rags was a staple in the African American...hell, in *any* community. Like Jordan's, those with any fashion sense or a collector of wearable art, had a Randy Rag hanging in their closet or framed on their wall. Randy Malcom was a legend. Married to an NBA star turned successful restaurateur, it was rumored she had

303

made *him* sign a prenup. Gurl came to him with that much bank.

Ms. Randy's full lips, glossed in a natural tone that went well with her ebony skin, parted in a wide smile. "I brought some samples for you two— "Deja squealed and I shot her a disapproving look. My assistant didn't notice. She hung onto every word coming from Ms. Randy's mouth. "My driver Mike is getting them from the Rover."

"Oh, thank you, Ms. Randy!" Deja clapped her hands over her mouth, looking like a five-year-old that said a dirty word. "Oh, may I call you that?"

I was never one to get between a person and their idol, but Deja was working my nerves. I needed to get these meetings started so I could leave early and mentally prepare myself for the next day.

Fat chance of that.

With a happy, pregnant woman in the room, it would take me all night to get into the right mind for what awaited me tomorrow.

"Thank you, Deja," I said, with a sweet tone but a stern look. "That will be all."

Without removing her eyes from my visitor, she whined, "But Ms. Randy hasn't had a thing to drink. What would—"

"Thank you Deja, you can leave...*now*."

She pouted, throwing a quick glance in my direction. "Don't you want me to take notes. I can—"

Paying for It

I swiveled my neck and spoke through gritted teeth, "Gurl, if you don't leave right this minute..."

With pursed lips full of disappointment, Deja left, softly closing the door behind her.

"I'm sorry about that Ms. Malcom." To her, queen of an empire, I probably seemed like a real rube.

Her genuine smile lit up her large brown eyes, putting me at ease. "Call me Randy, please."

I nodded and scooted the cart closer. "What would you like to drink?"

Randy pulled some crackers from her Hermès Birkin. The one which cost fifty million times more than my mom's car was worth. "Just some water please," she replied, opening the wrapper with an expert hand. I always needed to use scissors.

I pulled a bottle of Fiji from the bottom rack of the cart, unscrewed the top, and poured her a glass. "Would you like some ice?"

"Nah, that's fine." I placed the glass on a napkin and she snatched it up. Thirst and pregnancy must be a thing because she drained that glass in almost one go. As she tilted it higher, the water almost gone, she jumped. Liquid dribbled onto her cream linen tunic and a few spots landed on her white linen pants.

She smacked her lips and wiped her palm over her chin. I relaxed even further at her *real folk* actions. This woman wasn't a snob or some rich bitch. She was just like me.

"Whoa," Randy said, fanning herself. "I needed that. Damn hormones."

Against my better judgement, I opened the pregnancy can of worms. "Is it tough?"

Randy rolled her eyes and tsk-ed behind her teeth. "Yes, I was pregnant with Finlay in the summer as well." I followed Randy on Insta and I 'd seen pics of her adorable two-year-old son. Curly blonde hair like his daddy, he had the cutest baby grin I had ever seen. Randy shook her head and resumed her fanning. I had a mind to get up and tell Deja to turn down the air. "Damn if I didn't forget about the heat and how it affects me, but I wouldn't trade being pregnant for the world."

"What's so good about it?" That sounded shitty and petulant, but I didn't mean it is such.

Randy smiled. "Well, it's the wondering I like the best. Wondering what the baby will sound like...look like...who he/she/they will take after..." Randy's eyes went dreamy. I assumed she was off in baby land, but I was wrong. When she came back, she gave me an impish grin. "I just met you, and we haven't even done any kind of business, but I sense you are a real woman, like me." Randy looked over her shoulder for eavesdroppers. Finding none, she said with a half laugh, "Shondra, sex when you are pregnant...." She fanned herself harder, "is out of this damn world. My husband...well, let's just say, not fitting behind the wheel wasn't the only reason I was late. "She stopped fanning herself, and slapped the table, letting out a string of cackles.

Just like Ms. Jenkins used to do.

Paying for It

Of course, that set me thinking on that day in the park and...

Axel.

For some unknown reason, tears sprang to my eyes. My eyelashes worked overtime to blink them back.

Randy didn't notice my discomfort as her head had turned to the door at Deja's loud mouth exclaiming, "Oh, I want this," and "This is just too cute!"

I sighed and heaved myself up and pushed my ex (*could I even call him that?*) to the back of mind. I'd pull him out as I did each night, revisiting the good times we'd experienced in D.C. right before my world imploded from the inside out.

Randy, already unscrewing another bottle and munching on the cracker hanging from her mouth, nodded. "Shondra, do you have kids?"

I gave her a fake, wistful smile. "No. Not yet."

Especially after tomorrow.

I wasn't married with a good husband like Randy. My company wasn't a household name like hers. I fought and struggled every day, just to keep my head above water. How could I bring a child into that?

CHAPTER SIXTY

SHONDRA

Six years ago

"Just relax," he rubbed my forearm, trying to warm it up.

Easy for him to say "relax" when his teeth weren't chattering from nervousness. He didn't have a thin hospital gown on his legs in stirrups, getting ready to do away with a part of *himself*.

Art, or the IV-Man as I called him, wasn't a bad vision to fall asleep to with his dark hair, china-blue eyes, and a defined physique under his green scrubs.

But men were *off* my radar, including handsome IV nurses.

"How are you doing?"

"I'm fine."

Fine enough to keep going.

I tried not to think of Randy and her huge bump. Our meeting had lasted the rest of the morning, and way into the early afternoon. We had gone mostly off topic with her hilarious tales of motherhood. The antics her little boy got up to were precious.

Didn't sway my decision.

No, not at all...

Well... maybe a little. While I waited in the lobby, a woman had come in with her baby on her shoulder. By his blue onesie, I gathered he was a boy. He had dark skin, enormous eyes, and a head full of hair that curled at the edges. Thrown up formula dribbled down his chin as he squalled his head off, yet he was a cute little thing.

The mother smiled and cooed at her screaming child, comforting him with pats on the back. Our eyes met over her son's shoulder and her look of knowing—pity mixed with a sorrow—directed my gaze to the floor.

Her glance shook my decision and made my resolve waiver.

But only for a minute, just like Randy's glorious tales of motherhood had.

If I didn't cut all ties to Axel, I could never move on. With his baby inside of me, forgetting him would be a task beyond my reach. Day in and day out, all I could think about was *him*. Axel was my first thought upon waking and the last before I closed my eyes . . . until he appeared in my dreams.

I had to wonder: *Would it take a lifetime to forget him?*

"Shondra, you doing, okay?" Art asked, rubbing my hand in comforting circles.

I nodded, thoughts whirling through my head of blue onesies, babies with tons of blonde hair, and sweet drool-y grins...

Maybe...

Could Axel and I... try to find a way through everything? I gave him up for the love his father had for him, but what about my love? Didn't it count?

"Okay, Shondra, I found a vein. You'll feel a little prick, all right? Do you want me to count it down or just do it?"

I gazed up to the cracked ceiling tile. Focusing on the biggest jagged line, I gritted my teeth. "Just do it, please."

"That's my brave girl."

It wasn't a little prick, but a big one, and the pain had me crying out behind my clenched jaw. If Art didn't have my arm strapped down, I would have ripped it from his grasp.

He patted my shoulder and released the rubber tourniquet with his other hand.

"You did well, Shondra." His dark brows furrowed as he noticed the pain on my face. "I can give you something to relax if you'd like?"

Hell yeah, I'd like. I'd like that very much.

"Yes, please."

Art took a needle filled with solution from his kit and injected it into the IV knob. Within seconds, I felt like a cloud in the sky and just as high. I drifted...floated on the breeze, headed towards the sun, all my burdens buried deep within the muck of the earth.

I must have nodded off as Art shook me awake with a few nudges to my shoulder. "They're on their way to get you."

The startled look I gave him prompted him to provide reassurances. "I promise within an hour you'll be back to normal."

Normal? Was there ever such a word for one like me? Forcibly kissed at eight. Saw a man killed at fourteen. Pregnant at twenty. My story wasn't different from many people's, however tragic. I knew I wasn't unique. Far more people had suffered worse than me and they'd gotten up to fight another day and here I was . . .

Here I was doing . . . *what?*

A bubbly brunette appeared at the door. "Okay, Ms. Williams, we're ready for you."

Art checked the fluid in the IV one more time, flicking the bag to get the solution to flow faster. A rush of cold slithered down my vein. I whimpered at sensation.

"Did that hurt?" The brunette asked, a kindly smile on her face.

Would *it*. . . the baby feel pain? Would Axel ever forgive me if he found out? Could I live with the knowledge of what I was about to do?

"I'm...I'm... fine."

She nodded, and the bed moved.

Was I fine? What if I put a stop to the abortion?

Before we rounded the last corner, Uncle Nassau appeared at my side, hitching a ride. His bald head gleamed while his silver teeth flashed. He leaned in close, kissing distance. His breath smelled of beer, cigarettes . . . and blood.

"Do it, gurl. These people invested a lot of time on yo' ass. You can't be selfish and keep 'em waiting. Damn baby won't love you, anyway.

My baby.

Axel's baby.

Clear as day, I saw Axel in the hotel room, tangled in the sheet, leaning against the headboard with a brilliant smile on his tanned face. *"Whatever happens, happens, angel."*

Uncle Nassau blocked him out by pressing his forehead against mine. My eyes crossed, trying to focus.

"You want to spend rest of yo' life looking after a kid? No help 'cept from Vee? Gurl has her own mess to deal with."

Vee...

Another child neglected and unwanted.

Not my child. Things would be so different. . .

The anesthesiologist, a soccer-mom type with streaks of gray in her hair, held a scuba mask over my face. Air hissed and sputtered around it. "Ms. Williams, we're ready to begin, okay? Breathe deep and this will be over soon."

Begin . . .

Over?

What am I doing?

Randy was right. I wondered too, although I never admitted it. But as I lay on the table...in viewing distance of the knives that would remove part of me, I let the thoughts take shape...take hold.

What would he sound like? Who would he look like? When would he know I loved him? Did he feel it even now?

I loved him. I did.

And I had changed my mind.

***

The last few months had been hell, but I never regretted my decision, even when I swallowed bile to keep Vee and my mother from discovering my secret. The growing baby inside of me gave me a purpose not even my business nor taking care of Vee had done. *The baby,* not the father, was my focus.

I wasn't showing. . . yet. My bulk did a good job of hiding my pregnancy. As long as I kept my morning (and evening) sickness to myself, no one ever suspected a thing.

The bathroom door handle rattled. "Sho, are you going to be long? I need to get to school and the bus will be here in a minute."

I flushed the toilet and took a piece of paper towel from the roller above the sink to wipe the spittle from my chin. "I'll take you to school, Vee," I said, unlocking the door.

We brushed our teeth together, Vee nearly dribbling toothpaste on her sweater as she related all she had to do that day during her college classes.

Paying for It

Vee rinsed her toothbrush in the cold water, then cupped her hands under the stream to drink. I made as if to spit in her hair and she squealed, skittering away, water dripping from her mouth.

I laughed, spraying toothpaste at the mirror. It was times like these that I forgot Axel was engaged.

I avoided calling him in the beginning because of the Tabitha Moore Scandal William had told me about. I didn't want to read in black and white that Axel had confronted and skewered the mother of his child in front of their peers. If he had done that to a petite, privileged girl, what would he do to me?

The week I got my first clear sonogram at five months, when I saw our son for the first time, I took the plunge and looked up the Facebook page of Tabitha Moore.

The parent's description wasn't of Axel, at least not the Axel I knew but of a "Wealthy stud with ash blond hair, a face suited for a magazine cover, and the lean body of a rocker."

Axel *didn't* have a rocker body type. I'd met him when he was sixteen, and he'd sported a "football buff" physique even back then.

Why had William lied to me?

CHAPTER SIXTY-ONE

SHONDRA

Six years ago

I should have known he was up to something devious. By the way he was talking—he had it in for Axel. Maybe William wanted me to doubt Axel, so I'd leave him.

Hurt him.

Had I really wasted time we could have shared over a lie?

That night I'd called him misdialing three times because of shaky hands. I clutched my growing stomach when the correct number rang. The baby kicked in a series of fast flutters. A calm built from perseverance floated from the top of my head to the tips of my toes.

All was fine. I'd made it through the first step. I could make it a little far—

"Hello," said a female voice slurred with sleep.

I sat in near darkness at the kitchen table with the only light coming from my cell. The clock above the microwave had already struck midnight. Yeah, it was late. Too late for a friendly date to still be over for anything but hot and heavy sex.

Thank God I used the "unknown number" feature.

Paying for It

The baby kicked again. My all-consuming love for him gave me the wherewithal to continue. "Um. Is Axel there?"

"He's sleep. Shall I wake him? Wait... who is this?"

I had no right to bristle at her tone; I had woken her up after all. But why had she answered his phone in the first place? Axel never let me near his cell during those days we spent together.

"Who is this?" I countered, swiveling my neck in agitation.

"This is his fiancée."

Shut down, Sho. Way down.

"He's engaged?" I asked, my tone coming out flatter than a ruined crepe full of holes and bubbles.

"Yes, since the end of June." The woman sighed. "Look, he's off the market. I'm sorry about it. I really am. Get over him, okay? Goodnight."

The line went dead and so did my heart.

As much as I wanted to, I gave his fiancée props for the sincere sympathy I'd heard in her voice. Had it been me, I would've cussed a bitch out.

I sat at the table, filtering through the mistakes I had made and the regret and anguish it would cost me and my unborn child. The seat grew hard like a brick and my tailbone throbbed, but still I sat until light slanted through the blinds and the coffee pot started its morning percolation. All night I thought of every scenario of how to come out on top with my baby in my arms and my man by my side. In the end, just as the pot steamed the last of the water. I booked a ticket for Boston.

***

Late October in Boston was everything I expected. The weather, crisp and cool, had a hint of a sea breeze in the air. It helped to clear my senses. The blinding sun dappled through the colorful foliage of the trees, making the city come alive with color.

Despite my errand, confronting Axel and his unsuspecting fiancée with the news of his impending fatherhood, excitement coursed through me. I'd made the right step forward. I'd swallowed my fears and put it all on the line. By the end of the day, best-case scenario, Axel and I would have an amicable plan to raise our child in place.

I gave up on the hope of us being together. As I's sat on that hard chair, reasoning took over and the knowledge hurt like hell. He never loved me as much as I' loved him. How could he when he'd gotten engaged within two weeks after my departure?

Maybe William had a point after all?

That thought, above all others, convinced me not to fight for Axel. I carried the best part of him, and that was all that mattered. I loved my little boy. I would be the mother to him mine had never been to me. One who freely gave hugs and lots of kisses and smiles that lit up my face at everything he did.

Given the father and the stories Paul had told me of his younger years, I would probably be a haggard mess by the time the terrible twos were over, but hell, I didn't

317

care. I welcomed the opportunity to hold my baby in my arms, comforting him and keeping him from the evils of the world until he was strong enough to face them on his own.

But I had to not only get through to Axel, I had to face the baby's grandfather as well.

I dreaded the thought of confronting Paul. I'd promised him to stay away from Axel, and less than six months later, I planned on breaking that promise with life-changing news.

Yes, my company was skyrocketing with Randy's mentorship and investment. She was not only my role model in business, but in motherhood as well. Her little daughter, Aja, was adorable, and the way Randy managed not only one but two kids under five, and a company three times the size of mine, I knew I could have it all too.

Paul could react any type of way to the pregnancy news, I didn't care. I was more worried about how to pay him back for the money he'd given the She-Witch to drop Vegas's custody case. I had some money in the bank, but the six figures Paul had laid out for Vegas would take more than that chunk of change.

Billionaire status eluded me, but becoming a millionaire within a few years, hovered on the horizon. Still, I owed Paul something for helping me, I just wondered how he would make me pay for it?

I'd find out soon enough.

Paying for It

With my influx of funds, I could have afforded any hotel, but I booked the Airbnb room I'd stayed in for Axel's graduation, hoping it would bring me luck.

This time the owner was home. She handed over the key with minimal fuss, unlike the previous time when the chatty neighbor almost made me miss Axel's name being called.

I headed toward the room in the basement, careful to take one stone stair at a time. The wind had picked up, and the air had turned cooler since my ride from the airport. As I opened the door, a gust nearly knocked it from my hand.

It was a sign. A foul wind on the horizon...one filled with evil.

"Shondra!" William appeared at the top of the stairs, and the sun filtering around his outline, hid his face in shadows.

I was too shocked to speak. I should have expected Paul Hammersmythe getting in contact with me once I called his son.

I put it down to a pregnant woman's forgetfulness.

William bounded down the steps and I envied his lithe movements."Mr. Hammersmythe wants to see you, Shondra."

"Well, I don't want to see him. Not this time." I turned to close the door in his face, but he inserted his foot, poking his head in to give me a sweet smile.

"Come, on Shondra. It won't be as rough as the last time. He really just wants to say 'hello' and besides, I'll be there to hold your hand." William gave me such a cheeky grin I had to laugh.

There was always something so familiar about William. Even when he acted like a dick and slandered Axel, I couldn't help but like him.

William waited inside the door while I debated the pros and cons. I finally reasoned that at least this time, I knew what I was up against and I had to meet him eventually, I might as well do it now, rather than later.

"Okay, William. I'll meet him. But I warn you, when I've heard enough, I'm leaving."

He grinned. "I'll escort you myself... anytime you're ready to go."

He walked up the steps ahead of me, his feet heavy on the concrete.

I was just placing my left foot on the top stair and my right on the one below it when William turned...

and pushed me.

CHAPTER SIXTY-TWO

SHONDRA

Six years ago

Lying in my hospital bed, I felt the hurt.

All over.

Inside and out.

The pain floated and drifted and squeezed when I moved.

When I thought.

When I cried.

Which was *a lot*.

Buckets and lakes. Rivers and oceans.

I wanted my tears to wash me clean.

It would take years before that happened.

***

Paul was there, off and on. A big hazy shadow and a smooth, comforting voice.

William had been there as well. Just the once.

I'd come up from a drug induced fog and his pale face and mop of brown hair hovered over me like some dark spirit. His face inches from mine.

Paying for It

My throat burned with the terror of my screams. They peeled like midnight alarms into the light colored bedroom, nearly drowning out his "I didn't knows" and "I'm sorrys".

Paul came with two burly guards dressed in white.

The guards hauled William up by the armpits. Curses spilled from his mouth as they dragged him away, his feet kicking up from the ground.

Over William's little girl shrieks, Paul told "plane", "island" and "tonight."

Plane?

Where to?

Where was my baby?

Paul swam into view. He placed a warm hand on my forehead, smoothing my hair back in a fatherly gesture. His brown eyes full of knowing and sorrow.

I knew then that they mirrored my own.

He was there to tell me . . .

The truth.

The finality.

The end before the beginning.

I wanted to close my ears. I even welcomed William's distant squalls at that point. Anything to block out the words that crushed me. I tried to scream again, but I had nothing left to give. No sound would eke from my raw, scratchy throat. I could only stare at Paul in growing horror as his voice cut through the death of my heart.

"My grandson is gone. We couldn't save him."

***

I listened mutely, my face set in stone as Paul related the events that ultimately led to the demise of my baby. A baby I didn't want in the beginning, but whose loss nearly killed me in the end.

"William was Marjorie's child."

Paul's eyes flickered to my face as if the revelation would shock me.

It didn't.

I lay there numb.

Unseeing.

Unfeeling.

Uncaring.

"At fifteen, a family friend... a trusted family friend raped her. A neighbor boy." His clasped hands clenched and his eyes grew hard, as hard as a rough-hewn rock. "She didn't believe in aborting an innocent child, so she gave William up for adoption."

Paul took a moment to gulp whatever emotion he'd been feeling into his gullet. His Adam's apple bobbed and wobbled like a cork above the water's surface, with a mammoth fish tugging on the hook below.

Did he miss his wife like I missed my baby? Was he happy that his wife had given away the monster that had killed his flesh and blood?

I didn't know. And I didn't care enough to ask.

Paying for It

From the expressions that morphed his face, Paul, through sheer will, went on with his exercise in futility.

"Ah. Um, William had his adoption records opened three years ago when he turned twenty-one. In his search for Marjorie. . . he found me." Paul shook his head as if in denial. "I should've known he was sick. I mean, his father was. *Had* to be. I should've done more due diligence on the kid. Dug deeper into his background. But he was my wife's son. Her boy. I couldn't . . . couldn't turn him away."

At the time, the parallel of Marjorie's life and mine, both victims of sex crimes, was lost on me. All I could do was ask, "Why?"

"William was jealous of his half-brother. Jealous Axel had grown up with Marjorie and me. I mean, the boy—William—had a suitable home, from what I could gather. The adopted son of a strict military father and a stay at home mom. They loved him, but they had noted a few things..." Paul trailed off and shook his head as if he were clearing it. "I don't know why...I guess in his sad and twisted mind, William thought that if he prevented the meeting between you two, Axel would marry his fiancée and come to regret losing you." He grew angry then, a sight to behold with his flushed face and flashing eyes. "I wish the boy would've come to me. I would've told him Axel wasn't going to marry that girl because..."His eyes flicker to mine and then away. "Well, it doesn't matter." He ran a hand through his mane of hair, then scrubbed it down the side of his face. "Shondra, I never should have interfered with you two. God knows I will regret doing so for...damn forever."

Paying for It

Paul banged his hands on his thighs and rose from his seat, his gaze on the ceiling. "What assholes we are—rich men and their money—controlling lives like chess pieces." He hung his head. I hoped in shame....in remorse. "I'm going to pay for this. In the next life, if not this one."

He raised his head. His eyes had brimmed and go red around the edges.

Paul placed his palms on top of my clenched fists as he begged for understanding. "William didn't know. . . *We* didn't know about the baby. I'm-I'm so sorry, Shondra."

I offered no words of comfort to the man who held my hands in his as he spilled huge tears over them.

I had none to give to him *or* myself.

***

Jacob Charles Hammersmythe was laid to rest on the Vermont family estate, ten days after he was born. The heavens opened up, raining down its wrath, for the fifteen minutes it took to cover his impossibly small coffin with freshly plowed dirt.

I'd picked out his name from the ancient family bible I'd found on the second floor of the Hammersmythe library. It listed the Hammersythe's births and deaths from their days in England, right down to the last descendant in America—Axel.

I wanted to connect Jacob, even if by name, to roots and stability—two things I never had. I might not have a heritage, but my child would.

Paying for It

Paul and I had flown to Vermont after I'd spent a week convalescing in Boston. During my recovery period, the missing pieces of what happened, and the aftermath came together like pieces in a macabre puzzle.

After the incident, I was unaware of my surroundings or what happened. All I remembered was that William had pushed me.

I was *unaware* Paul had waited in the car with the driver while he sent William to get me. *Unaware* that I'd screamed when I fell from the top step. *Unaware* that the driver had tackled William on the lawn while the Airbnb hostess, a nurse practitioner, attended to my baby while remained unconscious and . . . *unaware.*

Paul had promised the hostess a big payoff for her silence and he ensured I was seen by the best, and most discreet, OBGYN money could buy.

Paul informed me that even after our talk, the talk that ended with Axel and I, he'd followed my movements just as he followed his son's.

It wasn't just lip service that he'd taken a liking to me. He'd thought I'd make a brilliant match for Axel and I'd impressed him so much with keeping my word, taking care of Vee, and excelling in my business he soon realized he'd made a mistake.

He'd sent William to collect me that day in Boston so he could apologize for steering me off. Paul wanted me to go to his son with a clean conscience.

Paying for It

Come to find out, William had other plans. According to Paul, William *wanted* Axel to suffer. He thought by incapacitating me, Axel hurt like William had hurt all those years growing up without his birth mother's love.

To my mind, William's reasoning was weak thinking by an even weaker man.

Axel had let me go without a second thought. What did William ever think to achieve by doing *me* harm? And my baby harm? Axel wouldn't care. He never did.

He wasn't a man of his word after all. Axel had promised if there was a child, he'd stand by me.

Well, he *lied.*

Axel was at fault *even more* than William. He hadn't lifted a finger to save our relationship. If he had, I would've never lost my child.

My Jacob.

My baby.

So was my thinking. I was full of bitter anger, hurt, and resentment. And I'd laid it all at the doorstep of the half-brothers—William, the killer, and Axel, the sperm donor.

***

Just before I left for Chicago, Paul came to me. So far, I'd successfully avoided telling Vee what had happened with fake cheer and distracting her with news about my upcoming trip to China. Paul had set things up for me in Shanghai to study with a world-renowned mixologist.

When I was ready or of course.

327

Paying for It

I was ready. More than. Getting away from it all was what I needed. Six weeks in China, just concentrating on myself and healing, was exactly what I needed.

"William can't hurt anyone anymore," Paul said, walking into the room. "I put him in a safe place where he can get the help he needs." Paul shifted his weight to the balls of his feet. "I hope you understand, Shondra... we can't go to the police with this. I don't want our name blighted with scandal. It would — "

"As long as Axel never finds out, I won't say a word." I didn't want him to know. Ever. I couldn't bear what would be his indifference.

CHAPTER SIXTY-THREE

VEGAS

Present day

Sho claimed in the morning that she had news to tell me. Since Terrance had my car, I'd suggested she pick me up from work and we have a heart to heart at the hotel bar near the house.

I figured her news had to do with her burgeoning relationship with Tony and she needed to spill. I was down for that. If my girl required an ear to bend, it was the least I could do. Sho had listened to me talk about my fears concerning Jae time and time again. Matter of fact, we had stayed up late the night before discussing the meeting Jae had planned.

Shondra was selfless like that, always taking care of others before taking care of herself. Her dealings with Axel and his father, and all of those years of having my back, proved that.

"So, what do you have to tell me?" I asked, buckling my seatbelt.

Shondra shook her head, "I'll wait until we're settled at the bar with a drink in my hand."

"That serious, huh," I said with a tease in my voice.

Shondra's lips molded into a thin line, preventing her from answering. She pressed the car forward from the

329

hospital parking lot and into the snarl of Chicago's infamous bumper to bumper traffic. "This mess will cut into our time," she said, muttering a few choice curses.

I hastened to ease her stress, "Don't worry about it, Sho."

Shondra had promised to get me home early in order to give Kae her bath. The little badun' had taken to hiding when the nanny tried to round her up for "tub time."

Kae was a creature of habit. If Aunt Sho or I wasn't there to dress or bathe her, she would make it very difficult for anyone else to do it. My shift tomorrow was perfect—seven to four. I could have breakfast with Sho and my baby. Then it was off to work for nine long hours of rounds, patient care and *fun*—now that Shelia Caldwell had taken her ass to a conference.

Even after six weeks of putting up Dr. Caldwell's snarky attitude, the belittling of my work, and her overall negative demeanor, I still loved my job. I'd made more than a few friends, and the other doctors respected me, complimenting my knowledge more than a few times. My colleagues and I also commiserated with each other as I wasn't the only one to suffer Shelia's wrath.

Two other residents, women of course, all young, talented, and pretty, suffered from her stank-a-tude. When the She-Devil was on duty, she worked us like indentured servants. We suffered through in silence, taking pleasure in tearing up the good doctor by inventing alternative names to call her behind her back.

One of my fellow laborers, Gertrude Eisenberg's grandniece, came up with the perfect nickname- Shelia the Squeela. Granted, Shelia had a cultured voice when talking down to us, but it rose to a high pitch when she flirted with men. Not idle gossip, I'd seen it with my own eyes, and hearing of her many, many, many affairs. During my meeting with Jae, I planned to find out *exactly* what he knew and how much. I didn't want Kae exposed to such a woman, and if Jae couldn't agree with that . . . he'd see Kae under supervision.

"You still nervous about seeing Jameson tomorrow?" Shondra asked, turning off the expressway.

"No, not really." It was mostly the truth. I didn't expect Jae and I to magically come together. He had his wife, and I had Terrence—the man who loved me enough to be okay with *any* closure I might need, up to an including sex.

I hadn't read between the lines. Terrance had given his blessing in plain words.

The next day after the fundraiser, I'd told him I'd run into Jae. He kissed me on the forehead in that absentminded way of his and said, "*Whatever you need to do Vegas, including goodbye sex, is fine with me. I want you to be free of all past ghosts, so that when we are married, you will be truly mine.*"

At first, incredulity shocked me into silence as I processed his words. Once I did, I got scared. Not because of what would happen if I followed through with his suggestion, but what if I didn't *want* to say goodbye?

Shondra put her blinker on and slid over into the next lane as a white truck with tires bigger than body let us in.

Shondra waved to the driver. He flashed his lights in return.

"What about you, Sho? How are you getting on with Tony?"

"That's what I wanted to talk to you about." She fell silent, her eyes focused on the road.

"Well? Don't leave me hanging."

CHAPTER SIXTY-FOUR

VEGAS

Present day

"Wait for the bar, Vee. I told you I need that drink first." Again, her mouth set into a thin strip. I let it be. With this traffic, she needed to concentrate.

I pursed my lips and crossed my arms over my chest. Gazing out the window, I willed my mind to go blank. All too soon, thoughts of my upcoming meeting with Jae crept in like a cat from the rain, wary and disturbed.

Tomorrow, Jae would learn about his daughter.

I asked myself for the millionth time, *what would his reaction be?*

"What's that sigh for, Vee?"

"Did I sigh? I'm sorry."

"It's about Jae. You *are* nervous. Tell the truth."

"Yeah, I guess I am," I said, letting out another sigh. "What if he rejects us, Sho?" I said, voicing my biggest fear.

"Then he is the biggest fool on the planet."

I laughed. "Yeah, he would be, right?"

"*Tru* that."

Paying for It

The steering wheel spun under Shondra's hands as she rounded the corner to the bar, stopping short when the light changed to yellow. A car honked. Shondra looked in the rearview mirror, giving the driver behind us a narrowed-eyed glare. After an exaggerated eye roll to the offender, she turned her attention to me. "Vee, you really don't need to worry. Jae wouldn't bother to stop me in a crowded restaurant to ask about you if he didn't care."

"I suppose," I said, infusing a modicum of doubt in my voice. Since I'd spoken to Jae, I'd wavered between hope for the future and the memories of the past.

That one night, the one that gave us our miracle, had blown me away. I had fallen like a meteor from the sky, and the implosion—finding out that Jae was still married—had left a crater in my heart no one could fill. Not even Terrence. And knowing that he never would, I'd decided that after my meeting with Jae, for better or worse, I'd give Terrence his ring back and wish him well.

***

The valet, a sandy hair freckle faced man-boy, took down Shondra's information with a wide smile. He gave her the "I'm interested in you" look that followed my girl everywhere she went.

"Anything else you need, ma'am?"

"No, I'm fine," she said, knocking him back a step with the wattage in her smile.

He ripped off her claim ticket with a flourish, scribbling something on the back. "My name is Trent." He placed the ticket in her palm and winked." Anything you need, you just call."

Paying for It

"Thank you, Trent."

We headed through the turnstile doors with Trent still staring after my girl.

The wide doorway of the bar area gave us an excellent view of the spectacle. A college aged guy had just slammed Jae against the bar.

"Let him at me, dude. With that foo-foo drink he was slurping down, what harm could he do?" He pushed what could only be Axel in his chest.

"Bo Johnson!" Shondra screamed. "What do you think you're doing?"

Every head swiveled towards us. The college guy backed away from Axel as if he'd been scalded.

"Ms. Williams, I—"

"Vee—" Jae said, pushing away from the bar.

"Jae—" I'd already moved forward, ignoring his dark look of worry.

"Shondra—" Axel said, outpacing Jae.

Shondra skittered away from Axel's outstretched hands to approach Bo, whose head hung like an anchor between his shoulders. Axel stared after her with such a look of hurt and bewilderment, my heart went out to him.

Jae wrapped me up in a tight embrace, and I forgot everything else.

"Are you, okay?" he asked as if I'd taken a punch.

"I should be asking you that."

Paying for It

He pulled up, stretching his back and shoulders. "Everything is in working order, doctor." He brushed the curls from my forehead and placed a quick kiss, smack in the middle.

Hot damn!

This was no dry Terence kiss. My knees shook and my core clenched, a shiver of pure pleasure went down my spine.

It must have affected him too as he stepped back with a disbelieving look on his face.

Was that bad or good? What is he thinking?

If he wants nothing to do with us...

I didn't get to finish that thought as Shondra walked, no *stomped* past us, pushing Bo out of the door with Axel trailing behind.

Jae's worried look popped up again. "We'd better—"

"Let's go," I said, finishing for him.

Jae pulled out his wallet. The bartender held up a hand. "Axel took care of it. See you next week?"

Jae nodded, pulling me along with him.

As we exited the doors, one patron said, "Damn, that would've been a good fight. My money was on the sweatpants guy."

Shondra berated Bo while Axel stood to the side, his arms folded across his chest.

Paying for It

"Bo, haven't you learned your lesson? Duke just got you out of a mess last week, and here you go, starting something else."

"I know Ms. Williams, I know." Bo kicked at a pebble on the walkway. "He'd be pissed if he found out. You won't tell him, will you?"

Shondra let out a huff. "I should, just so he could hand you your ass on a platter."

"Like I would've done," Axel said, loud and proud.

Bo bristled, but under Shondra's glare he held his tongue.

Shondra threw her ex a warning from over her shoulder, "Axel . . . "

His name spoken from her lips was apparently the "in" he needed. He moved to stand slightly in front of her, as if Bo posed a problem. "Sho, who is this idiot?"

Shondra reached out to pull Axel back, but in the end, she let her hand drop. Instead she stepped forward, angling her body an ocean away from his. "Bo is Duke's cousin, and he works as a head trainer in one of his gyms. . . when he's not landing himself in trouble."

Bo blushed under the sodium lighting. "Aww, come on now, it was only twice that—"

Shondra held up a hand, "I know, I heard." She moved in towards Bo, grabbed his hand, and led him a slight distance away, speaking to him in quiet whispers.

I shivered in my jacket, and Jae pulled me closer. I sank into his warmth like butter on freshly made pancakes.

337

Paying for It

Axel shot a steely glance at the pair, cursing under his breath. Jae placed a hand on his shoulder. Whether to shore him up or hold him back, I wasn't sure.

"Take it easy, bro," Jae whispered.

"Fuck, I will. If he so much as—"

"Bo! Bo! Are you coming back inside?"

Bo popped his head up, focusing on the petite girl with the oversized lips standing in the turnstile door. He jerked his head towards the valet area. "We're leaving, Samantha. Let's go."

She passed by us in a cloud of expensive perfume and complaining mumbles of a "sucky evening."

Shondra gave Bo a hug, a pat on the back, and released him into the care of his date. She then turned back to us. "Vee, I'm going home. Do you want to come with?" She gave Jae a pointed look, "Or will you catch a ride?"

"Can I come?" Jae asked with the enthusiasm of a six-year-old headed for a sleepover.

A sleepover with Jae is just what I need.

"You're my ride, Jameson." Axel said, staring at Shondra's profile hard enough to leave an imprint.

"You took a Lyft here, didn't you?" Jae said, a touch of impatience in his voice.

"I'll ride with you and call one from Shondra's place, 'cause I didn't bring my phone."

Only a fool couldn't see through what Axel was trying to do. He wanted to go to Shondra's place and chat up my girl as much as Jae seemed eager to chat with me.

338

Shondra scoffed, "Isn't that your phone in your front pocket?"

Axel didn't blink. "Nah, I'm just happy to see you."

Shondra turned her head from us, but with her long hair in a ponytail we could all see the big smile curving her cheek. When she regained control, she started walking toward the valet, throwing over her shoulder as if she didn't care, "Come on then . . . if you must."

CHAPTER SIXTY-FIVE

VEGAS

Present day

Some moments happen just as they should. From the beginning of time, these moments are pre-ordained by the universe to play out in a certain way and no other.

***

Jae and I left Sho and Axel at the valet. Sho had dragged her eyes from Axel's stormy ones to give me a nod as if to say, "do what you need to do." She knew where I was headed and what I had to reveal.

It was long overdue.

We walked to Jae's car as silent as the night.

He drove while I spouted off directions to the house like my heart wasn't in my throat, threatening to choke me. The closer we came to Jae learning of Kae's existence, the more difficult it became to draw a full breath.

Vivid images of Jae's reaction, his wife's, and my daughter's future, swirled darkly in my mind.

Jae's anger.

His wife's derisive laughter.

Courtroom drama.

Paying for It

"Turn left here and stay in the right lane. At the end of the street you'll see it. Number 21562. There'll be a large plaque by the gate," I said calmly, as if everything were right in the world.

Jae didn't buy it.

"What's wrong, Vee? You seem tense."

So much for pretending.

If I'd lied and said everything was all right, he'd remember later. A little thing, sure, but it would eventually add up in lawyer's fees and have a negative influence on the judge's decision.

Stop it! You don't know he'll take it that far.

Jae might not, but his wife would.

Shelia Caldwell was a nasty piece of work. I'd seen her in action with staff, visitors, and even with patients.

One guy, an eighteen-year-old with terminal cancer, cried in the ICU after Dr. Caldwell had left his bedside. She'd told him in no uncertain terms there wasn't any hope, and he should start making preparations.

Bitch was *all* heart.

Jae pulled up to the keypad box, his eyes full of concern. "Vee? Are you okay? Talk to me."

"The code is 59638."

Jae punched in the numbers. The heavy metal gate with delicate fleur-de-lis majestically swung back against the twelve-foot hedge.

Paying for It

As he turned in the driver's seat, a piece of dark hair fell into his eyes. He brushed it back with an impatient hand. "That's not an answer to my question, Vee."

I cleared my throat. The heart-sized lump moved lower, but only by an inch or two. "Don't block the gate. Pull into the drive and I'll tell you."

As he drove, hands clenched at the wheel, I began with the beginning *or ending* of it all.

"Do you remember at the Bakers' party when I said I needed to tell you something? Do you remember that?"

Jae blew out a breath and parked the car with a heavy foot, jerking us in our seat belts. He reached out a trembling finger and pressed the button to turn off the engine.

The silence in the car grew deafening and the tension between us swelled along with it. I couldn't remember a time when I was so uncomfortable. Only the day when my aunt had to beg my father to take me in, compared. If the earth had opened up and swallowed me whole, I would've considered myself lucky.

With a hard profile and a flat voice, Jae said, "Do you have anything to drink inside? Something strong? I think I'm going to need it."

At my nod, we exited the car in silence. Jae followed behind me, dragging his feet along the concrete as if the gravity of Jupiter held him captive.

I unlocked the front door as if in a dream. I knew instinctively that *somehow* Jae guessed what I was going to tell him. Why else would he have changed from worry to unbridled anger? The fury undulated from him in a dark wave of heat that felt like a furnace at my back.

My heart fell from my throat and oozed into my toes.

His reaction spoke volumes.

He didn't want Kae.

He didn't want me.

There wasn't ever going to be an *us*. At least not in this lifetime.

Here goes nuthin'.

I pushed open the door and landed right into a time-stood-still moment of chaos.

A naked Kae scampered down the hall, her arms outstretched. A chubby fist clutched the tie of her pink bathrobe. It trailed behind her like a unicorn's tail. Big crocodile tears ran down her face.

"M-m-m . . ."

My stomach rolled. Kae was going to say the word that would validate her father's anger.

"M-m-m . . . mama. . ."

CHAPTER SIXTY-SIX

VEGAS

Present day

Anxiety pushed my knees to the floor.

Kae barreled into me. On unsteady legs, I teetered backward.

Sturdy hands kept us from falling.

Hands . . . then a broad chest at my back. Strong arms circled around us. A small tousled head nestled on my left shoulder while a larger one rested on the right.

And both shook with uncontrollable sobs.

***

I had a hard time dragging Jae out of Kae's room. He would have slept there by her crib if I would have let him. Since she ran into my arms in the hallway, he only had eyes for her.

It was time to find out what he was thinking. That if the revelation he experienced drew us closer or further apart. If it were the latter. I'd move on, but I had to *know*. I'd waited long enough.

I took his hand in mine. He didn't pull away, so I saw it as a good sign. I led him to the library—neutral ground and far from the temptation of my bedroom.

344

Paying for It

He let go as if he just noticed I was touching him. He walked over to the couch, shifting from foot to foot as if he were deciding to sit or not. After a moment, the weight of meeting his daughter carried him downward. Jae put his elbows on his knees and hung his forearms between his legs. His hair fell into his eyes as he dipped his head, and there it remained when he looked up at me.

"Why didn't you tell me, Vee?"

I took in the sadness of his dark eyes that seemed to sink under his black hair. "I was all set to do so, Jae... until I found out you were still married."

"I'm not married. We just pretend we are because that's what Shelia wants. She doesn't like failure, and she sees our divorce as such. It also gives her an easy out for all her affairs." At my shocked look, he gives me a wry grin. "Yeah, I know all about them, and to quote Axel, *I don't give a fuck.* Not since I met you."

"Jae..." What do I say? How can we be together? Where do we begin?

His eyes go round as he looks at me. "Did I say something wrong? Do you not want us to be together? Do you not want me?" He doesn't wait for my answer, but rises from the couch. In two strides he stands in my space, towering over me as I meet his gaze. "Tell me, Vee."

"I-I thought you were angry at me. I thought—"

I could no longer doubt his intentions or his sincerity as he lifted me from the floor and covered his mouth with mine. I wrapped my arms around his neck, pressing into

345

him. Jae chuckled against my throat as he carried me to the couch.

I reveled at being in his embrace—it was all I ever dreamed of and all I ever wanted.

And now that the truth is out, and he accepts us, Shelia Caldwell can go—

"Oh! I didn't know you have company, Ms. Shipley. I'm so sorry."

Jae smiled into my neck as I addressed the embarrassed nanny. "Don't worry about it, Kindra. Kae is asleep so you can go to bed now."

Poor Kindra.

She had apologized profusely when I brought her a half asleep Kae. I forwent Kae's bath and put her to bed. Since I laid her down, she didn't make a fuss. The little booger.

When I came back downstairs, I thought Jae had left. My heart spun out of control until I heard him in the kitchen. There, I found him drinking glass after glass of water. His throat worked furiously as he chugged down the liquid as if he were forcing the news of being a father down his throat.

"Well goodnight, Ms. Shipley. Sir." Kindra quickly turned and escaped upstairs.

As soon as she left the room, Jae started on my neck, nipping and nuzzling, biting and sucking...

I found it hard to concentrate, let alone speak, but I had to. "Jae," I said, scrambling out of his embrace. "We need to talk." There was Terrence to consider and Shelia, of course. I didn't give a hang about her, but Terrence didn't deserve my betrayal, even though he'd given me permission...*his blessing* to sleep with Jae.

We sat on the couch. At my insistence, we put a respectable distance between us.

"Jae?" I asked, pulling a cushion onto my lap, "What are we going to do?" That was the question that would unlock all the answers and with them, the consequences.

Jae's smiling face grew somber, as if the sun hid behind a dark cloud. He pulled out his phone and tapped the screen. With a grimace, he showed me what he'd pulled up.

I stared up at him in confusion. Unease filtered through my bowels and held my stomach in a vice like grip. "Why are you showing me this kind of website, Jae?"

He took a deep breath and said, "This is what I do, Vee."

It took me an hour to go through each page. The images I saw burned my retinas more than once. There were thousands upon thousands of pictures.

"How long have you been doing this for?" I handed him his phone. Our fingers touched and quickly withdrew mine. His eyes flashed hurt. I hastened to reassure him. "Jae, I'm no prude. But I did not know you, um, you did this?" I posed it as a question because I was still trying to wrap my head around what I just saw.

Jae designed sex toys.

Hundreds of sex toys and many pieces of clothing too. Mainly with the female form in mind.

Shelia and Jae were "still married" because that witch had threatened to expose him. She promised to "out" him in front of his peers, his parents, and the media if he so much as breathed a word about their divorce.

"Yes, Vegas," he said shortly, his tone terse. "I did. *I do*." Jae put his phone back in his pocket, making a show of concentrating on that instead of looking at me. "Is what I do a problem for you?"

His startled eyes met my mischievous ones as I sat in his lap and circled my arms around his neck.

"It's only a problem, Jae, if you don't show me how to use some of those things."

ACT FIVE

You try and tear me down.
I still rise.
You try and shut me up.
I still speak.
You try and hurt me
I love you back.

CHAPTER SIXTY-SEVEN

AXEL

Three years ago

"Honey, I'm home!" My fiancée Hadley slammed the front door and the rattle of plastic grocery bags let me know she needed help. I rose from my chair at the kitchen table and Hadley came like a gangbuster from around the corner with a bright smile. She never failed to brighten my day with her infectious energy.

She refused my outstretched hand with a shake of her head and headed to the kitchen, laying the bags down with a drawn-out groan.

I rolled my eyes at her theatrics. She laughed and held up a package of meat. "I'm making pepper steak tonight. Will you join us for dinner?"

Pepper steak was Julia's favorite. Hadley cooked it every time she came into town.

I shook my head. "I'll probably stick around long enough to say "hi" and then head to the library." Spying a familiar snack in her grocery haul, I opened the bag of corn chips. In between bites, I reflected on my life post-Shondra. All I did was study, sleep, workout, and study some more.

What else is there to do?

350

Paying for It

Hadley straightened from putting dishwashing liquid under the sink and gave me a disapproving look, throwing her blond hair over her shoulder.

The action reminded me of Shondra so much, my gut clenched.

"Stay here and eat with us, Axel." Hadley blinked her brown eyes and clasped her hands together, rocking on her heels with the force of her plea. "Come on, you know Julia wants to spend some time with you."

In between bites I said, "*Suuuure* she does. Why would Julia come all the way from Florida to spend time with me?"

"Because she loves your muscles." Hadley stole the chip bag from my hand and gave me a lewd wink.

I struck a bodybuilder's pose. "Tell her I'm waiting for her anytime she is ready."

"Easy, stud," she said, thumping me on the shoulder.

When our laughter died down, Hadley's face grew serious. I recognized the look. She was gearing up for a preach on the need for me to socialize more. My fake fiancée didn't disappoint. She rattled on about my self-imposed hermit status. I tuned her out, thinking on how we first met.

Hadley and I had interned for different Congressmen in DC. Since I didn't hit on her and she didn't hit on me, we started talking in between assignments. We quickly found out we had a lot in common such as: staying ripped, skiing, love of the law, and the need to hide our true selves.

351

Paying for It

One night—over *a lot* of drinks—I learned of Hadley's predicament.

Like me, Hadley had to hide her true self—her true desires.

Since I hadn't done a very good at job hiding mine, I lost Shondra. Hadley, however, was desperately trying to hold on to hers—her girlfriend, Julia.

Hadley's Grandpa, a wealthy bastard, controlled the lives of his descendants with an iron fist. If someone crossed the old fart, they got booted from his will as soon as Gramps hit the speed dial for his lawyer. Hadley's grandfather was a well-documented homophobe, and she was deathly afraid of student loans; therefore, she had to keep her relationship with Julia on the down low.

Enter me, post-Shondra.

The ache in my heart, caused by the agony of losing my angel, threatened to cave my world in. Sleep had evaded me most nights, and if I ate, it didn't register.

Hadley's friendship and subsequent confession pulled me out of my zombie-like state.
Her need of a "beard" had given me *a purpose*. I'd become her champion like a knight of old and save her from a life of penury.

With Tennessee whiskey sloshing in our veins, I took Hadley home, telling her of my plan in the Uber to the amusement of our silent driver.

I proposed as we stumbled from the car and by the time we fell into bed, fully clothed, she'd said "yes". The next day, I went to the first jewelry store I saw, and bought her a ring.

I never regretted my decision. Hadley shielded me even as I did her. She provided me a convenient excuse for turning down dates. I even let her answer my phone so she could play the jealous fiancée. She did an outstanding job. After the first six months, the calls from randoms trickled down to nothing.

Our arrangement had started out with me saving her, but in fact, she had saved *me*.

"Axel? Are you listening?"

I smiled at her need for my attention. It was funny how she sometimes acted like a real fiancée.

"Suuuure, *honey*. I'm listening."

Hadley grimaced, giving me the side-eye. "Look, Axel, even if you're saving yourself for Shondra, you can still go out and have some fun. Right?"

Hadley told her story in one night, a sad story in one night while mine took the entire summer to spill. Regret and guilt kept me from telling Jameson about Sho, but with Hadley, both of us embroiled in similar circumstances, I told her *everything*—from the day I met Shondra in the park to our break up in D.C.

In the beginning, Hadley encouraged me to contact Shondra and get her back, pointing out long-distance relationships *could* work. I refused, afraid of rejection.

What a pussy.

Paying for It

"Hadley, I don't want 'fun'. I want to pass the bar, move to Chicago, and get my world back." Now that I'd fulfilled my obligation to my mom's memory, I was free to go after Sho. It was all I thought about.

Under Hadley's disapproving glare, I gathered my books from the kitchen table and stuffed them in my backpack. "I'm headed out, don't wait up."

Hadley balled up a plastic bag and threw it, missing me by a mile. "Don't worry, we won't!" she shouted, and I ignored her deep sigh which followed me out the door.

***

I pinched the bridge of my nose and closed my eyes. They had grown bleary from reading and re-reading my study material. Graduation was next week, and the last step to becoming a lawyer, taking the Illinois bar the week after that. I'd been studying my ass off, wanting to make Shondra proud by passing with flying colors.

Shondra . . .

Would she want to see me?

Was she with someone else?

Over the years, I played out every scenario of our reunion, and during my weakest moments, I'd dial her number, hanging up when she answered. Sometimes, just her voice was enough to see me through another day.

I'd neglected to keep up with her personal life—too painful, but I had kept up with her business, reading all the on-line information I could. She got a mentor and went to China for a few weeks. When she came back, she introduced a new line of fragrances. The upscale department stores had snapped them up and from then on, Shondra rested on easy street.

I'm so damn proud of her.

I should call her and tell her so.

What can a call hurt?

Everything . . .

Damn straight.

If she was with someone else. . . *intimate* with someone else, it would hurt like a slow death. That was why I hung up when she answered, I didn't want to know the truth.

After all this time, when we met, it had to be face-to-face. I wanted to study her expression. That way I'd know if she were still interested by the depth of feeling in her eyes.

All I have to do is get through this week. Then make the move to Chicago, and then take the bar—

"Hi," said a female voice.

I jumped in my chair, my eyes flying open.

"I'm sorry to have startled you," she said in a soft voice.

The woman was a vision. Petite with natural curls, her skin tone was a few shades darker and redder in hue than Shondra's. She wore ripped jeans and a white peasant blouse with a turquoise backpack full of books on her shoulder.

"No problem." I said, packing up to leave. "I'm just surprised someone besides me is here at ..." I checked my Apple watch for the time, "... 10:50 on a Friday at night."

Paying for It

"Oh? I'm in here a lot." She threaded an arm through the other loop of her bag. "I've noticed you stay later than me most nights." Smiling, she took me in from head to toe.

As cute as she was, I had zero interest. "It's been a long day," I said. "I best head home to my fiancée."

Like everything in my narrow world, the disappointment on her face was a reminder of how Shondra looked the night she left.

I walked the girl to her bike, reveling in the balmy night by slowing my pace to take in the sticky heat and the ocean scent.

Just like graduation night with Shondra.

The heat. . .

The sweat. . .

Her mouth . . .

Her hands . . .

Damn.

Daytime was a struggle, but nights made them bearable. I'd lie in bed, stroking one out as I thought about all we shared. I relived every touch, every stroke, every moan...

"Thanks for being a gentleman," the girl said, caressing my hand as I handed over her bag I'd volunteered to carry.

I gave her a nod and turned to leave, eager to get home and perform my nightly ritual. Self-gratification had kept me faithful these past three years. It was all I needed to get by.

Paying for It

CHAPTER SIXTY-EIGHT

AXEL

Three years ago

Julia and Hadley lay entwined under a blanket on the couch. Sharp jealousy coupled with an all too familiar ache burgeoned in my chest. The TV flickered with some sit-com; the volume set on low. I grabbed the remote from the floor near Hadley's yellow sneaker and hit the power button with my thumb. The apartment drowned in darkness.

I welcomed the gloom. It kept me from seeing Hadley so content and at ease with her lover, reminding me of what I lost.

The ache spread throughout my torso. I pulled at my T-shirt, trying to relieve the pain and the thought of calling Shondra rose in my mind.

I shouldn't.

I couldn't.

I will.

My phone was in my hand, pressing number one on my speed dial. When it connected, I promised myself to hang up when she answered as all I needed to hear was her breezy "hello" to reassure me everything was right with the world.

Paying for It

Too late, I thought when I realized I hadn't hidden my number.

"Hello, Axel," Shondra said with a voice made from sunshine and sugar. "I'm glad you called."

***

My father had grown smaller since I'd last spent time with him—the night we had dinner before my last graduation. Since that time, I had thought more about the garlic bread shards than I'd thought of him.

He'd left early that day, right after the Dean called my name. Said he had a situation that needed to be handled. I hadn't admitted it, but that shit hurt. What could be more important than seeing your only child graduate?

For my law school graduation, he planned to take me out to dinner. Me *and* Shondra. I politely declined for both of us. The bridge between my father no longer existed. Burned beyond all recognition, shit was nothing but ash. Nothing left to build on, and as far I was concerned, only raging water passed underneath our father-son bond.

Besides, Shondra and I had our own plans, and they included nothing more than room service and an enormous bed at a five-star hotel.

My peers and I filed into the seats, waiting for the speeches to end and our names to be called. I swiveled my head this way and that to find Sho among the throng of relatives and well-wishers.

It was easy.

She sat next to my father, plucking the graduation program from his hands like they were old friends. He leaned over to tell her something, and she laughed.

Fucking strange. When did they become buddy-buddy?

I thought she'd wanted to stay clear of him as much as me.

I kept craning my neck to look back at them as they smiled and talked to each other. The announcer had to call my name twice before I tore my eyes away.

***

Shondra gave me the side-eye when I hugged my father with one arm, thanked him for coming, and led her away. "Axel, you didn't have to run your father off like that. He wanted to spend time with you."

I forgave her expression because she looked damn good in her fuchsia dress and silver sandals. That shit would soon be on the floor of our hotel suite and damn if I could wait.

"He's coming to Chicago to settle the property I bought. I'll spend time with him then." I wouldn't have to suffer his presence after that. I'd be in charge of my trust. With major wealth came major power. The power to cut dead weight out of my life for good.

I would be my own man. A man who only needed to win back his woman to make his life complete.

"Look, Shondra," I said, pulling her into my arms. "I don't want to worry about him. I want to discuss what's going to happen with us?" We had fallen back into how we were, right before my father's ultimatum had fucked up my life. The familiarity and ease were there, just as it had been in the beginning, and I would not ruin it with subjects that still rankled me raw.

I didn't even bring up how close Shondra and my father were with each other.

At that time, I didn't care.

I'd pay for my lack of curiosity later.

Shondra lifted a brow and her fuchsia lips pouted. "Us, Axel? Is there still an us?"

"Of course, there is. There always will be, Shondra. I'm done with my father's rule. I've graduated and I'm my own man. No one can ever separate us again."

There was something behind her eyes I should have noted. Something I hadn't seen before—a slow anger just below the surface. I was so caught up in the love and lust I felt that only afterward on reflection did I see the signs of her scheme to hurt me once again.

***

Shondra didn't want room service. She didn't even want to talk about Hadley or our future.

She started her attack as we rode up in the elevator to our suite. Nothing but hands, lips and fingers. They were all over. Everywhere and anywhere I had dreamed about for three long years.

Once behind closed doors, we didn't even make it to the bedroom. She tore off my blue shirt with impatient hands, causing the buttons to fly helter-skelter over the carpet.

Paying for It

Her exquisite fingers scrambled at the belt of my khakis until they were down around my knees.

Shondra nipped at my chest. Little pecks that were too quick to leave marks on my skin, but made their way deep into my heart.

"Ease up, Sho. We have all the time in the world," I said as she sank to her knees.

She pulled at my tanks just enough to release me. "Time passes all too quickly, Axel." She ran her fingers gently down my length and then back up again. I sucked in a breath and willed my eyes to stay open. I wanted to watch everything she was going to do to me.

As she flipped her hair behind her shoulders, she gave me a clue. "We'd better make the most of it while we can."

I was far from disagreeing as she took me in her mouth.

***

I'd returned her earlier favor. Twice.

Finally, having her under my mouth again was like getting a high from the most addictive drug in the world. I never wanted the feeling to end, but all good things must.

With a vengeance.

We lay with our hands entwined. She was on my chest, listening to the now steady beat of my heart. It had taken a long time for my pulse to return to normal. I was about to rev it up again when she asked a question.

Paying for It

"Why do you help Hadley in the kitchen and you never helped me?"

Since the night I ghost dialed her, or *thought* I had. Shondra and I talked every day via Face Time. She met Hadley over the Internet and her girlfriend Julia as well. She wanted to see my daily life and my place in Boston.

I showed her everything.

We talked while I was in the shower. When I went to the gym. While Hadley and I cooked. Even when I spread my books on the kitchen table and claimed I was studying. We talked all the time as much as we could.

And I fucking loved her eyes on me.

"I didn't help you because I was too busy watching you. Every single move you made. I love watching you, Sho, especially when you're doing something so simple as stirring a pot or seasoning a meal. And when you sneak a taste...*fuck* Shondra. You don't know how I love seeing your eyes close and that sweet tongue of yours licking at your lips.

She raised off of me, gazing intently into my eyes. There was a softness there, a forgiveness perhaps, but I couldn't tell as she closed them too quickly.

Shondra lay back on the pillow, tugging the covers down past her hips. Her legs parted ever so slightly. A whisper of thighs on the sheets.

I moved down the length of her, placing soft kisses as I went.

She giggled when I pulled up the blanket and covered my head.

Paying for It

She groaned when I delved into her center...

In the morning she'd left. No note. No apology. No nothing.

I sat in the room all day. Waiting for a sign. A signal. A lightning bolt.

The hotel called asking if I wanted a late checkout. I told them to fuck off.

I waited until midnight. I gave love one day to get it right. It didn't. For the second time she'd let me down and cast me aside to twist in the cold, dark wind.

From then on, I was dead inside. Dead because I no longer believed in love everlasting.

CHAPTER SIXTY-NINE

AXEL

Present day

"Back already?" The valet gave Shondra a wolfish smile, checking her out from head to toe.

Is this prick really trying to flirt with her? Does he have any respect? I'm standing right here.

I gave the bastard my worst stare. He caught my look and nearly dropped the claim ticket Shondra tried to hand to him. He fumbled a save and beat a hasty retreat.

Sho whipped around just as I straightened my face.

"Stop it, Axel," she said in a whisper. "You're showing too much of your alpha tonight."

I cocked a brow and looked her up and down. "Just how you like it, Sho."

Vegas and Jameson passed by. Vegas looked like she was going to intervene in our one-sided squabble. Shondra took a moment from glowering at me to give her girl a nod. After a concerned glance, Vegas kept moving. Jameson had a few surprises for her and I hoped she would be ready to receive them. My boy was betting *everything* that she would.

The happy couple disappeared into the parking lot and a second later the valet drove up in Shondra's car. He didn't even wait for a tip, just hightailed it back to his podium.

As he should.

We got in the car and she started in before I had a chance to open my mouth. "I'm taking you home, Axel."

I didn't argue. I had a few plans of my own. "Sure, Shondra. Thanks."

She set the car in drive and peeled out of the parking lot. When dealing with a testy Sho, I found it best to say as little as possible. She needed time to cool down, and I was happy to comply. A happier Sho would listen to what I had to say.

I wanted to start over. Forget the past. Put it behind us. Tabitha Moore, my father's ultimatum, her leaving me in Boston and last December...fuck it. We needed to see if there was an us left to salvage and tonight would be the beginning of that discovery.

Even if she had been with Tony.

I doubted it though. Shondra wasn't that kind of woman. If she waited for me all these years since D.C....since my graduation night ...it would take more than a few weeks for her to sleep with him. It would take...

A trip to Europe.

I'd find out—one way or the other. But first, I had to get her upstairs...to my teeny, tiny place.

Paying for It

When I first looked at properties in Chicago, I viewed a home in her neighborhood. I wanted to be close. After the night she left me, I didn't bother looking for a bigger place.

"You need to get in the right hand lane."

Shondra nodded, keeping her gaze on the cars ahead.

Giving Shondra directions was my excuse to stare at her profile. I still recognized the girl from the park bench, and damn if she had only gotten better. The years ahead would be very kind to Sho, and I hoped to be right there with her, growing old together.

"Turn right at the light," I said, watching how the street lamps touched the planes of her face. My eyes slowly traveled down her body. She always looked fantastic, but her weight loss made her healthier, and in turn, she'd be around a whole lot longer. To me, Shondra resembled a living hour glass. One I wanted to turn over and over, touching and tasting every delicious inch.

Damn! She still has me.

Hell, she always *did*.

***

Getting Shondra to come up with me was relatively easy. I told her she had to see the river lit up at night. She hesitated only a second before agreeing. I left her on the balcony and told her I was going to take a quick shower.

It was on my lips to ask her to join me.

Wistful thinking.

Paying for It

I was done in under ten minutes, purposefully leaving my shirt off and spritzing her favorite aroma in the bedroom. I hadn't used my sandalwood scent when we were apart. Shit brought back too many memories.

I came in to the living room just in time to see her walk from the balcony and take a seat on the couch. She was regal in the way she moved and sat, just like a queen with a roomful of adoring subjects.

Count me among them. Forever and always.

No matter how many randoms I slept with, no matter what shit I said about Shondra, no matter how many times I made myself relive the hurt she had inflicted on me, *nothing* could set me free. I spent the past three years trying my damnedest to let her go.

A futile effort.

Last Christmas, when I was forced to work with her, all of the old feelings that lay dormant like spring flowers under the ground, blossomed once more. I'd told Jameson that Shondra kept changing the terms, but she hadn't.

I had.

I'd stretched out negotiations for that chemical lab because I *liked* the look on her face when I'd break off to text and talk to randoms. I'd watch her fume from the corner of my eye while I made plans with women I never intended to keep. I wanted *Shondra* to make the first move since she was the one that had *left* me.

Moving forward had to come from her.

CHAPTER SEVENTY

AXEL

Present day

When she finally decided to show me her true feelings, her act was once more fueled by trickery and spite. Not wanting any interruptions, I took her to a hotel and switched off my phone. As soon as I closed the door, just like on my graduation night...*both of them*, we were on each other. Clothes ripping. Teeth nipping. Hair pulling...

We didn't even make it to the bedroom.

The walls, the couch, and the kitchen table felt our weight. When we finally collapsed on the bed, once more descending from the atmosphere to land softly back on ground, I made the promise of a ring and a happy ever after.

It was then she decided to come clean.

And fuck, did her confession hurt.

To break our never ending cycle of destruction, I kicked her out, vowing thereafter to distance myself.

And I did. And I tried. And I failed.

Shondra. . . my gorgeous, courageous angel, had set the bar so high, no woman I'd ever met could vault over it. The randoms I had never measured up to the criteria.

Paying for It

Too small. Too tall. Too big. Too thin. Not smart enough. Not challenging enough. The list went on and on. Randoms *didn't* get me. They never did. Not one of them had chipped past my bravado and saw the real man inside.

Only Shondra knew my darkness. Only she knew my light. And she accepted both.

I came further into view and her grew wide. She liked what she saw, even though she tried to hide it by turning her head.

"You want something to drink?"

She nodded. Before I turn, I saw her tucking her plush bottom lip under her teeth.

Oh, yeah.

Back in the living room, I hand her a bottled water, whisper touching every bit of her hand I could. Then I sat down—practically in her lap.

"Move over, Axel," she said in her *reserved for sex* voice. The tone she defaulted to when she was ready for *more.*

I didn't snooze on it. I laid on the charm to seal the deal. "Now why would I do that?"

She took a drink, slightly bumping my chest with her elbow. My heart sped up even faster at the contact. I watched her look around the room, unable to peel my eyes away. "You have a nice place," she said, letting a small smile grace the lips I wanted to suck between teeth.

"You don't think it's too small?"

She scoffs. "Nothing about you, Axel, is small." Her lip fell under her teeth again and I started to grow...

"I'll take you on a tour." I took the bottle from her hand and drew her up.

Without heels, Shondra came to my chin. It was all I could do not to wrap my arms around her and hold her in that old familiar way, with her head on my shoulder, her body molded to mine. In the end, I cautioned myself against it.

Too much. Too soon.

The tour was short. The powder room, the living room and open kitchen, my home office...and lastly, my bedroom.

She went to stand by the window, pulling the gauzy curtain back to look out on the river and the twinkling lights of the Shore.

"Your place really is great, Axel. I love the view."

I came up behind her, my body pressing close to hers. Wrapping my arms around her middle, I rested my chin on her shoulder and whispered, "Did you sleep with him? Did you sleep with Tony?"

At the Bakers' party when she told me I was the only man she'd ever known, the news hit me like a sucker punch to the throat. I couldn't believe that she thought so much of me she hadn't let another man near her.

Then she turned around, said we were over, and not a day later, she moved on with someone else.

Paying for It

Nothing compared to the dismal hole I crawled in when I learned she was dating Tony. After all I did for him...never outing him to *anyone* that he was the father of Tabitha's baby...

By the time the test results came out, Dad had taken care of it, and since everyone in our circle assumed it was me, I kept it that way, promising Tony I would keep my mouth shut. His family was deeply religious. He would have been ostracized if they learned he'd had a child without the benefit of marriage.

Shondra dropped the curtain and turned in my arms. "No, I haven't slept with him."

I let out a breath of sweet relief. No sooner was it breezing past my lips when she said, "But I did tell him I'm ready to take our relationship further when he gets back from his parent's place in Kentucky."

I removed my hands from her waist and stepped back. Long ago on that park bench, I promised never to lie to her. I'd also sworn never to kiss and tell, but for Shondra, I would. The promise I made to an ex-friend became invalid the moment he went after what was mine. "Do you remember that night in D.C. when you'd asked me about Tabitha Moore?"

Shondra closed her eyes. She tilted her head down and shook it in denial. Her ponytail whispering over her back sounded like a soft wind threading through the trees. "He told me, Axel. He told me how you used and discarded Tabitha after a few nights and when Tony went to console her, one thing led to another." She lifted her head to shoot off sparks into my eyes. "Either you or Tony could've been the father. We'll never know because after

what happened in the common room she. . . she got rid . .
." Shondra pushed past me. I followed her into the living
room where she grabbed her bag and slung it over her
shoulder.

I stopped her from walking out of the door and out of
my life by turning her around and speaking the truth,
"What Tony told you was a lie. I've never had any
children, Shondra. Not with *any* woman. I have the copy
of the DNA test to prove it. You're the only person
I've *never* used a condom with."

Her brow scrunched in confusion. "Tony said there
wasn't a DNA test... Did he...did he lie to me?"

"Yeah, Sho. He did. Tony always went after the women
I... uh, finished with."

Her face grew dark with anger. "Just like me..."

"No, Sho. *Not* like you. Those ramdoms...hell, I
couldn't give a fuck, but you..." I shook my head,
wishing Tony was there to punch in the throat. "If it had
been you coming to me...telling me you were pregnant,
nothing would..."

Shondra's eyes filled with tears. Her mouth trembled.
"Axel. . . I." She covered her face with her hands, hiding
her expression. "Oh God, help me. I'm sorry. So Sorry.
You don't know how many times I wanted to tell you . .
."

The hammer came down. The lights went out. My legs
were strong like iron, but they nearly buckled underneath
me. The disquiet that rose from my toes dried my mouth,
cramped my stomach, and put a hurt in my heart.

373

Paying for It

I knew.

I knew what would come out of her mouth and I didn't want to hear it. I wasn't ready. *Nothing* could make me ready. Once the words were said they could never be unsaid and I'd have to live with what happened. I'd wake up ten years. . .*twenty years* from now and relive this moment, remembering just how the agony had oozed into my nerves and scraped the life from my cells.

Since the tidal wave of disaster was already on shore, I might as well let it consume me. "Please don't tell me. . ." I wanted to swallow my tongue to keep from speaking the words but I had to hear her say them so I could finally let her go. "Did you . . .did you get rid of our child?"

Shondra looked up at me, her tears doing nothing to mask her shock and hurt. "I *lost* him, Axel. I lost our baby."

I fell. Shondra was there to help. The pain was akin to learning of my mother's death, only this time, I didn't shed my tears in private. Shondra saw me as raw and as unsure and as vulnerable as I'd ever been. And during all of that, I let her arms comfort me even while my overwhelming grief blotted out my senses.

CHAPTER SEVENTY-ONE

SHONDRA

Present day

Axel threw a bag on the bed. He stuffed a pair of jeans, a couple of T-shirts, some socks and underwear into it. The sound of the zipper closing, got me moving. That *zzzzrrrrp* tore a hole big enough through my grief to stop Axel in what would be the biggest mistake of his life.

I snatched the bag form the bed, crossing my arms around it, stepping back until I reached the door.

Axel looked startled for a moment. But just for a moment. "Stop playing games, Sho, and give me the bag."

"Don't do it, Axel. Don't go to the island." After we'd both cried a river of tears, I told him what happened. I told him how his half-brother had pushed me down the steps because of his misguided sense of justice. I told him how his father and I buried his child in his mother's grave. I told him how I'd written Jacob's name in the Hammersmythe family bible, giving his short life substance and meaning. He had existed. He was real.

Axel had sat silent through it all, the tears flowing from his eyes and onto his bare chest, doing nothing to stave the flow or wipe them away. When I was done, my voice was hoarse with grief. Axel had gotten up, calm as you please, and started to pack.

I knew where he was going. I knew what he was set to do.

He was going to kill William. A poor sick bastard, who according to Paul, had reverted to a child-like state. He was much like Vee's daddy with Alzheimer's— a blank canvas in a dark room.

"That's not what I'm going to do. Now, give me the bag." He was so reasonable, so eerily calm, that I believed him and handed it over.

He disappeared into his closet to get dressed. We headed out when he was done. Him in the lead and me following behind.

As we headed to the parking garage, something—a niggling doubt—made me ask, just to make sure, "If you aren't going to the island, where are you going?"

He didn't answer. His jaw was clenched too hard to do so. I made another effort when we got to his car, a sleek Maserati with a custom paintjob that matched his eyes.

"Axel, tell me. Where are you going?"

He opened the door and tossed his bag in the back seat. He then looked at me over the low roof. "I'm going to Vermont. I'm going to confront my father, then sever all ties. And then I'm going to the island to kill the bastard that killed my son. We can talk when I get back."

Without a word, I opened the passenger door and slipped inside.

Paying for It

I didn't consider my business. I didn't consider Vee. I didn't consider taking any luggage or toiletries. And Tony? I'd deal with him when I came back.

Axel needed me, and I wasn't going to let him down.

"Okay," I said. "Let's go." It would take a strong mind and will to haul Axel away from revenge, and I that I *didn't* have, but I could at least do my best to stop him from ruining his life.

Axel stared at me a moment before a slight smile graced his lips. "That's why love you, Sho."

He got in, started the engine, and putting his foot to the pedal, we drove away into the night.

***

Vermont was breathtaking in all its fall glory. The abscission of the leaves was almost over, but what remained on the trees was nonetheless striking.

Axel drove the rental car at a grandfatherly pace. It seemed he was in no hurry to rush into a confrontation with his father... or view the place where his son was buried.

We didn't talk...much. Same as when we spent the night in the hotel near the airport in Vermont before driving out early this morning. Axel didn't say a word when we entered the hotel room. He'd delved between the covers of one of the full-sized beds and turned his back to me. I took up residence on the other, sleep evading me for a long, long, time. In the morning, I woke to find Axel wrapped around me like a blanket. His arm on top of my breasts and one leg over both of mine. I eased from his embrace and went to the nearest Wal-Mart to buy what I needed. A far cry from my labels at home, but the clothing I picked out would do.

I got a thrill from being able to fit into the sizes they carried. As inconsequential as that was compared to what we were dealing with, it was the only joy I experienced for the entire trip.

Last night, when we'd gotten to O'Hare, we were able to catch the last flight out. However, there was only one business class ticket left. Axel insisted I take it, claiming he was happy to sit in coach. When he'd left me to walk to the back, I made a few calls.

The first was to Deja, telling her I was leaving town for a few days. She knew what was on the burners and would put fires out when needed.

Then I called Vee. She answered on third ring. Her voice was different, lighter than air and breezier than the wind on the Lake Shore.

It seemed through the darkness of the night, at least some light had shone through.

Jae and her must have worked things out.

I damn sure hated to disturb them, but Axel needed his friend...

And Jae could get hold of a jet.

He was there waiting for us when we arrived.

The ancient butler was coming around the corner, followed by Jae. Axel didn't see him at first as he was busy setting his bag down but when he looked, there wasn't a friendly greeting in his eyes. In fact, those chips of blue grew steely as they registered his friend. He didn't greet Jae, but turned to me instead.

"Sho—"

I shook my head to warn him off. Murder was a private conversation. The last time I was here, it seemed like there was a staff member for every room, and although they'd probably signed a non-disclosure agreement, something could always slip out. "Not here, Axel. Let's go somewhere we can talk privately."

He dipped his head and whispered, "Then take me to him."

Axel walked slightly ahead while Jae and I shot worried glances at each other. The sorrow which trickled up from the soles of my feet to rest in my chest was nearly overwhelming. What kept me from caving, was Axel. *He* had just lost his son. To be there for him like he needed me to be, I had to compartmentalized my grief in the face of his.

***

The grave site had changed.

Paul had put a small plaque in the middle of Marjorie's grave. Jacob's name, date of birth, and death date were recorded on a slab of pure white stone. There were no guarantees that Axel would come here and visit his mother's grave, but if he had, *which he now was,* he would know or quickly guess something was different. *Amiss.*

I guessed Paul was ready to tell him the story if he asked, but I had beat him to the punch.

Jae and I stood on either side, ready to catch him if he fell. However, Axel chose to express his emotions, we were ready to support him— within reason.

It was about to get unreasonable.

Paul came out, his face a flushed red. Little puffs of wheezed air escaped from his mouth. Paul and I talked at least once a week, but I hadn't seen him in well over two years and he looked like he had found the weight I had lost.

I knew all about emotional eating, and I, in him, recognized a fellow binger. He *had* to be. Paul was always a big man, but seeing him, with his belly as wide as he was tall, shocked me.

"Axel," Paul wheezed, coming to stand in between me and his son. "I wanted—"

He never got to finish what he was about to say.

"Save it, Dad. Just save it. This time is for me and *my* son."

And with that, Paul wisely hung his head, clasped his hands, and left his son alone.

CHAPTER SEVENTY-TWO

VEGAS

Present day

Our reunion had been short-lived, but oh-so-sweet. When Shondra called, she asked me to put her on speaker so she could fill Jae in at the same time.

Her news floored us.

No wonder Shondra doted on Kae so much. No wonder I saw sadness fill her eyes every October. I shuddered to think what she went through, practically alone.

Later, when she returned home, we'd talk about why she didn't come to me, why she didn't want to share her burden.

But I already had an idea.

Shondra was a rock. Time and time again, she took care of everyone but herself. She put her life on hold for her mother, for me, and even for Axel. She didn't allow herself to crumble because we needed her.

Enough was enough.

When all this was over, I was going to fight to make sure my girl had a happily ever after. I was going to make sure she ended up with a man who'd make her happy and put her above himself.

As things stood, I wasn't sure Axel was the one.

Jae ended the call with his pilot and turned to me. He wanted to stay... with *us*, but his friend was about to make a life altering mistake and I couldn't fault him for wanting to go.

I touched my lips to his, intending it to be a light kiss goodbye, but there were too many lost years in which we could have gotten to know one another and too many regrets that we didn't.

Too much damn time wasted.

I arched into him. He must have expected it as he didn't stumble, instead he pressed me even closer, bending my back into the crook of his arm. Peace, the kind I only knew that night with him, danced through me like the slow swirl of his tongue in my mouth.

I moaned, loud enough to wake the dead.

He nibbled on my bottom lip in sweet chastisement, his hands gripping my sides. "Vee, don't do that again. I'll never leave if you do."

Years of pining for the other, our daily thoughts and nightly dreams had brought us to this moment. We had spent little time together, and the odds were against us going for the long haul, but somehow... someway, I knew we would.

   ***

Paying for It

I'd called Terrence to meet me for an early dinner at a café near the hospital. He sounded resigned when we'd hung up. Or maybe tired. February was right around the corner and his campaign for mayor was in full swing.

We'd been to this café before. He always got the mushroom burger, and I was just about to order it when someone slipped into my booth.

Gertrude Eisenberg. The woman who was funding most Terrence's campaign.

Her showing up startled me to say the least, but I hid it well behind a puzzled smile. "Mrs. Eisenberg? What are you doing here?"

Her steely eyes met mine. "I think it's time you and I had a chat, don't you?"

I hadn't a clue what she was talking about. We'd met once at a fundraiser; the same night I saw Jae. After that, I'd only heard about her through Terrence.

Mrs. Eisenberg recommended...

Mrs. Eisenberg said...

Mrs. Eisenberg told me to...

I thought little it until she was sitting across from me, pinning me down like a bug with a needle through its belly.

She has a hold over him.

"What do you want, Mrs. Eisenberg? Where is Terrence?"

She didn't answer me. At least not right away. She sat back and became the epitome of ease by folding one hand over the other. "I want to tell you a story," she said, studying the enormous diamond on her left-ring finger, "and by the end, you'll understand." Her eyes met mine once more. This time there was steel, but also a hint of amusement. I sat back, heartily wishing the café served popcorn.

"Let me start from the beginning, shall I?"

I nodded. Wondering just what she had to say.

CHAPTER SEVENTY-THREE

VEGAS

Present day

"My grandson, Abel, was, and still is a handful. He lives for sports, the more extreme the better. Matter of fact, he IS rock climbing in Sedona right now."

The server came to our table, breaking off her story. He offered to take our drink orders—hot tea for me and water with lemon for Mrs. Eisenberg. Mrs. Eisenberg picked up my menu, studied it for a moment, and asked for the Cobb salad. I switched my order from the chicken wings to the same.

I didn't think a greasy meal would go well with her revelation.

The server left and Mrs. Eisenberg picked up where she left off. "As I said, my grandson has always been fond of sports. When he was fifteen, he wanted to play varsity football. All summer he... what do the young people call it?" She snapped her fingers when the word came to her. "He wanted to 'beef up.'" Mrs. Eisenberg rolled her eyes. "That sounds more like a cholesterol problem than getting into shape." I giggled, and she gave me a small smile. "He went to the gym, every day, week after week. On this one particular day, he was there for over four hours, lifting weights nonstop."

Unease crept in. I had a feeling where the conversation was going, but I still couldn't connect how her grandson, and even herself, had anything to do with Terrence and me.

I would soon find out.

"When he came home that day, his mother said he'd stumbled from his jeep, nearly collapsing on the driveway. She had to call a few of her staff to help him into bed. She said he looked like a giant, his muscles swelled up to almost twice their normal size. He said his lower back hurt. He'd been doing a lot of abdominal work and these side-twisty things." Mrs. Eisenberg mimicked a gym-body twisting to the side, arms up high, and her hands holding a phantom medicine ball. She lowered her arms and folded them across her narrow chest. "He'd thought he'd overdone it, but it was... much worse than that."

"Was it Rhabdo?" I asked. Rhabdomyolysis is when broken down muscles, usually from exercise, release a muscle enzyme into the bloodstream that can ultimately cause kidney failure if it not caught and treated. It is a rare syndrome and only detectable by a blood test.

The server appearing at our table prevented from Mrs. Eisenberg from answering. He set the tea down, told us our meal would be out shortly, and asked us if we needed anything else to which Mrs. Eisenberg replied, "Privacy, please."

The server nodded and scurried off. I bit back a laugh at his surprised expression. Mrs. Eisenberg was a feisty ol' gal.

Paying for It

As my tea seeped in the pot, she confirmed my suspicions. "Yes, it was. We rushed him to St. Vincent's right away." She took a sip of water. Setting the glass down, her lips curled. "I'm sure by now you've guessed who his doctor was."

"Dr. Caldwell?"

"Yes!" Her arms flew wide and a feral look came into her eyes. I shrank back. Mrs. Eisenberg, this diminutive woman, had morphed into a 90-pound gremlin. Her dark expression put fear into my soul. I'd pressed so far into the cushions of the booth, I thought I'd indent.

"That dumb bitch misdiagnosed him at first—fair enough, it was easy to do — but when another doctor tried to contradict her, she took him off my grandson's rounds. Abel suffered for a day and a half, writhing in pain, until she finally saw the light after dusting off her medical books and reading up on his condition. Of course, that quack took full credit for saving his life. If she'd waited any longer, Abel would've gone into kidney failure and been on a dialysis machine, or worse."

I leaned forward, placing my hands on the table. My heart raced in my chest. This woman had something up her sleeve... but what did that have to do with me?

"You must wonder why I told you?"

Again, I nodded, my heart racing.

"Terrence told me about you, you know. I don't back losers and Terrence comes from winning stock, at least in the political sense. As far as being a man... well, Terrence has a low, and I'm talking almost *non-existent* sex drive.

387

When I vetted him, he said he would rather eat rocks than fuck."

No wonder he wasn't so interested in intimacy.

She waved her hand as if to say she couldn't care less. "His sex drive, or lack of, didn't bother me. What mattered were the *rumors* circulating about him. We couldn't have that. Things are getting better for the LGBTQ community, but even in this day and age, we still need small-minded people and their money to get candidates elected, and once they are, they can change things from the inside out."

"So you had Terrence call me... and propose?" I was more shocked I was taking her revelations as calmly as I did. Others might have expressed their outrage at their life being upended.

Not so.

I wasn't mad, not even a little perturbed. How could I be when those that loved me were by my side? Dallas had been rough on me and Kae, what with little support and no one I considered family. No, I didn't even *think* about complaining.

"Sorry dear," she said in a *sorry, not sorry voice*, "but we needed someone like you until I could wrap up a few of our more conservative donors. All I asked is that he get a woman who wasn't flashy, had a decent job and good manners, and I'd have no problem getting him elected mayor come February. He said he knew a woman who would fit my criteria, and... well, I asked him to call you." She gave me a sweet, grandmotherly smile that was so sincere, I took that as an apology instead. "Proposing was *his* idea, though. I guess Terrence thought he should go whole hog to keep you with him." She lifted her gaze to the ceiling for a second and returned it to me. "As if your job, which *I arranged*, wasn't enough to keep you in Chicago. Men—pffft." She let out a wicked chuckle. "Little did I know you and Shelia have a connection." At my wide-eyed look, she giggled like a five-year-old. "Oh, I know about you and Jameson. When I saw him take you from the room during Terrence's fundraiser, I made it my business to find out all I could. I knew for some time he hated his wife...*ex-wife* almost as much as I do." Her blue eyes turned stormy with fury. "I would have destroyed her by now, but with my fingers in all sorts of political pies, I couldn't chance anything coming back on me." She gave me a conspiratorial wink. "I don't mind ruining a life, I just have to make sure doing so is in my best interest."

CHAPTER SEVENTY-FOUR

JAMESON

Present day

Axel and his father headed to the back of the plane, I assumed to talk things out. Estranged since the summer he'd graduated with his bachelor's, Axel and his father hadn't spoken. I always thought it was because he got engaged to a girl Paul didn't approve of. Then when he broke it off with Hadley after she graduated, I knew that couldn't be the reason. Axel, closed lipped about everything personal, never revealed the reason. I see he had kept more hidden than I had ever imagined.

Then again, so had I. Axel knew about my sex toy business. Although he wasn't my lawyer, he looked over each and every one of my contracts as a favor to me. And yes, he knew about Shelia from the start. He encouraged me to celebrate my divorce in any manner I needed to.

And I damn glad I took his advice. I met Vegas and my life...my faith in *decency* was restored. Shelia had all but broken it with her affairs. I bet even now she was with someone at her "conference." I didn't give a damn. I was moving forward with Vegas and Kae...my beautiful baby girl.

"Jae, is there a place where I can make a few calls?"

Paying for It

"Sure, I have a small office just past the lavatory." My jet wasn't as big as they came, but with a lounge area, a full sized bathroom, and an office, it wasn't half bad.

Shondra gave me a smile of thanks. When she was out of earshot, I called Vegas.

"Hey," she said. Then she giggled.

"What?"

"You won't believe the conversation I had. I still can't believe it happened."

Weary as I was, adrenaline shot through my system, giving me a second wind. "What's going on, Vegas?"

She told me. At the end of her wild tale, all I could do was laugh.

***

We arrived on Paul's private island in the afternoon, closer to dinner time than to lunch. The balmy breeze carried the salt of the ocean and tossed everyone's hair. I had got a few winks of sleep, despite Axel's raised voice.

He had berated his father for allowing William to live, and that "he would do something about it."

I let them be. The conversation of Axel gaining control over his life was long overdue. It was best to let them hash it out, get all their grievances out in the open *before* we got to the island.

Axel needed to break free from his father's clutches once and for all, same as I needed to break free from Shelia's. Vegas told me of Mrs. Eisenberg's desire to help. I planned to take her up on it as soon as I returned.

Paying for It

***

When the plane stopped, we all piled out and stepped into the limo. A contrite Paul and angry Axel sat opposite a silent Shondra and a concerned me. On the way to confront William, reality hit—

My brother might get himself into serious trouble.

"Axel, man, are you okay?"

The ice-blue eyes he turned on me were flat...deadly.

He wasn't. Not at all.

"I'm done talking, Jameson. It's best if you leave me alone."

Paul shifted slightly away from his son. Shondra let out a small sigh. I stared at my friend until the harsh intensity of his gaze made me look away. All I could do was try to hold Axel back when the time came.

We headed up to the third floor. I walked in front along with Mr. Jones, William's burly caretaker. Shondra was next, and Paul and Axel brought up the rear. Paul murmured to his son. Snatches of Paul's pleas for calm floated to me.

"—he's sick."

"— your half-brother."

"Think about what your mother—"

We had reached the landing when Axel whirled on his father. His face a mask of fury. "Don't... under any circumstances bring Mom into this. Had she known what kind of sick bastard he was, she would have gotten rid of him."

Paying for It

Shondra stepped to him, placing a hand on his arm, which bulged from tension. "I've forgiven him, Axel. You should too. You can't blame a person who has a mental illness. That's like blaming a baby for catching a house on fire."

Axel looked at her with eyes full of pain. "Sho, how can you forgive the guy who killed our son?"

"It wasn't easy. I blamed him...and... I blamed a lot of other people."

Axel stepped back. His eyes went glassy. "You blamed me?"

"I did."

Axel sucked in a breath as if he were lacking oxygen.

Shondra wrapped her arms around him and said, "Will you forgive me? For leaving you? For walking away? Will you forgive me for all the bad I've done?"

Axel was stiff in her arms, his muscles cording and bunching. I was ready to intervene when he wrapped his arms around her and kissed her hair. "Only if you forgive me, Sho. I should have fought for you instead of letting you go. You are my life, always have been."

A door down the corridor opened, and the person we all came here to see emerged from the gloom. His shaggy curls stuck to his head like corkscrews, and his beard resembled the matted fur of a farmyard animal. His gray T-shirt fell off one shoulder and his blue sweatpants hung loosely on his gaunt frame. "Oh! Guests! Are you here to see me?" He waved us forward with childlike glee. "Then let's get started."

Paying for It

William and his room smelled. The strong, sickly sweet odor on top barely masked the dead animal smell underneath. Shondra smelled it too. Her eyes grew wide and filled with fear. Paul and Axel seemed oblivious. They gazed around the room, taking in the décor of cream, light blue and white. Paul, in low tones, asked the caretaker a question while Axel stood on Shondra's right side with his arms crossed over his chest.

No one sat, not even when William offered us the window seat close to his bed.

He shrugged off our refusal and pulled open the French doors that led to a small balcony. The view overlooked the ocean waves, which rocketed against the shore many feet below.

Paul's mansion was on a cliff and the scenery was beautiful for miles. I suspected Paul gave William this room to instill peace to his step-son's maniacal mind.

Despite the situation, I almost relaxed. *Almost.* The burly caretaker placed himself between the two brothers and tensed, ready for action. Still, I doubted if he alone could hold Axel back once he got going.

William clapped his hands, smiling. "So we're all together as a family! You too, Shondra. After a long glance in her direction, he turned and pointed a finger at me. "I don't know you."

His gaze was calculating and cold, quiet unlike the friendly one he wore when he invited us to his room.

"I'm Jameson. Axel's friend."

"Best friend," Axel murmured, flicking me a smile that soon faded under the glare he held for his half-brother.

It cheered my heart Axel was thinking along those lines and not rushing William like I thought he would.

Or maybe...it was all a ploy to relax us into thinking he wouldn't.

I moved closer to the burly caretaker, pining my eyes on Axel. This position put me at a disadvantage, given most of my back was to William. Seeing as how he'd attacked Sho, I'd rather have him in my sights, but my duty to protect my best friend was more important.

"Well, that is nice. Wonderful! I never had one of those." William shrugged and pulled at his four-inch beard. The way his hands tangled the strands, I understood why it was so messy. William carried on, his eyes tearing, "I was always the loner, the outcast. The weird one in the corner."

Axel grunts. "Is that why you hurt, Sho? Is that why you killed my child?"

William's bottom lip quivered, and his eyes overflowed with tears. "I'm sorry for that. So sorry."

It was then that everything happened in fast motion.

Axel moved forward. Shondra screamed, whirled, and held onto his arm, digging her heels in to the carpet. Paul stepped away from the fray. The caretaker and I surged forward, pinning a snarling Axel back. William cackled, enraging Axel even more. He strained in our grasp with the strength of ten men.

We lost ground.

Paying for It

Sho and I pleaded with Axel to remain calm.

I looked to Paul for help, but he had his attention on someone else. He gave William a nod and as we continue to struggle with Axel, I heard William say, "Yes! Yes! It's time!"

Ignoring the bizarre exchange between William and Paul, I turned my head to make sure William wasn't sneaking up on us.

He wasn't.

William, quicker than a bolt of lightning, ran to the balcony and sat on the railing, his hands white knuckling the cold dark metal. The sky behind him was a brilliant blue. Wispy clouds moved along with the wind in a hurried pace. A lone seagull wailed overhead.

With a smile, William let go, throwing his body backward. He didn't even let out a scream...

***

We had to wait a day and a half before the authorities cleared us to leave the island. There were no authorities on the private island, so they had to fly in from the nearest capital.

Vegas, that giving soul, cried more than anyone when I told her the news. Out of the quintet that were witnesses to Williams self-destruction, not one of us shed a tear.

And I hated that. Hated that I couldn't mourn William's passing as a human being, despite what he had done. But as a father, I didn't have it in me.

396

CHAPTER SEVENTY-FIVE

AXEL

Present day

Shondra, Vee, and I arrived at Shelia's birthday party an hour after it started. Place was packed. I rubbed my hands in glee. The more people that witnessed her downfall, the better. We strolled in as a group, and chatting her and there, we made our way ever closer to the birthday...*girl*.

Shelia was thirty and had been for the last five or six years. She held court center stage to a group of men vying for her attention. I could understand why they did so. Shelia was cheap, easy, and could promise them a quick ride with no strings attached. Just what a married woman could offer.

"These decorations, I hate to admit, are lovely", Vee said to Shondra. My angel nodded, looking around the room. Yeah, Shelia had spared no expense. White chrysanthemums and pink roses flown in from the Netherlands rose majestically from crystal vases exploding with eucalyptus and leather leaf. Blush tablecloths were the backdrop for the silver plates and heavy silverware. The gift table groaned under the weight of presents even though Shelia, the philanthropist, had asked for monetary gifts to her favorite charity.

Herself.

Paying for It

A pile of envelopes from those who followed her crass wishes, poked from the top of cream tulle bag. Most of the gifts were from Jameson, but they weren't for his *wife*. They were for the people who came to the party.

A wrapped package from his spring collection for everyone who'd RSVP'd.

After Shelia's speech in which she thanked everyone for coming, Jameson planned to make one of his own. With the waitstaff distributing the party favors, he would unmask Shelia for the cheating, blackmailing bitch she was.

My phone was fully charged and ready to record.

"Ladies, why don't we go to the bar?"

Shondra nodded her agreement.

Vee, however, had other plans. "Axel, I'll catch up with you two later. I want to find Jae." She looked around the room, already on the hunt for her man. "I want to make sure he is okay."

We wished her well and off she went, lost in the crowd within seconds. With my arm firmly around my woman's waist, I led her to the bar. On the way, we ran into her jilted-never-lover, Tony.

He narrowed his eyes, and his lips curled into a sneer. "You move fast, Shondra."

She stiffened at my side, and I pulled her closer. Before she could respond, I did it for her. "Fuck off, Tony. Shondra made her choice, and you weren't it."

"Yeah, so she said." He then *mumbled* something loud enough for us to hear.

It wasn't nice.

I opened my mouth to react, but Shondra beat me to it.

"What did you say?" She placed her size nine stiletto on his shiny Italian shoe and put on the pressure.

Tony winced in pain, his eyes tearing up and his mouth trembling.

"Don't you ever use that word around me." She removed her foot from on top of his after she pushed a bit harder to make sure he got the message.

"He's said worse about you," Tony whined, nodding his head in my direction.

"Unlike you," Shrondra said, leaning close to Tony's pain-filled face, "Axel has always been transparent. You, on the other hand, lied about Tabitha."

His face turned from pale to lobster red in under a second. "How do you know?"

"In all the years I've known Axel, he has always told me the truth."

Tony opened his mouth to refute her claim, but snapped it close under my glower.

His shoulders slumped. He knew he had lost. "When he tires of you, don't come looking for me." After one last look filled with longing and regret, Tony limped away.

I shuddered, remembering how I'd almost lost Shondra for good. Tony, with his manufactured lies, had nearly convinced her he was a good guy. Damn prick had always coveted what was mine, and now he was paying for his mistakes in underestimating Shondra's regard...her *faith* in me.

No other man would get a chance to do the same. Shondra was mine. In fact, when the time was right, I would happily go down on one knee and make Shondra my wife. I was more than ready to say my vows before God and the world. I was ready to move on.

Wrapping my arms around my angel, I hugged her close. "Are you always going to cause trouble wherever we go?"

"Yeah, I might," she said, cutting off my retort by planting a juicy kiss on my lips.

I groaned into her mouth. We had yet to bring things up to speed. We've kissed and cuddled, nothing else. After the funeral of William, over a month ago, we agreed to go slow, grieve if we had to.

And that I did.

I shed more tears over my son, but not a damn one for William.

Shondra, however, wanted time to process William's death. Learning of my father's role in how my half-brother died had put a pall on our reunion.

Dear old dad had hired a hypnotist, one Dr. Kamara, under the guise of helping William get better. In reality, the man encouraged William to orchestrate his own destruction during their sessions.

Paying for It

When I showed up, ready to throw my half-brother from the balcony, my dad gave William a nod, *the signal* to make amends for the innocent life he took.

And the poor bastard ran with it, straight to the rocks below.

Paul Hammersmythe was all about revenge.

And if anyone hurt me and mine, I, Axel Sexton-Hammersmythe, would be just as ruthless.

***

JAMESON

My overwhelming feeling of disgust at Shelia's blatant display of sluttiness changed when Vee came into view.

Her beautiful face filled me with contentment...and purpose.

After my speech, we would be out in the open. Free to express our love for the world to see. Vee and I had already discussed living arrangements. We would buy Shondra's old house, and Axel and Sho would move into their new one, right across the street.

Vee approached and stood an arm's length away. I ached to hold her. To keep things civil until the "unmasking," Vee and I agreed to stay apart. If Shelia caught wind of our budding relationship, she would pounce on us with both feet.

I struggled to resist my urges when Vee came close. Close enough for me to smell her perfume, feel the heat of her skin, study the curve of her mouth...

I told caution to go to hell and pulled Vee in, kissing her forehead in front of anyone who cared to look.

She squirmed in my arms. "Jae, what are you doing? I thought we would wait—"

I closed her mouth by sweeping my tongue along the seam of her lips. She parted them and I went to town, nearly bending her in half with the force of my passion. A few shocked gasps from those around us registered in my mind.

But did I stop?

Hell no.

I'd waited long enough. Too damn long.

"Ahem."

That was Shelia clearing her throat in that damn way I hated. Thank heaven it was the last time I'd ever have to put up with it.

Vee broke our kiss by stepping away. Disappointment flooded me...until she reached down to take my hand.

"Jameson? What are you doing?" Shelia hissed, her blue eyes pointing daggers at Vee.

"What I should have done a long time ago." I saw Axel move inside my peripheral vision, his phone held aloft. My eyes shifted to Shondra. She directed the staff to hand out the gifts. Most people took them dumbly, too busy staring at the blowup of my fake marriage.

***

VEGAS

Paying for It

No way was I leaving my man, the father of my child, to deal with his crazy ex on his own. I took his hand and stood by his side. My rightful place.

Shelia looked ready to chew nails. Her face was an alarming shade of red and her eyes brimmed with fire. I held her damning gaze, refusing to lower my eyes like I had when my stepmother berated me. When my father didn't stand up for me. When Terrance left me.

I had found myself in Jae, and I would not give him up for anyone.

"What do you mean 'what you should have done a long time ago'? Have you been sleeping with this slut?" Shelia screamed.

Jae's fingers tightened on my hand as I surged forward. "You have some damn nerve calling me a slut."

"Easy, Vee, let me handle it." Smiling, Jae brushed his thumb across my cheek.

I conceded, giving him the lead to take out the trash.

Just inside the banquet room, Mrs. Gertrude Eisenberg, in a red tracksuit, stood with her arms folded much like Axel did when he expected a fight—feet planted, arms folded, and a deadly smile on a face that was almost wrinkle free.

Jae coughed once, then he spoke, his deep voice carrying throughout the room. "Can I have everyone's attention?" He needn't have asked. Shelia's screeching had all eyes riveted on us. Jae cleared his throat. "Shelia and I have lied to you for these past few years." Shelia let out a squeak of protest. Jae silenced her with a look so

403

dark it was a wonder the sun didn't hide. "We," he said, motioning between them, "divorced some time ago. I kept up the pretense we were together because my ex-wife blackmailed me into doing so."

There were a few shocked mummers from the general crowd and a few noises of disbelief from Shelia's admirers.

"You have in your hands the reason for her blackmail. I would ask that you open your packages now."

No one moved for a few seconds. I had started to think our plan wouldn't work when an elderly man set his champagne flute on a cocktail table and made quick work of opening his gift. A laugh rang out when he held up a blue, three ball butt plug. He studied it for a moment while his wife looked on, aghast. She blushingly slapped him on the arm when he said, "I haven't used one of these in years. Cindy, do you want to give it a go tonight?"

Laughing, the rustling of paper, and shocked exclamations filled the room. Shelia looked on with a sour expression. After a few minutes when no one condemned Jameson, she turned and hissed, "You think you have won? You haven't. Your bitch will feel my wrath. Just wait—"

Mrs. Eisenberg had sidled up to Shelia as she talked. She grabbed her arm in what looked like a rather powerful grip. "Consider yourself done at the hospital, my dear. The doctor, whom you blackmailed with sex into keeping quiet about your misdiagnosing, my grandson, has come clean. He and his wife are in counseling, and you are out on your fat ass. You can expect your license to be yanked within a week."

Shelia spun out of her grasp and ran from the room. No one went after her.

And just like that, she left our lives with less than a whimper.

***

Six months later...

SHONDRA

I opened the door.

Kae squealed when she entered our home, barreling for Axel. She loved that man almost as much as I did.

Axel squatted and threw his arms open wide. When she got close, he scooped her up and twirled her around. She giggled, kicking her feet. Jae and Vee came through the door, smiling. They often took a stroll in the evening and ended up at our house on their way home.

Vee and I left the guys with Kae, her arms wrapped around Axel's neck.

We walked into the kitchen. I put on the kettle and Vee got the Earl Grey. It had become our ritual of late. We also had plenty to discuss. Our double wedding was only a few weeks away.

"Shondra, I want your mom to walk us down the aisle. She practically raised me and you know Daddy..." she trailed off, looking out the window. Vee's father wasn't in any condition to do anything for anyone, least of all himself. His lucid days were no more. He existed until his day's end came upon him.

She'll like that, Vee. I'll ask her when I see her tomorrow." Mom had finally stopped working. For a long time, she didn't have to because I could have supported her. She insisted, telling me it gave her something to do to keep her mind off her past. About three months ago, she met a nice man at church. They started off talking, which led to dating, and now there was nothing he wouldn't do for her.

I was happy she finally found a semblance of peace.

Vee brightened. "I love the planning, but I can hardly wait for our day. What about you, Sho? Are you ready?"

Axel and Jae came into the kitchen. Kae was in her daddy's arms, her curly head on his shoulder and her eyes drooping closed.

Axel shifted his blues and locked them on me. And just like always, he made me want him with the promise he spoke without words.

Looking into the eyes of the man I knew I would love forever, I said, "Yes, Vee. I'm more than ready."

THE END.

Thanks so much for reading!

Find out about my other books and social media accounts at https://linktr.ee/author_jwylder